A Christmas Reunion

A Christmas Reunion

By Todd Aldrington

Edited by Emily Nemchick

Cover Design by Temiree

Also by Todd Aldrington

Available in paperback and ebook:

Todd and Colton:

Chasing Colton's Tail
Out on the Highway
Akio's House (with 'Return to New York')
White Christmas
Gone Day - Part 1
Gone Day – Part 2

Trick and Dolphin:

California Otters – Part 1
California Otters – Part 2 (due for release Summer 2024)

Chapter One

As soon as he saw it, Orson Brookfield decided that the Barstows' house really was the one from *Home Alone*, even if it was in New York and not Chicago, or wherever that Christmas flick was set. Orson suddenly wondered why the family in that film were otters rather than bears like the Barstows. Bears would have been funnier, and people wouldn't think all otters had those sorts of families and every Christmas was a slapstick laugh-a-minute.

Maybe I'd actually like being an otter, Orson thought, *if I'd ever known any who did Christmas like that. If they're out there somewhere, I wish they'd call me.*

The New York 'burbs' looked like any American movie suburbia to him, but now he felt the true cold of them, and it was the kind of cold that made him realise for the first time that movies could never truly make someone feel winter, or any season. Or smell Christmas. The icy breeze carried the smell of freshly cooked roasts and spiced biscuits. It was nothing like London here.

That was the best part. His father wasn't the mayor of New York and never would be.

The Barstows' house sounded like a movie set too.

The look on Julia Brookfield's face said, 'Oh my God, what *have* we done?'

We've escaped politics, Orson thought. *This is how regular families do Christmas.*

'How many bears live in this house, Richard?' Julia asked her husband.

'*Polar* bears,' Richard said, with that infuriating politician's accuracy that Orson always thought his father deliberately didn't switch off outside of the office. 'Five. Natasha, John, Ben, Ella and Sam.' He was most likely thinking the same thing as Orson: it wasn't a family of five tearing around in there.

Orson's smile widened. The Barstows had surely forgotten that they were hosting the Brookfields and had invited a brother or sister and cousins. Maybe they actually *were* going to go to France in the morning and would end up forgetting a kid. Orson went up and rang the bell.

Someone who clearly didn't live there and wasn't old enough to answer a door to a stranger opened up. 'Hi. You collecting for the poor?'

'Sure,' Orson said. 'Why not? Gimme your allowance, kid.' Cool, he'd even nailed how they called it that here instead of pocket money. 'Or do you want some poor otters to starve on the street this Christmas?'

'Errrr...' The kid bolted.

A teenage girl with a cynical look on her face, pierced nose and ears and a red boy's Superdry hoodie that was one size too big for her looked at him. 'Yeah, you're definitely Orson. Mom! Dad! The otters are here! They'll be right down. Kevin, put that back in the fridge right now!' She stalked towards the kitchen.

'Am I tripping?' Orson said to himself.

Natasha and John Barstow *weren't* right down. Another set of parents were instead. Mama was a brown bear, papa a heavy-set polar who Orson thought should be a trucker or a roadie for some rock band. It would be cool if it turned out he was a pro-gamer.

'Hi,' he said. 'I'm Cliff. I'm John's brother.' Surprisingly, he shook hands with Orson first. 'Orson, right? Better just say, please don't take it personally if one of my kids whines about not being allowed to bring their PS5. I told them it's Uncle John's house and he makes the rules.'

'Gameboooooy,' another bear who looked about eleven or twelve said in a laconic tone as he walked through. He had a polar's build but was brown, and he was waving the Gameboy like it was a security pass or an ID that carried diplomatic immunity.

'Urrrgh!' the mama bear said. 'Matthew! What did we say about this already?'

'"No Fun Allowed" or something, I dunno. Seth, you little douchebag! Where are my sneakers, you ass-hat?'

'Hey!' both parents yelled at once.

'I'm so sorry,' Mama Bear said. 'I'll be right back.'

'She's Holly, by the way,' Cliff said.

5

'Cool,' Orson said. 'I'm kicking Matthew's arse at Tetris later.'

'I think he's playing Zelda.'

'Forget about both,' Julia said. She introduced the family. There was pizza about to be delivered, but wine and snacks were already out. Soft drinks for Orson, of course, because it was obvious he was being lumped in with the kids when his mother looked at him.

'What, it's not eighteen to drink where we come from anymore, and I'm not twenty either?'

'You don't drink,' his mother said, as if to remind him he was lucky he didn't go to meetings for that along with everything else.

Orson shrugged and poured himself a grape soda. He'd never tried it before and thought it tasted like bubble gum. *I promised to behave,* he told himself, knowing he was looking for an open bottle of vodka he could add to it already. It was just like getting away from gaming: for a while, the world was going to feel a bit boring. He'd come to adjust to that. Christmas without booze might be better too.

John and Natasha came down dressed to go out. All the Barstow kids were in the local choir, and this Christmas Eve they were singing outside the church rather than in it. Outdoor nativity with carols. All this explained while an incessant amount of hugging went on, as if Orson's family saw them every Christmas and it hadn't been over fifteen years.

'I know,' John said to Richard. 'It's a full house you all weren't quite expecting. Little family crisis we had to help out with.'

'We burned our house down,' Matthew said, still glued to the Gameboy and not looking up. He was indeed playing Zelda. Orson heard the sound of a bomb exploding, then the world famous eight-note pinging of the secret door sound. It was still like a siren call.

'*Now* you're talking,' Orson said, grinning as he sat down, resisting it. 'I bet it was you. What kind of matches did you use?'

Matthew blew his overly long forehead fur away from his eyes. 'Iron left on.'

'It wasn't the iron, dipshit, it was the tumble dryer,' Ella said.

'Language in front of the kids,' Matthew said, even more deadpan. 'Feed me some pizza or something; my hands are busy.'

Orson was disappointed when Ella didn't simply shove it into her cousin's sarcastic little hole of a mouth. Maybe she would have done if Mama Bear Holly hadn't been watching.

'It was Mom's bra that caught fire,' another kid who Orson guessed was Seth said.

'For the last time,' Holly said. 'It was the boiler that started it. We're done talking about it; it's a miracle we all made it out alive, and we're going to go and thank God that we're all still here to enjoy this Christmas together later on.' She forcibly removed Matthew's

Gameboy from his hands now and ignored his response:

'Laaaame.'

'Don't worry, all our kids are rooming together to leave a guest room for you.'

Orson knew what this really meant, because Holly Barstow was looking at his parents when she said it. He was going to share a room with one of these kids? After a long-haul flight, with his body now tuned to half past fuck-knew-when o'clock? His parents weren't going to let him crash no matter how tired he said he was. Not now they'd seen that Gameboy in the house. Or how his face had so obviously lit up at the sound before he could stop himself reacting. He was going to watch the choir. Just like every Christmas back home.

Unless he could escape. There was one way. He took out his phone and searched for it.

'Where am I sleeping?' he said, wondering how to buy himself time while he flick-scanned Google. 'Could I maybe go do it now?'

'Don't be silly,' Richard said. 'You slept on the plane.'

It hadn't really been sleep; he'd just had his eyes shut.

'You'll be sleeping with us,' Julia said. 'These good people have had to put their family up for Christmas, so there isn't a spare room for you on your own anymore. But that's okay, isn't it?'

'Sure,' Orson said, forcing it out of himself. He'd never even slept in his parents' bedroom as a child. 'Or

8

I wouldn't mind just sleeping on the sofa. Couch. Whatever it's called here.'

'We understand sofa, otter-brain,' Ella said.

'Ella, don't be so rude,' John said. 'I tell you what, Ella can have the couch and Orson can have Ella's room.'

Sleeping in a teenage girl's room after she'd been kicked out? Watching the choir now seemed more bearable. The passive aggression that would come off of Ella Barstow, Orson thought, would bore holes through any wall.

'Oh, now don't let's have any upheaval,' Julia said. 'Really. It's no problem. We were the last guests to arrive, and rooms have already been shared out. It's fine like it is.'

Orson smiled. He'd found his get-out-of-jail card. By the time he got back from this, everyone would be asleep and the couch would be his. No choir either. He wasn't sure which victory was better. 'Dad, can I go to this?' He held it up.

His father looked torn. If he knew it was a deliberate play, he wouldn't dare to call it out. At least not right now.

'Well...let's just see. John, what time are we going out to hear the choir?'

'Seven, but Orson doesn't have to come if there's something else he'd rather do.' John Barstow looked like he knew exactly what this was.

'No,' Julia said. 'Whatever this thing is, we've been invited to something else.'

Richard moved in, slowly and quietly, as if he'd take his wife aside if he could find a discreet way of doing it. 'Orson wants to go to a meeting. Maybe it's a good idea.'

'*You* go to AA?' Ella said, looking at Orson. 'You're way too young to be an alcoholic.'

'I'm not an alcoholic,' Orson said, unable to resist conjuring up a barbed look for his mother. 'I just "don't drink". That's not what this meeting's for.'

'Narcotics then?' Ella said, her mouth half full of pizza. 'Is that what got you kicked out of college? Oh no, wait, *please* tell me it's a support group for addiction to se–'

'Young lady, any more being rude to another guest in this house and you'll be getting nothing under the tree tomorrow,' John said. 'I'm sorry, Orson. Whatever you go to meetings for, it's none of my family's business. They should all know better given what we've talked about before.'

Cliff, Orson thought, looked like a man used to riding this kind of thing out in silence. Especially right now, when he gave his brother a smile and a dismissive look.

'I'm not a sex addict,' Orson said, looking at Ella. 'For someone I barely knew existed, you seem to know an awful lot about me. Yeah, I got kicked out of college. I'll tell you the story later if you want.' *That's for telling me I can't even drink on Christmas Eve, Mum.*

'Orson is addicted to video games,' Julia said. 'He can't play them because he doesn't know when to stop, and it took an awful toll on his health for several years.

But things are better now. Fine, good idea, go to this Gamers Anonymous meeting. Richard, will you take him in the rental car? I don't want him getting a bus alone in New York.'

'Good call,' Cliff said. '*I'll* take him. I know New York better than anyone here and…well, you know.' He looked at Holly, and Orson saw something that passed for a sudden understanding.

'Yes,' Holly said. 'Perfect. Cliff doesn't sing and…well, this is nice. Happy to help out.'

'Hey, Gameboy,' Orson said, looking at Matthew. No surprise, Matthew looked up at being called that. 'You were trying to get the magic cape earlier, weren't you? You were looking in the wrong part of the map. I can't play myself, but I can show you where it is later.'

Now the stoic surliness broke. Matthew looked like it was Christmas Day and he'd just got a new, gold-plated Gameboy with some famous person's signature on it. 'I like you. You can have my room. I'll have the couch.'

'You'll have no such thing,' Holly said. 'The Gameboy or the couch.'

'Those matches you wanted to know about?' Matthew said, making a striking motion with his left hand. 'Zippo.'

'They make matches too?' Orson said.

'You bet your butt they do.'

'Well okay, but if I lost my butt in a bet then what would Mum smack when I've been naughty? My arse instead?'

11

The kids laughed. Seth and Kevin couldn't stop. Especially not after Sam, who shouldn't have been so amused by that at eleven years old, couldn't stop either. Julia looked like she'd given up, and Richard poured himself another glass of wine. Why, Orson thought, would the guy not admit that he wished he could go to Gamers Anonymous too just to avoid listening to another load of Christmas carols? This was supposed to be his holiday time, not time spent going to other people's events because it was expected of him.

His mother was giving him a cold look now. 'I never smacked your "arse",' she said, as if trying to say she wasn't sure what affronted her more, the word or the idea that she'd smacked his.

I made her wish she had, Orson thought, with the usual guilt that followed. After everything that happened, she'd sat in the intervention and looked like she'd wanted to full-on go for him. It was long past the point of a good old-school spanking.

'I want the couch,' Sam said suddenly. 'Orson can have my room. Long as he doesn't mind the pet tarantula.'

Orson blinked. 'Seriously?'

'Sam's into spiders,' John said. 'We bought him one for his birthday. He already wants to do a zoology degree one day. You know what, there's a thought. Why *don't* we give Orson Sam's room, and Sam can room with Seth and Kevin.'

'Three boys that age in a room together on Christmas Eve, John?' Natasha said. 'Really? They'd never get any sleep. I tell you what. You and I can get the blow-up double bed out and put it down here. Richard and Julia will have our bedroom, and Orson has the guest room they would have used.'

'I thought about it already,' John said, 'but it takes an awfully long time to blow that thing up.'

'Orson can room with me.'

The entire room stopped at that voice. Someone else had arrived, and it was like he'd been there for ages, just listening to this. There was an aura of tactical master about the whole entrance. The guy who watched the fight and then saved his moment for showing how he held the ultimate black belt. Through all of this, Orson couldn't believe he'd almost forgotten that Ben Barstow existed.

It must have been the movie house thing. How else could he have forgotten the entire reason he'd suggested this to his parents in the first place? The last time he and Ben had seen each other, they'd been eight, maybe just short of nine. What he was seeing now, no wonder it stopped a room.

'Heeey, there he is! How did the game go?' Cliff definitely had a 'there's my favourite nephew' voice and started the whole thing off. Bear hugs, noogies...even Ella exchanged happy banter, and Matthew had a hugging side to him.

Ben was dressed for ice hockey even when not at the rink. The stick and skates would have looked good with these clothes. He was from a family of big, stocky bears (Seth, Kevin and Sam actually *were* a bit fat), but he was an athlete. He probably worked out, ran, cycled, couldn't stop doing sports of any kind. Probably as stupidly gifted at all of them as he was at making people in a room come to him. He'd filled out like a grown-up bear should and stayed trim all at once.

'But surely you don't want Orson rooming with you,' Natasha said. 'I'm sorry, that sounded wrong. No offence, Orson, but Ben was having his girlfriend stay here this Christmas. Isn't Edie coming after all?'

'Her grandparents showed up unexpectedly,' he said. 'Grandma's got some kind of dementia, and this might be the last Christmas she remembers. I can't exactly argue with that. She's coming to see the choir later though. Orson can room with me; he can have my bed, and I'll put my sofa cushions on the floor. I'll take him to his meeting too.' He looked at Orson. 'Can I come in with you?'

'Come in with me?' Orson said, feeling like he'd stammered it out. 'Why the hell would you wanna do that?'

'Supportive friend?'

Orson glowed under his fur. 'Errrr...right. Yeah. Sure.'

'Awwwww!' Ella said.

'Oh, now come on, don't embarrass him,' Ben said. 'You gonna tell me *you've* got no issues? We won the game, by the way. Seven-two.' He mimed striking a puck with a stick, as if to say he'd scored, then came across the kitchen and geared up for what Orson was dreading. 'It's good to see you again, OtterSpotter.'

Everybody twittered, or laughed, as Ben hugged him, and Orson found enough of a hug for this boy he hardly knew. Who was now a man, even if he still looked young enough to have to show an ID card everywhere he went. Orson suspected Ben didn't drink though. After a sports victory like that, he should be smelling beer on his breath, and all he smelt was spiced tea.

I was the one who asked to come here, he thought. He'd made the deal. He'd wanted to see New York and see Ben Barstow again. He'd got the idea from a Gamers A session where everyone got talking about favourite memories. They said it might be good if he made 'seeing that bear again' a goal. So he floated it with his parents: clean up his life and become a normal functioning citizen like every other boring drone and in return they'd pay for him to go.

What had he been thinking when he let them add going on the trip with him as a condition?

It was simple, he still knew: money. They'd never pay for a trip like that if it meant he'd be out of their sight.

Was this a mistake? Orson thought.

Six months he'd gotten wrapped up in the idea that he'd filled the void of having his childhood BFF leave him with non-stop hours in front of a PlayStation, and this was the way to finally reverse the rot. He'd been *eight*, for God's sake. After a while, he'd gotten used to Ben not being there, and then he'd barely thought about him for years, until he'd been nineteen and sitting in that meeting, after spending two days sobering up in a jail cell, with one completely unrelated and unexpected thought: Why *hadn't* Ben Barstow ever kept in touch with him?

He wasn't asking tonight. He probably shouldn't ask at all.

When his parents planned the holiday, he didn't look at Ben's Facebook, or any other social media, because an almost total ban from anything he might play a game on hung over his head. All he'd wanted, after the initial infatuation with the idea of meeting Ben again had worn off slightly, was New York in front of him. For some reason, he didn't want it to be a place he just saw in movies anymore.

'Why don't you come and see my room?' Ben said. 'Unless you want the one with the tarantula.'

'Yours will be fine,' Orson said.

Ben's room, he thought, would have suited any gamer right down to the letter. His own sofa, coffee table, TV, sound system...this kid had it all, and it felt like he'd earned it rather than having Mom and Dad spoil him. They could have afforded to, but Orson felt like Ben had saved his own money for all of this. He decided not to ask. He wanted to imagine Ben was good with money.

Ben didn't game much, it turned out. He'd dabbled in having a Dreamcast once, but next-gen gaming hadn't felt like any kind of promised land to him. Orson remembered now that he had on one slightly drunken occasion gotten curious about Ben's social media after all only to find Ben didn't have any, or at least none that a stranger could find. In this room, Ben had books. Actual, physical books. He had a Mac too, but how he preferred to read was obvious. There was a Bible amongst them. No surprise.

Ben, Orson realised, had been staring at him while he stared around the room.

'Well, look at you,' he said. 'Look who you grew up to be. I still can't believe you're here.'

Orson shut the door. A little too hard despite trying not to make a bang, but he didn't care. 'Do *not* say that like there's anything nice or cool or good about what my life is and what I look like. I ruined my life. It's a disaster. You know what's going to happen later? I have to hand my phone over to my parents. They know my password. There are rules about what I can have on it. I can read the news and listen to music, and that's about it. I lost control of everything, and I only keep it by a seriously thin thread. You're going to end up wishing I'd never come here.'

'Ooookay. Long flight and you're tired. Why don't you take a nice deep breath, and we'll talk about how you're feeling right now?'

'Do *not* put your hands on my shoulders.'

Ben stopped halfway to doing exactly that, then looked like someone had just told him he was about to touch something with enough volts in it to throw him the length of a room. 'Okay. I'm Sorry. But you know what?'

'What?'

'When I had to move back here, I didn't get another friend I liked as much as you. Not for a long time. I didn't settle at my school well. I had to get to middle school and find out I was good at sports before I felt happy again. I'm sorry I never kept in touch. I don't really know why I didn't.'

Because that's all bullshit and you found the cool kids right off the bat. 'We were kids. It was just a kid friendship. You really do *not* want to know me now.'

'Why not?'

'Okay. Look at all this. Your life. How your family were around you. What's the plan for you next, college?'

Ben laughed like he couldn't help himself. 'You're the same age as me, Orson. I'm already at college. Second year. Sports scholarship. Home for the holidays.'

'There you go. Your whole life's the dream. I don't have any of this.'

Ben looked around himself too, as if finding all the reasons Orson had said what he'd said, like there was something in his head that made him want to launch straight into saying his life *wasn't* a dream. Just as Orson expected though, Ben simply said nothing after a moment of quiet.

'I'm a mess,' Orson said. 'I had one thing I liked. One thing I was good at. I was going to be an e-sports champion. People loved me. I only pretended to go to "college" and do computer science so I could have my own space to do everything. Now I've got nothing. I as much as touch a computer, I could end up sectioned, and I actually don't think I'm exaggerating. I did spend three days in a psych hospital once. I came to New York to escape from my life.'

Ben looked concerned. 'Escape how?'

'I don't know. Run. Disappear.' Would Ben believe him if he shared his fantasy? It was worth a try. 'I actually did have this idea about just disappearing into New York and living the rest of my life as an illegal immigrant, couch surfing with whoever I can buy off with gaming prize money. But maybe after I've at least spent Christmas sleeping in your bed for a couple of days. You won't tell on me, right? Not Captain Snowbear. He doesn't tell on his dead-eye gunner The OtterSpotter. Who else is gonna save the Great Ship Lightspeed?'

'You remember?'

'Course I remember.'

Ben looked dumbfounded. 'Well, OtterSpotter, I'm glad you at least said you wanted to go to that meeting. I *will* take you. Let me come in like I said. Nobody wants to be a loner in a place like New York. Trust me. I want to hear what you say when you're in a room full of people who really know what your life's like.'

'Do you know what gamers often go to Gaming Anonymous meetings for? To find people they can game with.'

Ben shrugged. 'It's your life. But you really think you can escape into New York and go AWOL with some stranger you hooked up with at a meeting?'

This adorably pious bear, Orson thought, perhaps needed a little taste of bad behaviour. Or the illusion of it. 'You think I'm out of my depth? Just watch.' *Who am I kidding? I've gotten used to being boring. I won't find the energy to do anything like what I used to even here. That room will suck it out of me, and that's the whole idea. That's what 'sobriety' is.*

'I don't know. But I think you'd have a better Christmas if you stayed here with us.'

Orson smiled, a bright idea coming through to him. 'Okay. Prove it. It's Christmas Eve, and the shops are still open for a few more hours. You know what I want for Christmas?'

'What?'

'I want some liquor. Scotch. And a packet of fags. Sorry, *cigarettes*. A proper American brand like Pal Mal or Camel or something. Get me that. I wanna go outside when the rest of your house is asleep and enjoy that. That's what I do at home sometimes when Mum and Dad have gone to bed. It's something to cling to. Give me that for Christmas.'

'I get it, my friend. I totally do. But it's gonna be a bit difficult to get hold of that with the busy evening we've got planned. When am I gonna get away?'

'Make it happen, Snowbear. Or I'm letting the Battletoads gun our ship down.'

'You know what's kinda fun?'

'What?'

'You really did become a dead-eye shot. First person shooters, right? That was your favourite thing. Maybe you really could have been a good gunner. You never thought about getting fit and joining the air force or something? Fly a real ship sometime?'

'What, me killing real people? Don't be soft. How did you know that about me anyway when you don't do social media?'

'I know what happened. Mom and Dad told me. Well, okay. That and I got talking to Kingsley again. That's why I thought of the air force thing. Did you know he became a navigator?'

'Oh *God*, Kingsley Osterman? Fuck, how could I *not* know? That sanctimonious twat of a stag. What did he tell you? Everything? Mum and Dad got him to be part of my intervention. It was excruciating. He was "the friend I should have listened to in the first place". Except that he...' Orson stopped, then sighed. 'Let's not talk about it. I've not talked to Kingsley for months. I should have, but I haven't. I just want to have one good Christmas before I try to talk to people again. Maybe.'

'He told me nothing, OtterSpotter. I just knew about the arrest. He said everything else that happened wasn't for anyone else to tell if you didn't want it.'

'Oh.'

'Yeah. I just got talking to him because I realised I'd missed him along with you.'

'Okay. But Ben, can you not call me OtterSpotter if we've got to talk about something serious? Actually, don't call me that at all. Especially not in front of your family again. Two, I don't want to talk about any of the last year full stop. It was humiliating. It was all over the fucking news, because of who Dad is. The mayor of London's son got arrested for that. Now I can never *not* be that person. People still ask me about it now. I can't even escape from it while I'm working as a waiter in a restaurant. Yeah, that's my job, by the way. Look at me. Look at who I grew up to be.'

'A waiter's a service people need, isn't it?'

'I bet you really do know everything, don't you? You know about the thing with the prime minister's son too?'

'I'm not judging you, Orson. People do crazy things sometimes. You think I'm a saint?'

'Funnily enough, yes.'

'Okay, I've never done what you did, but there's a different person under the golden boy sometimes.'

'Really. I can't wait to see him.'

'Orson.' Ben held up his hands. '*Can* I put these on your shoulders this time and get you to take that deep breath?'

'Yeah, go on. We're not going anywhere until I've at least pretended all my feelings will just melt away if...oh. Ooooooh, okay. I should have known.' Orson took the deep breath, feeling his friend's muscled fingers dig into his shoulders. 'Sports massage. Or therapy. Or something. You're doing a jock college degree.'

'Actually no, I just have good fingers. Deep breath again. And out. Feels good, doesn't it?'

'Yeah. Kinda.'

'Okay.' Ben took his hands away. 'I once needed a guy to do that to me too. Because I was worked up. I've known what it was like to have a head full of stuff I couldn't sort out. You were right. Captain Snowbear wouldn't tell on his gunner. So here's a secret you can have just to prove it. I sometimes wish I could be more like you. Because here's my secret: I kind of like bad boys. Or at least I think about them a lot when I'm imagining other stuff.'

'What do you mean?'

Ben smiled. 'What do you *think* I mean?'

Orson thought about those hands on his shoulders, and everything inside him squirmed. 'Seriously? Does your girlfriend know?'

Ben's smile widened. 'My girlfriend is my *best* friend. Edie likes girls. We both pretend we're in a relationship with each other because it suits both of us to do it. We love each other, but not like that. *She* became Captain Snowbear's new gunner once.'

'So that was it. Not well-adjusted at school my arse. You didn't just find the cool kids; you found a giiiiiiirl!'

'Yep. I *wanted* to get cooties.'

They both laughed.

'Edie's the friend I've still got all the way from middle school. We sleep in a bed together sometimes, but she doesn't want my penis and I've no interest in her vagina.'

'Are you actually, seriously coming out to a guy you really don't know at all?'

'Yeah. I guess I am.'

'Why haven't you told your family yet? Because I don't see them minding much. Not the guy who walked into that room and everybody went to him like he was their hero.'

'You know who that guy is? A straight white bear who's gonna marry another straight white bear like they think Edie is and keep the whole big family thing going. That's who the hockey team think their star is too, and the college with them. So does everyone who sees my college games on TV. I'm not ready to see how people react when it turns out I'm not that guy. I'm not ready to be out.'

'Then what are you telling me for?'

'I trust you. We're Snowbear and OtterSpotter again, even if I don't call you that anymore. Our lives are in each other's hands. For real this time.' Ben looked at his watch. 'I've gotta shower and get changed for going out. You can use the bathroom down the hall. Oh, no, I'm sorry, that's just bad manners. You use mine. You go first.'

Orson had somehow missed that Ben had an en-suite bathroom through the door on the other side of the room. It was never going to be a wardrobe through there, was it? 'Ben.'

'Yeah?'

'What are you studying at college?'

'Dentistry.'

'What? Seriously? *You're* going to be a dentist?'

'Yeah, why's that surprising? It's just like I said: good fingers.'

'You use your bathroom. I'll use the one down the corridor.'

In the bathroom down the corridor, wrapped in the towel he'd dug from the bottom of his suitcase, Orson looked at his own teeth in the mirror, mouth wide open. At least there was nothing wrong with those mostly.

A polar bear dentist though. What a terrifying idea, even if it was Ben Barstow, the Ned Flanders of bears. He probably wouldn't tell even if Orson did run away into New York somewhere.

Maybe he'd come after me, Orson thought. *That might make for a Christmas to talk about.*

Chapter Two

Getting this close to the centre of New York City should have meant the meeting was in some grand rehearsal hall, but instead this place felt more like a conference suite that was set up for something *like* gaming rather than a session for people avoiding it, right down to the big television screen and hotel carpet that probably got re-laid every three months.

At least it wasn't a dusty village hall from some parish in one of London's suburbs, one of those places where you went for cheap Christmas get-togethers with mostly older people and the smell of skin cream and out-of-fashion clothing mingled with stewing mulled wine and heated-up supermarket mince pies.

An NY Gamers A meeting, Orson decided, had a touch of irony and class all at once. He smiled at it and swished his tail as he went to take his seat.

Orson had the feeling that nobody in the meeting would have mentioned his accent even if he hadn't said he was from England. The melting pot of diversity here meant that where anyone was from or who their family were never got mentioned, let alone why someone talked the way they did. What was curious was how they all looked at Ben like they knew he didn't belong in here. They weren't going to come to him like his family had, like most people in rooms where he was completely unknown would probably come to him, because he couldn't have passed for fucked up even if he'd dressed like a hobo and walked in here stinking drunk.

Then of course, they got picked out as newcomers and asked to go first, and it was Ben the chair of the meeting looked at.

Ben handled it so seamlessly that Orson wanted to throttle him: he said he was there for Orson and was his ride – an unusual kind of tour guide to an unknown city. He said it all like he was middle aged and halfway through that dentistry career already. Everyone seemed to love him despite his apparent lack of problems.

Orson wanted to talk about how gaming addiction wasn't officially recognised by medical boards in either of the two countries represented in the room tonight, or how he came to this meeting to get out of hearing choir music. He even wanted to admit he'd prefer to hear everyone else talk so he could pick out who to slip his number to, with a note saying, 'Wanna check out an arcade? Call me.'

It would have Ben's phone number on it, which was why Orson had asked for it in the car. Ben gave it as if he knew what the game was but now was well on the way to proving he'd accepted the perfect gamble, because Orson simply couldn't do it, or voice the real thoughts in his head. Instead, he did the good behaviour version.

Orson was 'powerless over gaming'. He'd filled his years between ten and twenty taking advantage of how his parents let him be independent and manage his own time, what they called a 'long rehearsal for being grown up one day'. He could pull all-night sessions on MMRPGs or FPSs and still attend school bright eyed and bushy tailed once, then as that ability disappeared towards the end of his teenage, he'd propped himself up with MDMA (the gamer's favourite non-game acronym, as it was known), then speed or coke if he could get it, then any kind of uppers his gaming friends told him how to get hold of. Not hard to do when you went to a public school where everyone's parents had seemingly limitless money and many of them passed it on to their kids every birthday and Christmas, and they'd often throw drugs around their friend circle just to prove they could. That and when you're bored of being rich, you got your kicks from seeing who dared to do how much. (Orson decided not to name Kingsley Osterman, and wondered how much he'd confessed to in his interviews for joining the air force at officer-class.)

The alcohol loved Orson when he was on drugs. He made it through 6th form and got into Sussex to do computer science, but really that was because Brighton was a gaming hub, and he wanted the cheapest and most subsidised access to it that he could get. London's back door, and a front door to spending as many hours as he could stay awake getting that buzz that nothing else quite compared to.

His arrest on Christmas Eve exactly one year ago today ended it all. It was nothing that would have been newsworthy for most people. Just about anyone could get nicked for being drunk, high and naked running through a city centre if they tried hard enough. The news happened because his father was the mayor of London, and Orson's frequently intoxicated state of mind and almost total immersion in gaming had stopped him from seeing that a lot of tabloid journalists followed him with interest. The pictures were everywhere before Orson was sober again three days later. So was the statement he'd given to the police: 'I was so fucked up that I genuinely thought I was inside one of my games. I think it was Grand Theft Auto Vice City. I almost can't believe I didn't kill someone.'

Then there was the prime minister's son. Denied Oxford or Cambridge as usually befitted someone of that stature who'd gone to a London private school, Sussex had been a good home for him, and get this, the mayor's kid went there too. That's how they'd met. Their friendship ended three days after Orson's arrest.

Sydney Sheldon hadn't been arrested though. He'd gone to hospital. During the victim act that followed, he'd never acknowledged that he'd been a willing participant in what had happened, and at the time had found it as hilarious as everyone else. He'd blamed Orson, who by that stage was depressed and coming down enough to admit that he *had* done the poor guy some pretty serious damage, but none of it had ever been intended like everyone seemed to be suggesting. The only consolation was that all their other friends agreed that Syd was just a spineless rat about it all and destined to follow his father into politics, because he'd already mastered how not to take responsibility for his own actions. (Orson had never thought of it before, but he suddenly imagined Kingsley being the one who got the group together and said, 'Guys, this shit-show's not right, and I already told the police the truth, and now you're all going to as well', with that ever so subtle hint of how his family and money would be off-limits to anyone who didn't.)

Orson told his story, waiting for someone to have the flash in their eyes that said, 'Oh, you're *that* guy!' or perhaps actually say it, but nobody gave it to him. He got the looks he always did that seemed to say that he should be in AA or drugs rehab or anywhere but here, until he spelled it out for everyone: he stopped everything else straight away as soon as he was made to stop gaming. Apart from smoking. He still loved smoking, but he'd practically given that up too, against his will, after conceding that Mum and Dad knew best. Except it was better described as, 'They *think* I've given up, but I have to want to first, and I just kinda don't.' (He'd bet money Kingsley still smoked; it was popular in professions where your life was going to be on the line anyway, and that jammy bugger could pass any fitness test like he was immune to his lifestyle.)

These furs, Orson thought, were going to spend all night on him. He wasn't going to pretend he didn't want the attention. That was when he played the best card, the one he hadn't really been aware was there in his hand all along: he'd stuck with living at home under strict rules for a year because his parents did know what was good for him, and there was a bargain they'd struck – if he could stay clean for a year (or mostly clean, because they just about forgave him the crafty cigarette so long as he almost successfully hid it), they'd take a Christmas holiday to New York for him. They'd go and see the Barstows, who they'd known when Ben's father was on a five-year secondment to an English bank. It might have been JP Morgan; Orson couldn't remember and didn't care.

Ben was his best friend once. Everyone called him Benji back then, but to Orson he was Captain Snowbear, and the whole idea that he'd fed his parents had come from a meeting like this, where someone had asked what would make him happier than anything else if he managed to work for it and get it, and his 'sobriety' was key. Just for one hour (lunchbreak time), Orson would have killed to be the original OtterSpotter again, not the one he'd become when he'd chosen that name as his online handle for every game that had sucked him in, then sucked everything else out of his life. There was a way to restore a kind of purity, and that lightbulb had switched on over his head as soon as he'd shared it with a circle just like this one. That was how he knew these meetings counted for something even though some people were undecided or cynical about what gaming addiction actually was and what treatment had any effect. Orson had found his own kind of rehab.

Everyone loved it. What Orson loved, from the look on Ben's face, was the most unexpectedly joyous part of it: Ben had known nothing about the terms Orson's parents had imposed at all, that Orson himself had suggested. His family had so obviously told him that Orson was coming here for Christmas, and watch out because he'd had a few problems, but not the rest of it. There was never any doubt that Orson would come here, no mention of the possibility Orson could derail everything for himself.

The chair, a wolf called Drake, was all over it. 'Benji, how do *you* feel about this?'

Ben should have told him his name was Ben now, except he didn't, and Orson wasn't sure Ben had even registered the use of its childhood version. 'I...knew most of it,' Ben said, the pause ringing nicely in Orson's ears. 'Orson asked me if I knew about the prime minister's son earlier. I knew there was a practical joke gone wrong, that it got a little serious, but I actually don't know what happened.'

The circle were looking at Orson. He realised that in the trance he'd induced during the slow outpouring of his life story, he hadn't detailed it. 'I don't want to share,' he said. 'You can Google it later if you really want to know.' He decided not to look at Ben as if to accuse him of already having done so. 'The details don't matter. What matters is I hurt someone, and I blame gaming.'

He didn't; he blamed himself. He might have said sorry if Syd hadn't been such a prick about it all afterwards. It was the first time Orson had really learned the lesson that someone could handle something badly even when they were the one who'd gotten hurt. Blaming Orson and shaming him so publicly after he felt humiliated enough wasn't the action of someone who called themselves a friend. Not when Sydney Sheldon had suggested the idea for the forfeit himself and accepted the terms of the bet that came with it.

He watched the group, waited for the pressure to share, but none of them brought it. They asked questions about how he filled his time now that he no longer had gaming, or went to clubs, or did drugs, or had any online life at all. He answered it honestly: he worked as a waiter, he'd taken up running even though he sucked at it and seemed to be proof that otters weren't built for it, but really that was to make up for all the food, because Orson cooked. He could fill whole days with prepping elaborate dishes or learning new recipes, or just deep cleaning his parents' kitchen because he wanted it kept like the one at work. Did he want to become a chef? Maybe, but he wasn't sure he liked the environment of a kitchen that was literally its own kind of non-stop pressure cooker. Not to mention that the more the customers sent back perfect food and demanded to eat for free next time, the less liking he

33

had for people and the less he wanted any talent he had to serve society, but he cooked recreationally because it did bring him some happiness, and he secretly liked to think maybe he was as good as some of the pros at work. Maybe the customers wouldn't send *his* dishes back if they let him cook.

The longer he talked, the more convinced he became that Ben really didn't know what he'd done. Ben almost certainly wouldn't have come out to him if he had.

Unless, Orson thought, a barely suppressible shiver going through him, that was why he had.

'Actually, I wouldn't be a chef,' Orson said. 'If I had my way, I'd probably be a DJ. I like house music. I like mixing. I feel like any job I ever got would just be a means to an end. Getting more money to spend on music that I can turn into other music. Pretty hard to get employed to do that though. I guess I'll do it small-time. I like being a night owl. Club life would kind of work for me.'

A gazelle called Imelda asked him if he'd tried having any kind of conversation with his parents about where he wanted his life to go next. He said it was for the new year, and the conversation mercifully shifted towards her. It soon became Imelda's floor. She filled it with how her friends were all enablers.

At least she has friends left, Orson thought. Right now, he fancied that he had one, and he at least owed him keeping that phone number from the car private.

* * *

34

He waited until they were halfway back to Ben's house (a surprisingly long drive given that it was only twenty miles) before he decided to talk, but Ben beat him to it.

'Thanks for not giving anyone my number,' he said. 'That's what you were going to do, wasn't it? To get around how you'll have to give your phone to your parents and they'd know if someone texted it.'

'How do you know I didn't?'

'I just know.'

'You didn't know me coming here was conditional, did you?'

'No, I didn't know that.'

'You really *don't* know what happened with Syd, do you?'

'Mom and Dad said it would be better if I didn't know. I know they had a long talk with your parents about you coming here and there was a lot they had to understand, but in the end they understood. Or they maybe understood what everyone in that room seemed to. I don't know.'

Orson looked out of the window at the lights of New York City disappearing behind him. 'That's the line of no return, you realise that? Mom and Dad said no, so now you want to disobey.'

'Not all of us work that way, my friend.'

'Oh, come on. Stop being so fucking pious and just admit you want to know.'

'Yeah, okay, I'll bite. I'm curious. But before you tell me, is this going to spoil tonight because I realise you actually want to brag about this rather than repent for it?'

'I don't want to brag about it. I wasn't even going to tell you until I realised that on some level you might actually get why it's awkward. Like nobody else does.'

They pulled up at some traffic lights, and Ben looked at him for so long that he waited for a good ten seconds after the light had gone green. 'Yeah, okay. What happened?'

'You ever played on a Nintendo Wii? With that long bar-shaped controller it's got and the wrist-strap so you don't throw it across the room?'

'Yeah, I know the one.'

'Sydney made a bet with a friend of ours. It was a gaming bet. A challenge. I can't remember what game he was bragging that he could clock in one night with all the achievements, but I knew it was impossible. I knew Syd thought he was invincible, that he was genuinely that good. So I said there had to be a real forfeit if he lost. He came up with it himself. If he lost, he'd cover a Wii remote in Vaseline and shove it up his arse until it was completely inside him. Then he'd go out on the town for Friday night with it still there and keep it there until midnight.'

'Really? You're serious? Don't tell me he actually...' Ben slowed down for the next set of lights, which stayed red for an awfully long time, and he looked at Orson all the while.

'Yep. I'm the one who stuck it up him. Because he lost, and I just wanted to see him squirm all evening for being such an arrogant twat. Nobody else would do it; he thought he'd gotten away already because of it. He was laughing about how he lost but wouldn't have to honour his bet. I mean, what an arsehole, right? You make a bet, you honour it.'

'So you wanted to hurt him.' Ben looked like Orson had somehow hurt *him*.

'No, I didn't want to hurt Syd. When I think about it now, I think maybe I did it because I knew the others *would* hurt him if they got up the balls to try it. All I wanted was for him to admit he'd been stupid to think he was that good. I was better, and I'd never have made a bet like that.'

'You really don't remember what game it was?'

'Okay, it was Sonic Adventure 2. I was trying not to ruin that for you too, you dumb-arse. Although what the fuck, you don't game anyway, do you? I mean shit, who makes a bet that they can clock all the achievements in *that* in one night?'

'Ooookay, now I'm starting to get it.' Ben got a green light and pulled over near a 7-11 so he could keep looking at Orson. 'Let me see if I've got it right: Syd didn't think about the Chao Garden. There are at least five achievements related to it, aren't there? It would take about a day's worth of gaming to feed those things enough coloured bars to get them through the races and win.'

'You *do* game!'

'I've played that one. Sonic was probably the last gasp of harmless fun before all the nasty violent games took over.'

Orson smiled, then laughed, enjoying the release. He'd done how many meetings where this got talked about now? In none of them had he spoken the truth: that he still remembered that look on Syd's face and wanted to crack up. 'Syd realised how fucked he was when he clocked everything else and then saw those right at the end. That's when I held up the Wii-mote and asked for a tube of KY. Someone actually had one.'

Ben grinned. 'Was it Kingsley?'

'Yeah, right.' Orson thought for a moment. 'Did you *like* Kingsley? Even back then you kinda knew? Is that why you got back in touch with him?'

Ben looked a little bashful. 'Maybe.'

Orson laughed.

'No telling!' Ben said.

'I don't talk to him anymore, Benji. Why would he want to know me now?'

Ben looked like he might answer but then just said: 'That *is* a dumb bet. And a perfect example of why getting drunk's not a good thing.'

'Yeah. Isn't it. That's also why you and Kingsley would *never* have matched well even if he did like guys. He thought the whole thing was hilarious to begin with.'

'Were you laughing so much when it ended in...how *does* this story end?'

'Syd tried to keep the thing up his arse all night until he realised there was something seriously wrong. He

38

went into the toilets in a club and pulled it out of himself, and he bled like...yeah, I don't like thinking about it. Him unlocking that door and having to beg a bunch of other guys to call him an ambulance in a club toilet. There was blood everywhere, and a lot of people freaked out. It was bad. I shouldn't have let him keep it up there all night. I should have stopped at actually getting it in him in the first place. If I'd pulled it out, we'd have been okay.'

But I might not be here in New York right now.

Was he supposed to feel guilty about that? He didn't know. He wanted to know what Ben felt about it. He didn't know how to ask.

Orson thought of his Christmas present request and thought that if anyone needed a stiff drink and a smoke right now, Ben looked like he did.

'Orson, I'm not gonna judge you or anything, but why did you think I'd get this?'

Okay, nothing for it. 'Because you came out to me.'

Ben looked like he might grab the door handle and bail from his own car. 'What?'

'Come on, you *do* get it. Or if you don't, then just give me a minute before you have the freak-out I was starting to think you could never have. There were seven other guys in that room when Syd lost the bet. I was the only one who'd go through with the forfeit. There was a reason for that. All the times I've shared the whole disaster in a GA meeting, I've never said the one honest thing I could have. I did what I did to Syd because I knew there was a chance I might like it. I thought he might too. I wanted to see.'

'Seriously?'

'Syd's a good-looking otter. I wanted to see his bare arse. I wanted to touch it. I wanted to see his dick too. I wanted to see what putting something up his arse did to him. Okay, yeah, I wanted to see if everyone else in the room saw what happened when he liked it too. I thought he might get a boner, and if he did, I hoped he'd come. I knew there was a risk they'd see me enjoy it too. I didn't care. I was too fucking wasted.'

'So *you're* gay? This is how you're choosing to tell me?'

'I don't know, Benji. I've never done it with a guy. I've never kissed one either. I don't think I enjoyed doing that to Syd. But I think I might have if *he'd* liked it. If I'd taken it out of him and said that was enough instead of letting him walk around like that all night, we might just have had a conversation about it instead. I don't know who I am.'

Ben said nothing.

Just keep talking, Orson thought. *Save this somehow.* 'They say when you rehabilitate, it cracks you open and makes you discover things about yourself, and you get this deeper sense of who you are, but that's bullshit. I've never worked out the part of me that let me do that. This last year, I've not had time to try a relationship with anyone, let alone work out who I really want one with. I don't know anything. That's why I didn't want to share in that room tonight. That's why

I thought you'd get it. You'd been to the same place, just not like I did. A different way, maybe.'

Ben turned the engine off. 'Orson. Hey, come on, look at me.'

The only reason he did was because Ben had touched his face, just lightly, above his right ear.

'You're not a bad person. I *do* get it. You might have found a better way to explore that urge you had to see another guy's bottom, but hey, that's the one you picked. You were probably too messed up to realise there might be the consequences there ended up being. You already paid the price you did for it. But you got into the USA, right? So you didn't get a criminal record, and you didn't have to register as a sex offender. Right?'

It was the one mercy, Orson still knew, that the other seven furs who'd been in that room all independently told the police that Syd had consented to everything, and it had all been his idea in the first place. Yes, Orson encouraged him, but at no point did Syd say stop. He still thought what he had back in the meeting: it must have been Kingsley who talked them all round to telling the truth. Whatever else the guy was, he had the integrity the air force would have wanted. He explained it to Ben.

'But I know that doesn't make it okay,' he said. 'I'm not *that* fucked up.'

'Listen, if we've gotta close the door on this right now and never bring it up again, then fine,' Ben said. 'But here's the easy way to do it. You've already forgotten how I said I sometimes think about bad boys, haven't you?'

Orson's heart kick-started itself. 'Are you fucking hitting on me?'

'No, you big dummy. I'm telling you that nothing about that whole story really shocked me, and it doesn't make me want to kick you out of my house. I might have been a little surprised to begin with, but you were right: I get it. So what good would it do if I thought less of you?'

'Can you just take me back to your place so I can crash? I don't want your bed either; you didn't have to do that. Just give me your sofa cushions and the sleeping bag. Honestly, anything's good as long as it's not a plane seat right now.'

'Okay. You got it.'

Orson had known that a meeting like GA could take a good three hours and then some, but he was still surprised when he got in to find his parents already in bed and asleep, and all of Ben's siblings and cousins in bed at an hour that Ben described as 'uncharacteristically early'. John and Natasha had decided it was a good excuse for an early night. Orson realised he'd been up for what was now around 36 hours.

A lot of his tiredness had been induced by the last hour, since he'd made his real confession. The one before it had made him feel light enough in conscience to sleep. For once, a session of laying things bare had brought him the release it was supposed to.

Ben asked him if he still wanted the sofa cushions, and he said he did. Then he realised his parents hadn't stayed up late enough for him to surrender his phone, and he'd better surrender it anyway. He turned it off and put it on the big surface island in the middle of the kitchen.

'I wouldn't do that,' Ben said. 'One of the younger ones gets up first and finds that? You'll either never see it again or you'll be hunting for it for two hours while you try and get the one who hid it to own up. If you really have to, surrender it to me.'

'Okay, you take it.'

'What's your password?'

'Oh no you don't.'

'What do you think I'm going to do? Go gaming all night on it and drop you in it with Mom and Dad so they take you home first thing in the morning?'

'Nineteen eighty-nine.'

'Atta boy.' Ben pocketed the phone. 'When the Sega Genesis was released.'

'You remember?'

'Well, I wasn't alive back then and neither were you, but I remember you telling me. It was the password for our spaceship, remember?'

Orson had forgotten. He thought about it while they made his 'bed' up together. He decided not to bother with brushing his teeth or showering. He was happy enough to lie there listening to Ben do the same through the bathroom door, the bedside light still on. Only when he was lying down and ready to sleep even with the light

43

still on did Ben touch his shoulder. He hadn't heard him come back into the room.

'Hey.'

'Ummph. What is it?'

'Merry Christmas, OtterSpotter.' Ben was holding something for him. 'I *did* get you something a little more wholesome for tomorrow, but you can have that little extra you asked for now. Don't make too much noise going downstairs. The kids will wake up thinking you're Santa.'

Santa, Orson thought, would probably have eaten his heart out at the same thing. Ben had actually bought him a bottle of Bulleit and a packet of Camels. Good American blends, both of them, packed with enough alcohol and nicotine to turn his brain into a superhighway all night, no matter how tired he was.

'Plenty of ice in the freezer,' Ben said. 'You can find a light in the kitchen next to the gas range.'

'You actually got me these?' he said, still disbelieving that they were even in his hands.

'Well yeah, course I did. You asked for them, didn't you?'

'When did you get time? You've been with me all afternoon and all night. Did you sneak out of the meeting and I just didn't notice?'

'Yeah. That'll do. Or we'll just call it a secret only bears know.'

'Well, geez, thanks, Snowbear. I guess I'll be right back. Don't wait up; I might be a while.'

44

Orson didn't know he could descend stairs so quietly, or get ice out of the freezer without waking anyone else up. He didn't turn too many lights on, relying only on one from the kitchen surface. He found the keys on the hook and let himself quietly out of the back door, finding the long thing for lighting the gas range on his way out.

He went out onto the back porch, put his glass on the frosty picnic bench and cracked the bottle. The amazing smell of fresh liquor drifted into his nose. He fancied it had been so long that he could get a high just from inhaling with his nose over the end of the bottle. He poured, took a gulp, felt the burn in his throat and the warmth spread through his brain, and his life felt so much more like his own again that he almost forgot to open the cigarettes. He shook one loose and held the pack up, taking it out with his mouth. The click-snap of a lighter and he was home. One drag and his lungs filled with smoke, and he was better than home. He was himself.

Oh thank *God,* it felt so good. This was how Christmas was supposed to be. It no longer mattered that he'd been crazy enough to tell Ben that story, because Ben was his best friend all over again. Only a best friend would have realised how much he needed this despite it being bad for him. Bad really *was* good, and it was like Ben had somehow unexpectedly learned it, and Orson was the one person in his life that he wasn't afraid to show that side of himself to. Was Ben really just as trapped in pleasing his parents as Orson

45

suddenly wondered if he himself was? No matter right now; he could ask that tomorrow. What mattered was being alive and here to enjoy this whisky and this smoke, and think that at least he wasn't gaming. He was still on his ticket to being here with Ben.

A sound at the door stopped him, and he knew the shape stepping through even though he'd only met the guy that afternoon. Orson knew there was no time to do the schoolyard thing of putting the cigarette behind his back, which never worked anyway.

Cliff held a hand up to his lips. 'Shhh. It's okay, I got your back. You got a spare? How 'bout a light too?'

Orson gave him both, unable to resist a smile.

'Good,' Cliff said. 'Thanks. Now let's talk. If it'll help break the ice, how d'you think I knew you'd be out here eventually?'

'Ah,' Orson said, after letting a satisfied cloud of smoke out through his nose. 'You got me this. Ben asked you to.'

'Yuh-huh.'

'Of course. He'd never have asked John and Tasha. But good old truckin' Uncle Cliff? That's the ticket.'

'Yeah, not bad, almost. Right ballpark. I'm a cab driver. How d'you think I know the Apple as well as I said I did?'

'Oh. Yeah. Damn, that was slow of me.'

Cliff smiled and dragged on his smoke. 'I know Ben's secret too. He told me a year ago.'

Chapter Three

Orson stared into space. 'Why are you telling me you know?'

'Because he told me he'd told you earlier,' Cliff said. 'I could tell he was wondering if he shoulda. But I think he'll be alright. I think you've got his back. All I wanted to do was make sure. Because my brother and his wife aren't everything they appear to be. I think *you* are though.'

Was it a compliment? Considering that this guy had gone out of his way to buy an extra Christmas present, and for him, and what it was, Orson decided the smart thing to do was take it. 'Yeah, I got it.'

'Okay then,' Cliff said. 'Just in case it goes round in your otter head later, no I'm not suggesting you be his boyfriend. It didn't take much of a Google search to know you stuck something up someone's ass, but boys are boys, right? So it's okay; I think you and him were the friends kind of boys together once. *Months* he's been talking about how he was going to see you again. I know you won't fuck this up.'

'Was that a deliberate choice of words?' Orson said, enjoying another great cloud of smoke along with Cliff, who shrugged as he blew his out. 'Sorry, I should have offered; you want some whisky too?'

'Thanks, but I don't drink,' Cliff said. He leaned against the wall. 'You know why I didn't take Matthew's Gameboy away earlier, no matter what his mother said?'

Orson shrugged this time.

'Because I'm not sure about the whole protection thing your parents are doing. You've been not gaming for a year already. I haven't exactly known you long, but I know one thing: gaming and computers and smart phones aren't going away. So now's the time to learn how to be around it all, because you're gonna have to, and the thing is, I think you already know how to do that. That's why you went to that meeting instead of secretly paying my son a few bucks for an hour on the Nintendo.'

'I've gotta ask,' Orson said. 'How do you know so much about this?'

Cliff chuckled. 'You're out here because your mind's your own, kid. Use it.'

When it dropped into place, Orson knew it wasn't just new time zone plus drink equals dull brain. He felt sharper than he had in months, and still he wouldn't have got it, until a glimmer of it came through after he thought of what got said in the kitchen earlier. He looked at his drink and whispered, 'Shit.'

'Don't do what you're gonna,' Cliff said. 'You don't have to stop doing it or enjoying it just because I'm out here. I've been sober for five years. The smell doesn't bother me, and the worst thing someone can do is deliberately not drink just because I'm in a room. It's up to me. It's not up to anyone else to shield me from the world. So drink up and pour another one. I'll go get myself a decaf and then we can really talk. One for you too?'

'Coffee? Yeah sure, why not?'

Orson topped his whisky up and saved lighting another Camel until Cliff came back out so he could offer him one. The sharp bite of black coffee with no sugar was as welcoming as the burn of the whisky, and for a moment Orson felt like it had caffeine in it after all.

'I want you to ask yourself a question,' Cliff said. 'I don't know your parents, and I'm not going to judge, and that's why I don't want your answer. The question's this: how much of what they're doing to protect you is really for you?'

'To be honest?' Orson said. 'Pretty well most of it.'

'Yeah? Trust a New Yorker to know politicians right from the get-go, kid. I've had enough of them in the back seat. Yeah, make the joke if you wanna; I walked into that one, didn't I? Bottom line though, everything's about how they look, including their family, even when

49

they're doing something simple like taking a cab somewhere.'

'They care about me. It's all for me. Including this trip. You said you didn't want my answer, but there it is anyway. I needed help. They helped. They're still trying. Even if it's eighteen to drink where I come from and I'm twenty. I don't really care about that. It's not like I couldn't find a way to get a drink, is it? They'll drop that sort of crap sooner or later.'

'Okay then,' Cliff said, and Orson could tell he wasn't buying it. 'But if it's going to be later then you can make it sooner. Having an addiction problem doesn't make you wrong about everything, or make it that you can't call somebody else out when it's *their* crappy behaviour affecting you.'

'You're telling me to grow balls,' Orson said. 'I get it. But no offence, not all of us are cab drivers. Not all of us are used to being tough because constantly handling arsehole clients depends on it.' He sipped his drink. 'Sorry, that's probably a total stereotype.'

'No, it ain't,' Cliff said. 'And this is exactly what I mean. You *do* got enough balls to say stuff to people. It's not about growing a pair. It's using what you've got. I like you. Right down to the way you say "arsehole". I think you've got something going for you. This is what you might call Step Thirteen. Once your recovery's going well, own your life. Otherwise somebody else will. Think about all the circles you've sat in. You'll probably think the same thing I often do: lots of the people sitting in them don't own themselves. Or at least they don't yet.'

'Yeah, I've seen that,' Orson said. 'I don't think that's me though. But I know what you're gonna say.'

'Yeah? What am I gonna say?'

'Why didn't I come here on my own.'

'Yeah, okay, I hadn't thought of it, but why not?'

'I couldn't afford it on my own. I work as a waiter, and that's just when I work. I can't even afford to smoke or drink unless it's a gift. So Mum and Dad gave me a holiday. I needed it. I can't support myself. I should be able to by now, but I don't know that kind of self-control unless someone's keeping me in check. I've got stability because of them. They didn't have to keep supporting me. I know loads of other guys who would have been thrown out by now.'

'Okay then,' Cliff said. 'Stability. I got you. We all need it. But independence? I think you know that's different. Good. Something to work for. Come back and see Ben on your own next Christmas.'

Still not buying a word of it, Orson thought. He was too intoxicated on scotch and jetlag combined to care. 'Everybody's talking like I've got any idea who Ben even is now.'

'You've been here less than one night and you've already got something about him nobody else has got. That's not an accident.'

'No, it's not,' Orson said, deciding he'd voice what had crept into his head after the meeting and stayed there. 'He's been waiting for me because he thinks "who's this guy to judge?"'

'Maybe,' Cliff said. 'But we're getting off the point. You. You're not where ambition goes to die. Why not try being a chef? Can you cook? Learned anything from being in a restaurant?'

'Yeah, but they get paid shit too. What could I do that would ever afford me a ticket on my own back here?'

'How about those truckers you mentioned earlier? They're not badly paid. The riskier the cargo, the better the money. I don't know England, but I bet it's the same. Drive a petrol tanker. That's at least a ticket out of London and some time to yourself.'

'I've never driven. I don't even have a licence.'

'Then start. Get one. Even if you don't become a trucker, you've got some wheels of your own to go places, get some other job.'

It wasn't bad advice, Orson thought. He would have fallen asleep to it, but once he got back to Ben's room and put his head on the pillow, intoxicants and jetlag became such a heady mix that he was out in seconds.

* * *

The light behinds the curtains promised a bright and crisp morning. Ben was snoring in long, deep breaths, and Orson remembered what he knew from sleeping at Ben's house years ago: Ben was the walking dead in the morning. Orson closed his eyes and listened to his friend's snoring, and for a moment he was seven years old again, until the snoring stopped and Ben rolled over.

'You awake, Snowbear?'

'Murrrrrgh.'

'You want some ice water chucked over your head?'

'Murrrrrgh.'

'You want...' Orson stopped, thought, and grinned. 'You want me to get into your bed and be your teddy bear?'

'Murrrrrgh.'

A slight tingle went through Orson as he watched his friend lie there, somewhere between waking and sleeping. He thought about putting his hands on top of Ben, of pulling his ear to see if that woke him up, or scratching his head. Orson liked how he was the one who'd been drinking whisky and smoking to hotwire the effect of it, and Ben was the one who seemed hungover despite his sobriety.

'Where's the coffee machine downstairs? I'll make you some.'

'Murrrrrgh.'

'Hopeless bear,' Orson said, getting out of the makeshift bed on the floor, which he realised was covered by a very cosy and smooth duvet. He'd fallen asleep in his pants, and he wasn't sure where his suitcase was. Deciding he didn't want to go down in the same clothes he'd arrived in, he took Ben's dressing gown down from the hook and tried it on. It was like wearing the reaper's baggy hooded cloak, he thought.

He looked at himself in Ben's bathroom mirror and thought he looked more like a circus clown, right down to how the thing was a deep shade of pink.

He looked back at Ben, still comatose. 'Your family don't know you're gay? Fucking *look* at this thing!' Orson decided he was wearing it downstairs.

Natasha, already preparing a huge amount of scrambled eggs and toast, took one look at him and laughed. 'Sorry, but I've just *got* to take a picture of this! BRB!' She came back with the latest iPhone that looked like it had been unboxed that morning, and Orson realised it probably had; it seemed like such a fitting stocking filler for Ben's parents.

'I'm not sure where my suitcase is,' Orson said, after making himself look even more ridiculous for the photo by sitting on a barstool and smirking.

'I'm not sure either,' Natasha said. 'Hold on though, wait right there.' She came back with a present wrapped in Santa and elves paper. 'There you go, Merry Christmas. Open that one now.'

Orson opened a new set of pyjamas. They were nice quality cotton, a brand called Cinch that he'd never heard of. They were the right size for him too, and the familiar otter silhouette was on the species along with mink, pine marten and weasel. Why were otters always at the top? 'Thanks, Mrs Barstow. Oh, sorry, Dr.'

'Oh for God's sake, just called me Tasha.' She rubbed his head. 'It's lovely to see you again, Orson. It really is. Why don't you put those on right now? I'll turn around.'

'You've seen me naked already how many times?'

She turned around. 'You insisted your parents take you to a different doctor because I was your best friend's mom and it was "totally embarrassing".'

Orson put the pyjamas on. 'Oh. Yeah. I did. Dr Foster, the pine marten. She was nice. Mom thought I was being dumb when I wouldn't see you.'

'You weren't being dumb at all,' Tasha said. 'Are you dressed yet?'

'Oh, yeah, sorry.'

'Those look great on you. I wasn't quite sure what else to buy for you. Every guy needs clothes, right? Loungewear for a nice lazy holiday.'

'Can I help you make breakfast? I work in a restaurant, after all.'

'Sure. Now what does that tell you? A guest offers to help me but where are my family? Your parents are still dead to the world, by the way. Why don't you sneak out for a smoke before we make breakfast?'

Orson glowed under his fur. 'How did you know?'

'You left your cigarettes right there on the kitchen top. I'd have thought they were Cliff's, but when he sneaks a pack, he always has Marlboro.'

'Nice advice, Dr Barstow. You coming outside for a break?' He shook one loose and offered Tasha the pack.

'I've never smoked, but I'll bring my coffee out.'

In the daytime, Orson realised just how big and tidily kept their garden was. The garden back home would have been a mess if his parents didn't employ a gardener, and they only did that from time to time. This looked like it was kept with some actual love, like the Barstows did it themselves.

'Oh, this?' Tasha said. 'The kids do this with me at weekends. John sometimes helps if he's not working.'

'Bankers work weekends and doctors don't?'

'I'm a GP,' Tasha said. 'Of course I don't. We call it "family med" over here.'

Orson slowly blew smoke out around his head, liking how it drifted. 'Remember that Christmas when I had to go home sick from school and Mum and Dad were away and you looked after me for them? Ben was sick too, and you set up the beds in the TV room upstairs so we weren't bored.' Orson sniggered. 'You went to the school Christmas party to collect our gifts from Santa for us. They were plastic ray guns that lit up when you put batteries in them. Ben and I already had a set, and the two Santa gave us were broken.'

'I remember,' Tasha said. 'Vividly. Right down to Ben deciding to "renounce Santa".'

'Oh yeah. I just remember "Dear Lord, please can I stop vomiting my guts up tonight?"' *I wonder if he still thinks it worked*, Orson thought. *He never prayed for me to stop, and I managed to right when he did.*

'Orson,' Tasha said. 'Can I tell you something and we keep it between us that I told you this?'

Oh, bloody hell, she knew Ben's secret too? Yeah, who was Ben kidding? The pink dressing gown was probably just the start of the many tells his mother had picked up on. 'Yeah, sure. Our secret. Go on. Spill.'

56

'Gaming addiction isn't a medically recognised thing.' She nodded at his cigarette. 'I'm glad you're addicted to something else, because it means I think deep down you know the difference. Gaming took over your life, it made you someone you decided you no longer wanted to be, and it led you into drinking and a bit of drug use. I'm not judging you at all, but I don't think you're addicted to gaming. I think with awareness you could control it. Tell me something: within the games, did you pay for additional content all the time? Those in-app purchases you get in games?'

'Hardly ever.'

'Did you ever gamble within them? The pay-to-play features?'

'Are you kidding? Half the idea of getting to pro-gamer level was to make money, not waste it trying.'

'That's how games cause problems. Keeping people hooked on the stuff that's more like gambling. But that wasn't you, was it? You were one of the ones who probably could have beaten the house. Do you miss it? Like you feel you've lost a part of who you are?'

'Not really,' Orson said. 'If it was a part of me then I don't think it was a very good part. Taking a year away from it all made me see that.'

'Okay,' Tasha said. 'But you know what I remember? You once wanted to work for Sega. You always did like games, right from the first time Benji gave you Sonic the Hedgehog for your birthday. You remember? Your parents bought you a Dreamcast, and you wanted Sonic

57

Adventure, so Benji brought it to your ninth birthday party.'

'He was there for that? I thought you left when we were both eight.'

'No, it was nine.'

'See? I sometimes think I've damaged my brain, that my memory's shot.'

'Orson, your brain is absolutely fine,' Tasha said firmly. 'One year out with a birthday party memory's just an ordinary thing. You said you wanted to make games one day. Then you said it would mean you'd have to go to Japan, and learning Japanese was impossible, and I told you no, Sega have offices all over the world, and learning Japanese isn't impossible either. You were right back on it then. That was the dream. Did it really die?'

'How could I possibly make it come true now? You saw my parents when Matthew got that Gameboy out. I mention Sega in front of them, it's like I just said a dirty word at the dinner table.'

'I heard Clifford telling you maybe you should be a trucker last night,' Tasha said.

Everything inside Orson froze. 'You heard *all* that conversation?'

'No, just the end of it before you came in. When I came down for a glass of water. You'd be amazed how quiet a bear can be. I like Cliff; he's done well for himself getting sober and doing what he does.' Tasha looked upwards to see the closed windows and came closer to Orson. 'But you could do better than take that advice

58

from him. You've got a good brain. Keep using it. If you still want to think about games, then *keep* thinking about them. If you ever need advice, I'm still your friend's mom, and you probably still don't want me to see you in your underpants, but we can always talk. And remember one more thing.'

'Sure, what?'

'I graduated from medical school. Your mother didn't.' Tasha smiled. 'Would you like some more coffee? Maybe you should take some to Ben. He might be ready by now. Don't worry about his lack of response in the morning. He has Hibernation Syndrome. It's well known with bears. People-bears don't hibernate like animal-bears, but something in the way our brains are wired still makes us think we have to, and in the winter months, it results in a deeper than usual sleep that's harder to come out of. Ben sets his alarm for an hour before he has to get up to help him do it. During that hour, you could say just about anything to him and it wouldn't register.'

Hey Snowbear, did you ever want to show me your dick? Do you ever wish we'd played behind the storage sheds at school and not the climbing frame?

Orson managed not to shudder. That whole space at the top of the climbing frame would have been ruined forever.

What snapped him out of that thought was Ben, down to nothing but his pants, walking into the kitchen looking like he'd downed the entire bottle of scotch last night instead of giving it to Orson.

'Murrrrrrgh! I forgot to tell you, didn't I? I'm a totally proper bear in the morning.' He poured some coffee.

'Benjamin,' Tasha said. 'Look at you!'

'What? He stole my bathrobe.'

'Well, here it is. Put it on, for God's sake.' Tasha put it on him.

Orson didn't resist his laughter. 'Guess it's just as well you didn't have a morning boner, Snowbear.'

Tasha rolled her eyes. 'Boys. Do you still want to help me make breakfast, Orson?'

'Yeah, sure.'

'Hey Orson, you remember the dinner lady at our old school, Mrs Taverner?'

'The old bag? Oh yeah. I swear I saw her across the street about half a year ago in Oxford Street. She looked at me in disgust. Good. I'm glad she's disgusted by me. There's nothing she can send me to the headmaster for now. Remember when I wrote "munter" on the back of her jacket with a Tipp-Ex pen, and she wore it for a whole lunch break?'

'That was you?'

'I never fessed up either. Even when they pinned it on Grant Eastwood. You remember him, the weasel? I faked his handwriting. They both had it coming.'

Ben smiled. 'I just remember "Benjamin, *don't* pull Orson's tail!"'

'Yeeeaow!' Orson squeaked as Ben pulled his tail, reaching out from the stool. '*Damn*, Snowbear. If you *had* a half-decent tail, I'd totally pull yours back.'

60

The rest of the family, who had been stirring for an hour, all started to come in at once. 'What was *that?*' Holly said. 'That noise just now?'

'Benjamin pulled Orson's tail,' Tasha said. 'Supposedly for old times' sake.'

'Yeah,' Ella said. 'I bet he did.'

'Ella,' Tasha said. 'I've told you, we're not having any more of this. Your brother has a girlfriend. That's the end of it.'

Ella gave the eye-roll behind Natasha's back for *Sure it is, Mom.* She gave Orson a look. 'That *was* a pretty awesome noise though, otter-boy. Do it again.'

'It was just a squeak,' Orson said.

'I thought it was cool,' Matthew said, Gameboy recovered from his mother but on pause. 'Any idea how to get the angler key?

'Errrr... I think you've got to get the Pegasus boots first,' Orson said. 'You wanna hear me do that noise again? Okay then.'

All the kids started laughing before he'd even done it. 'That's nothing though; you should have heard what I once did when someone shut my tail in a car door. *That* was a noise.'

'And we've no need to hear it,' Julia Brookfield said, entering dressed like she'd been up for hours and obviously not wanting anyone to know she was the one who'd shut the car door. 'Why are you being so silly? I'm sorry, it's so nice to know my twenty-year-old son has grown up beyond silly noises.'

Yeah, Mum. Okay. Sorry I filled a house with laughter on Christmas Day. By the way, Tasha just reminded me you're not a doctor in a way that made it sound like she'd love to smack you one with a great big designer handbag and leave a great big Gucci logo dent in your forehead. Microbiologists who advise on government policy aren't doctors, Mum. She's got a point. When they marry the mayor of London, I guess it doesn't change that. 'Morning, Mum. Did you sleep well?'

'What's this?' She pointed at the packet of Camels he'd forgotten was tucked into the top of his pyjama pants. 'I thought you packed that up.'

'Yeah, well, one addiction at a time I guess, right? I'm helping Tasha make breakfast. You want some?'

'Did you say he could call you Tasha?'

'Of course I did,' Tasha said. 'Why wouldn't he, anyway?'

'Tell you what,' Orson said, looking at Seth, Kevin, Matthew and then at Ben. 'If you guys can set the breakfast table and do a good job, I'll make that noise for you one more time so you can laugh at it. How about that?'

It was obvious that Tasha and John, when he finally came in, had never seen their family set a table so fast in their lives.

Chapter Four

Orson hadn't cared about presents since his last birthday, when he'd expected his parents to ignore it along with him, then they'd bought him an iron and a board. He should have seen it coming after they'd told him if he could be neat for work then why was he always scruffy the rest of the time? He didn't want anything for Christmas and genuinely hadn't thought the Barstows would get him anything apart from perhaps some chocolate. Ben might have got him something other than last night's spur-of-the-moment gift, but Orson hadn't counted on it.

What surprised him, and got him caught up in not knowing why, was that they'd all bought him books. John and Tasha admitted they'd had to ask Ben for recommendations, but they thought he'd nailed it with a large set of science fiction books, which in Ben's words were the 'pew-pew-pew kind of sci-fi', which prompted Ella to eyeroll and ask why he didn't just say Star Wars.

Because fuck Star Wars. That was the look on Ben's face even if Orson knew he'd never have said it. This stuff was more the kinds of stories they'd once tried to write themselves in class, by someone who actually knew how to do it and did it for adults. Star Wars didn't have real sex in. That's what Ben's look really said, or at least Orson wanted it to.

The other side of Ben's family, more remarkably, had written Orson into their Christmas shopping list too, and Orson knew his face was a picture as soon as he opened their book: a hardback anthology of Sonic the Hedgehog comics.

'You know those are based on a video game, right?' Ella said to the whole room.

'It doesn't matter,' Tasha said. 'They're not *the* game.'

Matthew, holding a wrapped new-Gameboy-shaped box as if he was already playing it, blew hair out of his eyes and said, 'It's one of my old ones, and I don't read it anymore.'

Holly groaned. 'Urrrgh. *Matthew*!'

'It's cool,' Orson said. 'Thanks. Hand-me-downs are better. They have history.'

'There's a strawberry milkshake stain on page twenty-two,' Matthew said, the new box now unwrapped to find the latest style controller for the PS5 he hadn't been allowed to bring.

Ella looked like she just wanted to be out with a boyfriend her parents didn't know about. '"We're closing in five minutes. I'm not allowed to insult guests directly."'

'Megamind!' Orson said, before Ben could. The librarian. Matthew really was a young bear version of Bernard.

'Hey OtterSpotter,' Ella said. 'Catch.'

Another book. Could she out-do her cousin? She certainly looked like she was about to, Orson thought. Both her parents were looking at her smile, and they knew this was trouble.

'You bought Orson an extra present?' Tasha said.

'Well yeah,' Ella said, shrugging. 'Polite to guests and everything, isn't that what you always told me?'

It looked like a video game box, Orson realised. It was a book, but only he could feel that it was. He opened it. He stared. He laughed.

'Well...yeah! Okay, thanks. *Chasing Colton's Tail*. Wonder what the subtext there is.'

Everyone stared at it. Ben almost kept a straight face.

He's read this, Orson thought, and he kept looking at the male sportsman raccoon and the wiry fox on the cover, standing by a sports car. *Fuck, is this actually his secret copy and his sister found it and wrapped it up?*

'Errrm...' Richard Brookfield said. 'Right. Okay. What's it about?'

Orson turned it over and read the blurb. 'It's...about a guy who graduates high school and secretly he wants to go to the senior prom with another guy.'

'Ella, why did you buy this for Orson?' John Barstow said, in a way that promised a private lecture later that started with *'That was NOT an appropriate present to give a guest in front of this family, young lady.'*

Ella Barstow was on it like a pro already. 'I went into Borders and asked some nerd "Rec me a book about someone who turns their life around after figuring out they've been a massive asshat." That's the fox. I read it before wrapping it up.' She sat back against the couch and sipped her great big Starbucks cup of mocha. 'Just to make sure it was appropriate for the person I was giving it to. Relax, there's no gaming in it.'

'That's banned from my school library,' Matthew said, having probably not seen the cover.

'That's because you're in middle school, and it's unsuitable for your puny minor brain that doesn't even have hormones yet,' Ella said.

'That book *is* banned from a number of school libraries,' John said. 'I saw it on the church's list of books to look out for if you see your kids...well, never mind that; Orson's an adult. How did *you* buy this though?'

'No age limit on books, Daddy-oh.'

'Ella,' Tasha said. 'We'll have none of this if *you* want to receive anything.'

'This is a very good book for Orson, actually,' Julia said, in a way Orson found so grossly chipper and firm all at once that he could have strangled her. He put the book on top of his sci-fi books, then, realising John and probably Tasha and definitely his father wished he'd put it underneath them instead, moved it down there.

'Now, where's *our* present to the family? There it is. Richard, would you pass it here please?'

It was a vase. Orson thought it was...what was that word Kingsley had taught him once? A Cornish word that he'd looked up and found it had come to be Royal Navy slang? *Gopping*. Yeah, that vase was fucking gopping. *Minging*. It went with nothing in the Barstows' house, right down to how it had a Versace logo.

'Here Dad, I got you this,' Ben said to John, who was obviously looking at Orson's present from his daughter. John unwrapped the new jacket that Ben had surely tapped into his student loan to afford. It didn't quite seem to make John's thoughts go away, Orson thought. Ben had bought his whole family clothes, it turned out. Not exactly imaginative, but who ever really was with gifts?

'Here, that's for you.' Ben handed Orson another soft clothes package.

'But you already got me...' *Bloody hell, you were about to tell his entire family he bought you booze and fags for Christmas?* 'Thanks.'

'What did he already get you?' John said. 'Benjamin, you didn't actually get him a Switch, did you?'

Orson laughed. 'You were going to get me a Nintendo Switch?'

'It was a joke, Dad,' Ben said, and Orson now knew where Ella had learned such a fabulous eyeroll from. 'I bought him a drink last night on the way home from our meeting, that's all.'

Now Orson's mother looked even less happy. 'But he's...oh, never mind. Go on then, Orson, open your second present.'

What had caught Orson was that he hadn't realised Ben was twenty-one already. He'd been a September baby, one of the oldest kids in their year at school. Orson was June. Neither of his parents had told him off for buying a drink for someone underage. That was fine. As long as Ben hadn't bought that Switch. Or that gay book.

Orson hadn't read fiction since they'd been made to for English at school, but he was looking forward to trying that one. Especially after he opened his present from Ben. Socks, handkerchiefs, and the smoothest-looking underpants he'd ever seen. FCUK.

'Errrrr,' Orson said. 'Well...thanks. I'm...how did you know I needed new pants?' It was a dumb question, and he'd known it before he'd said it, but he had to say it before something worse came out of him.

'Every guy needs pants,' Ben said, shrugging and smirking at once.

'*Look* at those!' Sam said. 'There's a massive hole in the back!'

'Well, here's the thing,' Ella said. 'You see what's sticking out above his otter butt? It's called a great big tail, you moron.'

'Ella, we do *not* use that word in this house,' Tasha said.

'Yeah Ella,' Sam said. 'You moron.'

'Samuel,' John said.

'Otterpants!' Seth said, and then shriek-laughed.

'Seth, calm down and don't be silly,' Cliff said.

'Otterpants,' Matthew repeated, still in Bernard-mode, one hand in a great big bag of Haribo Megamix.

Orson opened the packet and held them up. 'Yeah. Nice. My big rudder butt will like these.'

Cliff looked at them, grinned and said: 'Are you sure that hole's not on the front?'

Now Matthew looked up, perplexed. 'Why would it be...oh. Yeah. Right.'

'Clifford!' Holly said as everyone in the room except Orson's mother either laughed or put their face in their hands and tried not to. Orson's father had to turn away.

'Oh God, this is excruciating!' Holly said. 'I'm so sorry, Orson. You must be so embarrassed.'

'Embarrassed?' Orson said. 'Has anybody got a t-shirt with Best Christmas Ever on it in caps?'

'Right then,' Tasha said, after the room slowly returned to quiet. 'Is everyone ready to be calm and sensible then? Good. Let's get our present for Richard and Julia out.'

Ben sniggered. 'Otterpants!'

'*Benjamin*! Oh for the love of God!' Tasha said, cracking up herself along with the youngsters. Orson's father was facing the room to laugh now. His mother repressed it, but at least she let herself smile. The kind that promised a talk on the plane home, perhaps. That smile always made that promise.

69

I'm going to stay an extra week, Orson promised himself. *Somehow. I'm getting that plane back by myself.*

Reality was still here though, despite everyone laughing at the best present he suddenly thought he'd ever had. He'd never go home alone.

His father, to his credit, waited until all the kids were playing with their new presents, the adults were reading or watching television and John and Tasha were in the kitchen. He waited for Orson to quietly (and unnoticed by Julia) slink out for another cigarette.

'You want one?' Orson said. 'Go on. Mum takes ages in the bathroom.'

'She's not in the bathroom. She had to take a phone call from work. She'll probably be on Zoom after it. I think they're worried about a virus that's in Australia at the moment. I might not be a biologist, but I still think it's nothing. Between you and me, she asked me last night what I'd do if we had to announce we were locking down London.'

His father did this sometimes. A little snippet of what seemed like insider politics, as if Orson worked for a newspaper. 'You're not though, are you?'

'Of course we're not.'

Good, because you'd never cope and neither would London. 'So you want one?'

'No, thanks.' He so obviously did. 'I wish you'd take better care of your health.'

70

'I'm not gaming, am I?' Orson said, knowing that whatever skill his father had as a diplomat, that always seemed to shut him up completely.

'Just don't read that book in front of the Barstows in their living room,' his father said. 'Please? They're not that sort of family. Ella didn't really think you'd like it; she did it as an act of rebellion, and I expect she'll be punished but we'll never know about it.'

'Punished for what? I thought everyone was supposed to love reading and go out of their way to promote it like English teachers.'

'This isn't about reading,' his father said. 'Look, Orson, I don't care if you're gay. I don't even care if Ella somehow actually knew it. Just don't display it. Not here. Please?'

'Dad, for the last time, I'm not gay just because I shoved a Wii-mote up Syd Sheldon's arse. If I actually was gay, that would have been enough to put me off. He stank like he never wiped it in his life. I bet he actually didn't. Mommy and Daddy always did it for him.'

'Don't spend this holiday thinking about how angry you still are at Sydney,' his father said. 'Forget about it all. That's what we came here for. I'm glad you were laughing at jokes about your underwear. Can we just stay doing that? Keep that gay book for private time. If you even want to read it.'

'I do.'

'That's fine. But privately.'

'*Okay*, Dad. Jesus, you're as bad as she is.'

'Don't disrespect your mother. She's been through a lot in the last three years, and we're lucky she still stuck with either of us. I'm not proud of my own behaviour either. We need this holiday together, and we need it to go well. It *is*. Will you help me keep it that way?'

'*Yes*, Dad. It's fine. I want it to be nice too.'

His father leaned in and whispered, 'John still can't cook to save his life. Why don't you go offer to help Tasha like you did this morning? She loved that. You'll be her hero if you do lunch too.'

He went to the kitchen and offered.

'That's very nice of you to offer, Orson,' John said, 'but don't worry. You go enjoy one of those sci-fi books Ben gave you. We've got this.'

'John, really,' Tasha said, 'for once in your life, take a day off from running round after this family. Go help Sam make that model plane; he's started it already. It'll get you away from the noise and the TV just like you always wish you could. Orson can cook with me.'

'Alright, you're the boss in here,' John said. 'God bless otters who work in kitchens today too.'

'God?' Orson said, once John had indeed taken the advice and gone upstairs. 'If God's up there, I don't think I'm exactly in any position to ask for his blessing.'

'Oh don't be silly,' Holly said. 'Of course you are, just like anyone else. Even if you're not sure he is. If you'd like to come to church with us later, just say.'

Orson decided not to rule it out. 'Does Ben go?'

Tasha looked like she was poised to say of course, then she looked around herself and,, finding her whole

72

family occupied, said quietly, 'I don't think Ben really believes, Orson. I think John knows, but it would upset him to actually hear it, so he doesn't ask. Neither do I. My husband is a little too into his faith for his own good sometimes. He'll let our daughter be as cheeky as she is because at least at heart she's a very devout believer. I know you'll find *that* hard to believe, but if she says grace, get ready to be included and even more embarrassed than you were about your underpants.'

'I wasn't embarrassed about my pants. Or that she bought me gay fiction. Even though I'm not.'

Tasha nodded and slid the oven door so it was just open a crack, letting the steam from the vegetables out. 'Between you and me, Orson, are you completely sure you're not? I'm not just talking about the incident with that boy; I know that's got nothing to do with it.'

Orson stopped stirring the gravy. 'Do people think I am because something about me makes them think it? Am I camp? Am I femmy? I really didn't think so.'

'You're you,' Tasha said. 'I didn't think it until my daughter did, but I almost felt like the idea fitted you somehow. But excuse me, it's really none of my business anyway.'

Orson helped her cook for another ten minutes. 'Tasha. Can I still call you Tasha?'

'Of course you can.'

'I don't know,' he said. 'If I am. Just between you and me. I've no real idea who I am. I was a gamer. That's who I was. Now I don't know anything. I don't know who I *want* to be either.'

'It's ripped right out of every cliched movie ever, but be yourself,' she said, putting her hands on his shoulders. 'No matter what. Even if you have to do it secretly for as long as it takes.'

'What does your faith say about this?'

'Faith itself? Nothing. Religion? I don't look to that for advice on these sorts of things. I'm a medical professional. Science does that part of my life.'

What would science do, Orson wondered, if her husband knew the truth about their son? She'd practically told him she did, over and over, and he spent the whole time they were preparing Christmas lunch waiting for her to say it, but she didn't. All Orson did to stop himself asking was remember what she'd said about how he kept Ben's secrets no matter what.

Ella didn't include him in her grace. She included her father having the sense to stay out of the kitchen this year, and it was close enough.

After lunch, she saw him reading the Sonic anthology, or rather pretending to. His parents were both upstairs, because his father was now taking a work conference call too, all apologies given profusely to the Barstow family, and Orson didn't feel like his father had to apologise for anything so long as both his parents got out of the way and he could start reading his gift from Ella, tucked behind the big hardback pages. She smiled and gave him the nod.

On his way to a bathroom break, she caught him in the hallway.

'Don't think I didn't notice. Your cheap-ass parents didn't buy *you* a gift.'

'Yes they did. They bought me the holiday.'

'I knew you'd say that.' She leaned in and whispered, 'I don't gotta tell you it's totally fucking weak, do I?'

He shouldn't have been surprised. He was. 'Don't disrespect my parents. I put them through a lot. I'm lucky they bought a holiday for me. You don't know anything about me. Especially not my real taste in books.'

'You don't *have* real taste in books because you don't *read* books,' she said. 'Yet. You'll get it though. Sooner or later.'

There was no point arguing with a teenager who'd crowned herself queen bitch, Orson thought. Let her keep the crown. She'd been two years old the last time he'd been around her much. He felt like he'd seen who she was now coming all along.

* * *

What Orson got later was the truth from Ben, once Christmas Day was over, with everyone in bed uncharacteristically early after too much alcohol, too much play or just too much excitement, so that the whole thing had become exhausting and sleepiness was catching. Orson had never been in bed by 8PM even as a child, but he welcomed it so he could carry on reading the book.

'I've read it too,' Ben said. 'I dared Ella to give it to you.'

'What? How did you do that so quickly after I told you I wasn't...wait, did *you* always think I was gay?'

'Of course I didn't; how would I have had any clue? I was saving that copy for someone at college. I bought it ages ago. After last night, I chose you instead. I thought it might help you work things out.'

'Oh.'

'Yeah.'

'You let your sister risk a bollocking from your parents for giving me this?'

'It was a dare. She accepted. Not my fault however it goes.'

'That was very naughty, Benjamin.'

'Yeah. Wasn't it.'

'I bet Colton's your hero. Bad boy.'

'Yeah. Kinda. Although actually, I like Obie. You don't get him until book three though. Wait till you get to Charlie though. That's book four. *That's* a dog.'

'You're into dogs?'

'Not really, no, but I was into that one.'

Orson's brain caught up. 'Wait, what? There's a whole series of these I've got to read now?'

'Well, you don't have to. Guess it depends if you find you're into it.'

'Nothing sexy's happened yet. The raccoon's only had his shirt off to get fur-styled for the prom; everybody does that. I've never thought I was into raccoons anyway.'

'Neither am I, but just wait. I'm gonna go brush my teeth. Don't forget yours, will you?'

'Benji, my teeth are fucked already.'

'I bet they're not. Even gamers remember to brush.'

'Wanna bet?'

Ben looked at him, standing over the makeshift bed on the floor. 'Okay, actually yeah, I do. Gonna let me take a look?'

'Sure, why not? It's cheaper than going to the dentist back home in London.'

'Hold on then, let me find my college bag.'

Not just an ordinary student backpack, the bag Ben picked up looked like it had been purpose-made to carry a whole range of dangerous, sharp-looking stuff that inspired racing nerves when put near someone's mouth. All he got from it was a mirror and a pen-light.

'You carry that around at college?'

'Not always. Depends what's on the timetable. Open wide then; let's take a look. Hmm, okay, not bad actually. Nice line; I'm guessing you never needed braces. You're a smoker, but it hasn't stained your teeth too much. No visible cavities. Your wisdom teeth came in straight and...oh yeah, you're an otter and you don't have them; that's your normal teeth. Oops. Rookie mistake. Gums look good, tongue looks good. Mind if I just feel your jawbone?'

'Aaaah!' Orson said, half laughing as Ben took the mirror out of his mouth. 'Seriously, how's your patient supposed to answer that when you're still poking about in there?'

'Close your mouth for a second, otter-boy. Lift your chin up a little. That's good.'

Those fingers, Orson thought, felt so delicate that Ben should have taken up micro-origami. For big bear hands, they could probably wire a circuit board worthy of any computer.

'Open and close for me,' Ben said, feeling the back of Orson's jaw. 'Nice. You have perfect bones and good teeth. You *do* brush.'

'Course I do. I actually did learn to do it with a controller in one hand.'

'What game can you play with just the d-pad or just the buttons?'

'Zelda.'

'Okay,' Ben said. 'Thanks for letting me check your teeth. I'm going to go get ready for bed.'

Those fingers though, Orson thought, waiting until Ben was in the en-suite out of his sight before he brushed his own clumsy hands along his jaw, trying to pretend he could be as delicate as Ben had been.

Ben hadn't shut the bathroom door. Orson saw the light on the carpet from within the bathroom and turned his head. He couldn't see through the door, but it was still open. Ben was brushing his teeth with the tap running. It stopped, and then he was getting undressed. Would he leave the door open and get in the shower before bed? Surely not.

He already showered, Orson thought.

Forget the book working anything out. Orson knew what he wanted to do. He couldn't. He sat there. He knew if he made any sound then Ben would hear it.

No matter. He could put Ben's dental torch and mirror back in that bag, because Ben had left them on the bed.

He got up and put them back in the bag, slowly, quietly, and turned his head.

Ben was pulling his pants on. Orson had missed the best part, but the rest was almost just as worth it. Ben was a spectacularly clean white all over, his fur thick with winter, his athlete's legs muscled from the motions of skating and his back a toned curve of muscle with the vague shape of his spine going up it. The butt under those pants was a smooth half-moon, the black of the pants Ben wore drawing out the shape of it on him.

Orson crept back into his bed and adjusted his own pants. He wasn't sure how long he'd stopped to look. He had a boner. He told himself it was the thrill of just having done something naughtier than gifting a forbidden book. He'd never tell Ben about it.

Ben *had* left the door open though. Was that another gift?

Ben came back into the room naked apart from his pants and walked right by Orson's bed, his backside close to Orson's face.

Orson's breath caught in his throat for a moment. Ben turned around as if nobody else was in the room as usual and got something out from the end of his bed. His pyjamas. He put them on.

'You wear pants under your PJ's?' Orson said.

'Yeah,' Ben said. 'You should try it. It's so much warmer that way.' He turned slightly, then snapped the elastic. 'Bear pants!'

'Oh, don't start again!' Orson said. 'I really wanted to just grab you and give you the hardest noogie of your life for giving me those pants.'

'Did you like them though?' Ben turned around.

Oh, fucking hell, the thick duvet over him was all that was saving him from real embarrassment now. Ben's front wasn't the product of working out but of just being a sporty bear, still with bear fat and his muscles not prominent, but so smooth, and his stomach a slightly protruding curve under his chest. Somehow, Orson kept his hands above the covers. 'Yeah. What kind are *you* wearing?'

'Same as you. They're my favourite. Except my tail's a little stump and not a rudder.' Ben turned around and twitched it, brushed it, and hooked his thumbs in his pants. He smiled at Orson warmly, and Orson realised he was smiling too. *Glowing.*

'You wanna see?'

'Do I wanna see what?' Orson said, staring.

'Me in my underpants,' Ben said.

I've already seen. 'Benji...is this normal to you?' Orson said. 'Okay, sorry, that wasn't what I...errr...'

'I'm a model,' Ben said. 'Makes me some money for college. This sportswear catalogue found me through the team. Took a while before they persuaded me to do pants only, but yeah, this is normal to me. Okay, I'll just admit it, I got those clothes I gave you for free. Special request, but they gave them to me. Sorry, I'm making you uncomfortable. You don't have to see me in my pants. I'm just used to being in front of a bunch of guys who kinda *like* that. They keep it decent during the shoot, but we all know they like an athletic white bear.'

'Yeah. I bet.'

Orson watched Ben put his top on, his hopes fading along with everything else, and decided it was better that way. Better, but he just blew something wonderful. What did he expect? He was always an idiot.

'I'm really sleepy,' Ben said. 'I can sleep with that little light on right there though if you want to keep reading. Night, OtterSpotter.'

'Night, Snowbear.'

Orson didn't want to read. He wanted to keep thinking about everything that had just happened. Maybe he hadn't blown it if he could imagine a different version of it. However much he'd damaged his health with gaming or anything else, he was sure of one thing: there was nothing wrong with downtown, and here he was proving it.

Without saying it, he willed and dared Ben to keep his eyes shut and his head down, then stripped his own pyjamas off, put on a set of the 'otterpants', and put the pyjamas on over them.

'You doing what I think you are?' Ben said.

'Yeah. Totally.'

'How is it?'

'You were totally right. Warm. Snug.'

'Told you.'

I'm also hard in these new pants. Right here. I'm going to 'jerk off'. Why don't the Americans just call it wanking like the rest of us do? That's what I'm doing. I'm having a wank in this bear's bedroom after I secretly looked at him in his pants and then he told me a hot model story which is probably true, and I blew my chance of seeing it all.

It didn't seem right in his friend's room, in this house, but he was having this. He waited until Ben's breathing told him his friend was asleep, then he decided he liked Ben's breathing, air slowly filling that athletic chest and then leaving it. He listened, trying to keep his own quiet, and then giving in and letting out a slow, deep sigh and giving a contented groan. Just softly, but it was good. He did it again, his back against the wall, the light long since off and only a few shadows within shadows making out the shape of the room. He was alone, hard, and going to get what felt like the first real pleasure he'd had in months. Better than last night. He'd finish, then he'd get that whisky out again and go downstairs and have the greatest drink and smoke of his –

'Hey, otter!' Ben was barely talking above a whisper, but he sounded excited.

Orson froze. 'Yeah?'

'Whatcha doing?'

'Nothing.'

'Really?'

'Yeah.'

'So you're not having fun with how you just found out you like pants under your PJ's?'

'I'm just trying to get comfortable.'

'Mmm. Okay.'

'I thought you were tired.'

'Mmm-hmm.'

'So you're going to sleep?'

'Uh-huh.'

Orson waited, still hard, still thinking about Ben as he listened to him breathing until he was convinced he was asleep. He began again, relieved, scratching the itch, and let himself sigh.

The light came back on. Ben stared at him with a great big smirking grin. 'Gotcha! I still rule at pretending to sleep!'

'Errrr...' Orson said, frozen with his right hand down under the duvet and his left gripping a handful of the duvet into a ball. 'Ooookay.'

'You were *totally* having fun with yourself!'

'Errrr...'

'You wanted to do something naughty in my room while I was asleep, huh?'

'Errrr...what's the right answer to this?' *Anything but that, you fuckwit!*

'Shhhh! Quiet!' Ben said, the grin on his face widening. 'You naughty boy! Self-pleasure, huh?' Ben tutted repeatedly, still grinning.

How much of this was an act? Had Ben never even wanked before? Some religious thing? Orson suddenly wouldn't put anything past him.

Fuck it then.

'Okay. Fine. I was wanking off. In your room. In the bed you made for me. You caught me. Happy now?'

Ben pulled himself into a pose, his head on his hand and his elbow on the bed. 'What were you thinking about?'

Just do it. Idiot as usual. 'Bears. Shirtless, fit bears. In their pants.'

'Alright then.' Without getting out of bed, Ben pulled the drawer below him open and dug into the back of it, pulling out a magazine. 'This'll help.'

Orson stared. The magazine actually did have 'Fit, shirtless bears' on the cover.

'You know,' Ben said, 'that bed down there on the floor looks awfully cold. Why don't you come up here? We'll do some reading together.'

For real? This was happening? Orson adjusted his pants, letting his still hard cock relax slightly, tip pinched in the elastic of his pyjama trousers, and got out of his bed.

'You don't have to hide that you have an erection, Orson. It's still obvious, and I like it anyway.' Ben rubbed the bed next to himself.

Orson sat on the edge of Ben's bed, then lay his legs along it, back against the headboard.

'You're going to get awfully cold like that,' Ben said. 'The heating goes off for the night in a minute. Here, let me.' He pulled his covers over Orson, then put his left arm around him. 'How's that?'

'Benji, I...it's...nice. This is nice.'

'Comfy?'

'Yeah. Your mattress is better than that one.' The bed was almost fiercely warm compared to what he'd just left. For a winter species, it was like this much warmth was really a guilty pleasure to Ben, as if he wasn't supposed to be wired to like it. The warmth was all his body heat, and Orson wondered if he'd ever been this warm outside of a sauna, then remembered he'd never been in one of those either.

Ben opened the magazine and turned the pages. 'He's nice. I like him. And him.'

'Yeah. *He* would.'

'He would, wouldn't he?' Ben stroked the top of Orson's head. Orson let him, tilting his head back slightly.

'Shirtless bears, huh?'

'Yeah.'

'Was it because you saw a *real* shirtless bear just now?'

'Yeah.'

'Was it me?'

'You know it was you.'

'Yeah, I do. I know it was me in *here*. What about in the bathroom? Did you take a peek? Even just a small one? You can tell me. Did ya look?'

'Yeah, I looked. I missed seeing your butt. Or anything else.'

'Mmm. Would you like to?'

'Would I like to?'

'Yeah. Would you?'

'Totally. Now?'

'Well, here's the thing.' Ben ruffled Orson's ears. 'We're going to save that for another day.'

Orson felt harder in his pants, a pleasurable urge to come soon washing through him as the skin on his shaft stretched as tight as he knew it could.

Ben turned the page. 'How about him?'

'Woah, yeah. That's a package right there.'

'I know him. His name's Ace.'

Orson laughed through his nostrils. 'That his real name, Snowbear? Or is that what you call him because it sounds like he's part of our crew?'

'That's the name he models by, look. There it is. I think it is a nickname though. But everyone calls him that.'

'So what's his real name?'

'I don't know. I've had sex with him though.'

'Really?'

'Yeah.'

'Who was top?'

'Me. Can you imagine me doing it with him?'

'He looks bigger than you.'

'He's actually smaller. He likes being hugged. He likes tip-play too. Do you?'

'I'm not sure.'

'May I?' Ben slid a hand down Orson's side, close to tickling him, until he reached the elastic of his pyjama bottoms.

'May you what?'

'Put my hand down your pants and feel how hard you are.'

'Yeah, Snowbear. Permission granted.'

'Good boy.' Ben took hold of him, and Orson gasped, almost releasing instantly. A few deep breaths later, he was still holding on as Ben pinched his tip, then stroked, then held Orson's cock in his fist. 'That's a nice erection, otter-boy. You liking this?'

'Yeah...oh *God* yeah!'

'Now, here's rule number one: you can't squeak when you finish. You a squeaker?'

'I...don't know. I've never squeaked when I did it myself, but I've kinda wanted to. I just never wanted anyone to hear the noise. Know what I mean?'

'Your parents? The guy in the room next door at college?'

'Uh-huh.'

'So you're quiet and private. Cool. Good practice for being in bed in a house full of good Christian bears when you're doing naughty, curious gay stuff with your old friend.' Ben stroked Orson's head with his free hand. Orson sighed deeply, harder than he'd thought he could possibly get, a feeling of impending relief welling up inside him that he refused to give in to too quickly. He just wanted Ben to keep talking like this.

Don't ruin it...don't ruin it...not yet...not YET...

'We need to be quiet or we're going to get found by the rest of the crew in this place, and then it's court-martial for both of us. So shhh! Quiet! Consider that an order. You wouldn't disobey my orders, would you?'

Orson breathed hard. 'No, Captain. Not you.'

'Oh, enough with the captain. Tonight, you can call me Benji. I'll use your name too. How about that?'

'Yeah.' He was trying not to breathe too noisily and hoping he wasn't failing. If he was, maybe Ben would put a hand over his mouth. Or they'd get right under the covers to muffle it. That much warmth...the idea of it made his heart thud so hard, the feeling of it went through his entire body as he heard it in his head.

'Squirt for me, Orson. Squirt hard.'

'Under your fresh covers?' He only just said it in one breath.

'In your pants. You put them on just like I said. Good boy. Squirt them full like I've wanted you to all day.'

Orson came hard, air rushing in and out of him, managing not to squeak or yell or groan in relief. He hoped it was quiet enough. He knew it probably wasn't. Fear of the door opening kept him staring at it, then up at the ceiling after it mercifully stayed closed, and all the while Ben was stroking his head and telling him, 'Shhhhshshsh! Nice and quiet. Keep going. That's it...that's it!'

His eyes closed, the tension left Orson's body, and he realised how floppy he was with relaxation, for the first time in as long as he could remember. Jerking off never got him this. It was always supposed to, but he couldn't reach it anymore. Until now. He wished his pants were wet with the pleasure so he could feel it against his crotch, but Ben had caught everything, his hand still tight, with Orson's tip nestled in the centre of his palm.

'Woah,' Orson said, his breathing now slowed. 'You just totally made me come.'

'Yeah, I did. You kept it quiet. Nice one, Otterpants. I didn't think you would.'

'I'm *called* Otterpants now? How many names do you need for me? And did you totally just use our childhood game and age it up and make it hot?'

'Yeah, I did.'

'How long have you been planning that for?'

'I haven't. I just thought of trying it now. Along with you, and how you totally do like shirtless bears. Was it me that set that off?'

'Of course it was, and you know it. You knew exactly what you were doing.'

'Yeah, okay, I did. So you took a peek while I was in the bathroom, huh? You into that?'

'Voyeurism? No way, it's creepy, and I don't like it at all. I don't know why I did that. Sorry. It just came over me.'

'Don't be sorry. I left the door open so you could do it if you wanted to. I *wanted* you to see me. I think you knew it. That's why you did it.'

Orson believed it. The relief was welcome. 'Yeah. Now we've got some clearing up to do. I can smell myself. Come stinks.'

'Uh-huh.' Ben grinned. 'Let me clean my hand off quickly, then you can take a shower. You won't wake the family up with it; it's quiet. They'll be fine.'

Orson took the hottest shower of his life, already feeling cold from getting out from under the covers.

What if the bedroom door had opened? After everything that he'd heard from Ben's family after unwrapping that book this morning, what the fuck *would* have happened if they'd just gotten caught?

Exactly the point. That was Ben's thing – thrill seeking. Bad boys and thrill seeking. He had the former in the house, in his room, and he went after the other, and all behind this polite, religious, studious bear act. Who maybe secretly was as un-religious as he was un-straight.

Who am I to judge someone for not wanting to let their family down? Orson thought. Ella was right. The buying of the holiday didn't feel like the gift it was supposed to, and even after what he'd just experienced, Orson couldn't say why not.

He went back into the room with a towel around him and put his pyjamas on before taking it off completely.

'Don't forget to dry your head,' Ben said, and then proceeded to do it for him. 'You'll get the pillow soaked.'

The fingers again. Harder on his head this time, but still Ben's touch.

'Hey Snowbear,' he said. 'You *are* hot with your shirt off.'

'Thanks.'

'So can I *take* it off you?'

'Mmm. Yeah, why not? Take it off me.'

Orson gently lifted it up, and Ben put his arms up and let him slide it off.

'Woah, Benji...wow. Just totally wow.'

'Touch me, Orson. Hug me.'

Orson embraced him and felt his warmth glow through the soft white fur. He nuzzled his head behind Ben's, closed his eyes, and sighed. When they came apart, Ben took hold of his head. 'Ever kissed a guy?'

Orson shook his head.

'Want to?'

Orson nodded. 'I'm an awful kisser.'

'Then let me show you, because I'm good.' Ben proved it. The stood there, lips together and tongues touching gently for a while, Orson holding on to the side of Ben's stomach, Ben's hands in the small of his back.

'Wanna sleep with me?' Ben said.

'Isn't that a little too dangerous?'

Ben lightly slapped him on the bottom and went over and put the chair from his desk under the door handle. 'We won't be bothered. But just in case.'

'How are you so sure?'

'They'd never think it could happen.'

'Apart from your mum. I think she might know.'

'I think she might too, sometimes. But she'll still never really *know*. She doesn't want to.' He picked up his shirt.

'Actually, you think you could leave it off?'

Ben smiled. 'I'd love to. But I think I'd get too cold.'

'Benji, how the fuck can you be cold? You're practically a natural source of geothermal heat in a bear's body. Seriously, your bed was a sauna just now, and it wasn't just because you were making me do hot stuff.'

'Am I? Okay, for your comfort, shirtless bear. Or I can just do underpants too if I'm too warm for you.' He took them off. 'Hey,' he said, his smile now a grin. 'How about you? How about we *both* just do designer pants?'

'Errrr...can I not?'

'Oh. Okay. Not for you? That's cool. Just me then.'

'Actually, maybe that bed you made down there for me's better. I seriously think I'll get too hot in there with you. Then we'll have to wash everything because I've sweated all night and made your bed stink, and then what's the story when you're shoving it all into the machine? Forget what you think about aquatic species being clean all the time. Otters can be real stink-bags. You should have smelled my room at uni.'

'Relax, it's cool. You're not ready for sleeping with me. It's fine.'

'Benji, I've never had sex with a guy. Real sex, like gay guys are meant to. You really have, right? With Ace. With other people.'

'Don't worry about it.' Ben touched his face. 'One step at a time. You like shirtless bears, and one just made you release. It was fun. Work the rest out slowly.'

'Okay.'

Slowly. We've got two weeks until this holiday's over. That's why he can't be my boyfriend no matter what we end up doing. I don't *know what I'm doing anyway. That's why we're getting into bed, putting our heads down, and doing it after he gave me a spectacular orgasm and I've given him nothing. I didn't even ask him if he was hard, if he wanted me to return the favour. How can I be around this unshakably nice bear and still be getting it all so wrong and have him like me? I should be sleeping with him right now. Instead, I had to have 'issues'.*

Idiot. Stupid piece of gaming-addicted shit. Never developed social skills because all you wanted to do was dissolve your already puny brain.

'I'm going downstairs,' Orson said. 'I want a drink.'

Ben was asleep for real this time, as though Orson had made it happen.

Chapter Five

With Ben in hibernation-whatever-it-was sleep again the next morning, Orson found himself learning how to make the perfect cup of mocha with Ella as his teacher. He'd never had ham and gravy with sourdough toast for breakfast either, until he saw her having it and wanted it too.

The cousins had found a Sky channel playing the Kung-fu Panda movies back-to-back and had started the first one, also calling a full-on pyjama party that was likely to last all day, a large duvet covering them all. Ella went and got her own, along with a second cup of mocha for both of them, which Orson wouldn't have asked for but felt strangely glad to receive, along with her next invitation:

'You coming under here, then?'

'Huh?'

'Join *in,* otter-butt.' She put her duvet over him. 'Not embarrassed, are you? Not wondering what Mom and Dad will think when they see us like this?' She smirked. 'Come on, what are *you* going to do to me?'

Orson didn't move, but inside his senses were all wriggling like snakes. He disguised everything with an eyeroll and a sigh and mouthed, 'I'm not gay!' at Ben's sister.

'What's that got to do with anything? I meant you're a decent guy. Who never had a sister. You're an only child, right?'

What did *that* have to do with anything? 'Yeah.'

'Well, this is kinda what having a sister is. Seeing as my brother's not up yet and I think at heart you're basically a big kid, why don't we just go with it, huh? Oh yeah, and I put you in my prayers last night. Actually, I kinda said an extra one for you.'

Oh brother. Okay, just be polite. 'What did you want God to do for me exactly?'

Ella shrugged. 'Some stuff about family. Like maybe yours could ease up and get off your back a little bit.'

Orson shook his head and smiled. 'Things aren't as bad as you think. Where are my mum and dad anyway? You've seen what Mum's like already; I can't wait to see what *she* says about me being under a duvet with her friends' teenage daughter.'

'Me neither, but I think we're gonna be waiting a while. Your parents went for a walk about an hour before you got up.'

'Right.'

Here it went then. When his parents went for walks together, it was because there were problems. When either of them went for one alone, it was usually to work out what to say during an impending together-walk.

They'd probably walk around 'the burbs' and still not figure anything out, so they'd get on a bus and then the subway, and then Central Park could play host to the Brookfield marriage drama, where Julia dragged up Richard's affairs and talked like she'd forgiven him but she was still unsure of why she was still with him, or she'd suspect a new one but not say it, trying to get it out of him by pretending there was some other issue, laying a guilt trap and waiting for him to confess. Orson never knew what was true when it came to his parents' marriage apart from two things: that they should have separated at least two years ago, and that they stayed together because they thought he needed them to.

Maybe this would be the walk where they realised that it was time to call it quits. A holiday from everything else could end in a much longer one from each other, and that would be fine. It might even be amicable. It would mean Orson not having to tell them the truth, and that would be the best part of it all. If he told them, then of course he'd be wrong. If they got to it on their own, he needn't be anything.

The TV ads were over. Tai-lung the snep was using his tail to pick a lock with a feather, the first stage in the most staggeringly impossible prison break ever committed to film. That, Orson thought, was what made it so wonderful.

Ben's hibernation soon ended with something not far from the same prison break urgency. He wasn't wearing the pink dressing gown because he was already dressed in hockey gear, save for the skates he was carrying. 'Morning, hi. Ella, have you seen my jacket?'

Ella shrugged. 'I dunno. Where did you leave it?'

'Your sports one?' Natasha came in. 'It's by the back door, where you always leave it. Where are you going? You don't have practice today; it's not on the calendar.'

'They called an extra one. I'm gonna be late already; I woke up too late to catch the text message. Can I have the car, please?'

'I'm going to need it in an hour. Don't worry, I'll drive you. Give me five minutes to get dressed.'

'Don't worry,' Ben said. 'I'll take the bus; I can make up some excuse. Or I'll just tell them I slept in and it's way late to be calling an extra session. Bye, love you!' He kissed his mother on the cheek and was out of the door. Then he barged back in and up the stairs, realising he had his skates but not his bag with everything else in it.

'That's strange,' Natasha said. 'That never happens.' She looked at the calendar, despite the explanation for the blank square that she found on 26th of December. Orson could just about make it out from where he was sitting. 'Everyone having fun?'

'Hey, Aunt Tasha, can we have some cake?' Seth said. 'Pleeeeease?'

'For breakfast?' Natasha said. 'Oh, I suppose so. It is Christmas. But nobody make themselves sick, okay? In fact, I'll cut you a piece each.'

She cut Orson one even though he hadn't asked. Looking at it and not being able to quite stomach it, it made him wonder if adults had more chance of being sick from rich food in the morning than kids did. He remembered how badly he once ate at breakfast every Saturday and Sunday morning in front of the television, up early enough to choose whatever he wanted. He sipped his second mocha, still hot, wondering why resisting the urge to get up and go outside for a cigarette seemed easier this morning. He wasn't sure he really wanted one.

'Hey Mom,' Ella said. 'Can we adopt Orson and give him a new family?'

Orson almost sprayed the room with coffee.

'Ella Barstow, what a thing to say!' Natasha looked horrified and stepped around to the side of the couch to put a hand on Orson's shoulder. 'I'm so sorry,' she said to him. 'Young lady, that was a completely...'

Orson looked at her as she tailed off. She was looking at the kids, who looked like they were about to run and hide. One of them had paused the TV, as if maybe not wanting to run so much as watch a more explosive show of Ella getting her arse kicked.

'No,' Natasha said. 'Let's not do this. I'm sorry. I *do* understand. You meant well. Even if you did totally embarrass our guest.'

'Well gee, Mom, I only meant to say I thought he was totally cool, like cool enough to be family. I wasn't dunking on *his* family or anything. I thought he'd get it, as I kind of joked about acting like his sister earlier.'

'I got it,' Orson said. 'It's okay, I just nearly showered your front room in coffee because...I dunno.'

Because I'm thinking of Ben's hot, white furry body and everything we did last night, and if you adopted me, what would the play be then? Giving his butt-virgin step-brother a nice kind initiation where big brother bear was the absolute boss despite the gentleness of those fingers?

Oh great. I can't move from this spot for at least ten minutes now, and if his sister pulls the duvet off me, I'm dead, and if I put a hand down there to adjust for comfort or hide it, I WON'T be hiding it...

'Orson, would you like to go and see Ben practice with his team? They don't mind family sitting in the stand to watch; I'm sure he would have invited you if he hadn't been in such a hurry. This whole holiday's supposed to be about him spending time with you.'

Oh yeah. Isn't it just. 'Errr...thanks, but...I kinda think he...ice hockey's not exactly my thing. And I'm not used to the cold. New York winter. Brrr! It's nice and warm under here, and I really like Kung-fu Panda. Maybe we can go and pick Ben up later and he can show me the best place to get a sandwich or something. I'll buy.' *You dumbshit, there isn't a practice. Whatever he's doing, you're going to blow the lid on it. You're shit-arse broke too.* 'Actually, I'll maybe take the bus too and go surprise him. If he wants me to. I'll text him.'

'Oh, yeah, *that's* going to be a surprise then,' Ella said.

'Okay, let's not worry for now then,' Natasha said.

At least he'd figured out how to save himself – his phone was in his pyjama pocket, and getting it provided a good enough amount of wriggling and awkwardness to quickly brush a hand over his dick to put it flat against his stomach, tip pointing at his belly button and held down by the elastic.

'*Your mum wants to pick you up later. If there's not really a practice, I'll let you know when to be at the rink. Gonna tell me what you're up to?*' After he'd texted it, he saw Ella holding up a QR code, and he knew what the game was: silent sister, texting so the kids couldn't hear anything. Orson added her WhatsApp.

'*There IS a practice, except it's not really a practice,*' she texted, with a link to the team's Facebook page. It was a party, where the team got together and played a few short, friendly games with anyone else who wanted to join in, picking two teams so each had a few members of the college team on it. Ben, Orson decided, had simply forgotten about it.

'*So why didn't he invite you?*' Ella texted after a few minutes of Orson watching the film and trying to pretend he wasn't asking the same question.

'*I can't skate, and I told him ice hockey isn't really my thing, I guess that's it.*'

'*Weird. All he went on about before you came was how much he wanted to take you to a rink to meet the team. He probably wanted to show off to you too. He said he wants to teach you skating if you'd never done it.*'

'*He was in a rush this morning. He probably thought I'd be happier not rushing with him when he saw us like this.*'

100

'As long as you're happy he's not been a jerk.'

Orson put his phone down. 'I'm happy.'

'Okay.'

They reached the bridge battle in the film before Orson got up to go to the bathroom and on the way back gave in to what he'd been drawn to since Natasha had looked at it. He went into the kitchen and looked at the Barstows' calendar on the fridge. It was larger than most of the ones you bought in the shops, with plenty of room on each day for five family members to put their important events. Each of them did it themselves, five sets of handwriting. In Natasha's there were also entries for the cousins. Orson knew he had been looking at it for too long to pass this off as pondering another cup of coffee. He went back to Ella, whose head hadn't turned, but he could tell she knew what he was doing.

Yeah. Families do this.

His parents had never put a calendar on the fridge. From his first day of secondary school, his parents had 'encouraged him to be responsible for organising himself', and that was it. From getting up, getting his own breakfast and catching the bus on time, getting his homework done, attending the only club he went to (computing), Orson's diary was in his head, and somehow he managed it. His parents only commented on it when his reports spoke of disorganisation with the subjects he couldn't be bothered with, which was half of them.

He wondered what else Ella had been thinking of when she'd not so much asked him as reminded him that he was an only child. A bit like Po the kung-fu panda, Orson thought. Whose 'dad' was a goose. It made him smile. If you accepted it, maybe your parents really could be anyone.

'Maybe I should run away to China and become a kung-fu otter,' he said as the moment everyone always spent the first film waiting for happened. 'Skidooosh!'

'Yeaaaaah, sure,' Matthew said. 'They should have done that film as Kung-fu Otter so he could do it in his otterpants of destiny.'

'Hey, douche-canoe,' Ella said. 'The pants jokes are yesterday already. We're making jokes about Orson's tail today. Got your tail!'

'Oi!' Orson laughed as she grabbed it. 'That's half my balance!'

'Yeah, that's why you're keeping your butt sat there and watching Two with us. Seriously though, *this* would be your kung-fu secret. If you spun round fast and smacked someone's ass with this thing, they wouldn't sit down for a month without using a rubber ring.'

Of all the things to get a response out of Matthew, Orson thought, it was *that* comment that made his eyes wide with awe?

'Yeeeeeow!' he said. The look that went with it, Orson thought, was either the wish that he could draw, or the actual plan to later, when kung-fu otter was going to be born on paper out of the most randomly arresting thought this kid had ever had: a rudder-butt tail as a weapon.

This was what families were for. Not writing on calendars. That was just everything that kept life moving to get to moments like this.

His mother came in halfway through Two, got halfway up the stairs with the kind of walk that was sure to end with a door slamming, regardless of whose house this was, and then she descended them again slowly. By the time she stood in the doorway to look at Orson under the duvet with Ella, she looked composed enough that even if it mattered to her, she wasn't going to let it.

'I have to take a conference call for work,' she said. 'I'm sorry, I'm not going to be around today. If you can drag yourself away from that for five minutes and turn the news on, that will explain everything. We might have to go back to England tonight.' She turned and went upstairs.

'Don't change the channel,' Ella said, as if anyone in the room besides her would have done it. She pulled up the news on her phone.

A moment later, she changed to the TV.

A virus that had broken out in the orient four weeks ago, thought to be contained, had arrived in the UK. Although not fatal in all cases, it was said to be more contagious than previously thought, and the containment protocols hadn't stopped the spread. Was it time for the UK to shut its borders? Probably not, so said Sydney Sheldon's father Patrick, ever the methodical figure, dressed in his usual suit and addressing every news channel, most likely preparing for a full address to the nation later, if it came to that.

He urged calm. He talked about how prepared the health service had been for this moment since before this thing even hit the news. A team of scientists, doctors and the chief physician would be holding a conference later to present the known facts about this illness and dispel the myths that were already circulating. People shouldn't speculate.

'What does your mom do again?' Ella said.

Orson wondered if the news had spooked her a little. 'Virologist.'

'I thought she was a doctor like Aunt Tasha,' Seth said.

'She went to medical school with her,' Orson said. 'To start with. She changed to biomedical science. She decided being a doctor wasn't what she wanted after all.' *Or maybe,* Orson thought, *she dropped out because it was medical school that made her realise that she just doesn't like people that much. Why care for a bunch of people you don't care about when there are other ways of showing off how smart you are?*

Natasha, Orson had always thought, had what his mother didn't have with other people.

'And your dad's the mayor, right?' Seth said.

'Of London, yeah.'

'You're not going home tonight,' Ella texted.

'Can we have Po back yet?' Matthew said.

Ella changed the channel back and sat back like she was thinking hard.

'I might not have any choice,' Orson replied.

'You do if they don't tell everybody abroad to get back before they can lock down. I don't think they'll do it. If your parents go, you can stay. We WANT you to stay. Especially Ben.'

'You try telling my mother that. You saw how she is. She wouldn't even let me have a drink.'

'Tell her yourself. Ben's been looking forward to this time with you for probably years. So now's your chance not to be a whiny fucking pussy. Don't get up and go sulk with me for saying it. I LIKE you, so stand up for yourself.'

'Okay,' Orson said, determined to stay focused on how she'd said she liked him and ignore the rest. He told himself not to ruin this morning for the kids, let alone give anyone a hint that he feared everything collapsing around him again. He hadn't even had a chance to figure last night out, with or without Ben to talk to about it. Whether he wanted it again or not he didn't know, just that he wasn't having his chance at getting somewhere with his feelings snatched away like this.

If Ella was right to tell him what she had, he knew he probably wouldn't act on it. He'd spend the whole journey home feeling like crying about how unfair everything seemed, but tears wouldn't come. It would just be the same numbness he thought he'd escaped from months ago. He'd shifted to all this in a matter of minutes, and this morning's fun was over.

Maybe it doesn't have to be.

He hated to admit it, but he was thinking of Patrick Sheldon's advice about calm and deciding it was good. This could just be nothing.

The front door opened and stayed open for a moment, a chill coming down the corridor that made the room slightly less cosy. After it thankfully closed again, cutting off the draft, his father came in, slower than his mother had.

'Have you seen the news this morning?' he said.

'Yeah, we saw it,' Orson said.

'Don't worry about this,' Richard Brookfield said. 'It's not going to stop our holiday.' Orson could tell his father didn't believe his own words. He'd become practiced at spotting these moments in his father's news appearances, and here was News-Dad in the room with him yet again. 'Your mother and I were having a difficult conversation at the time this landed; I think it put her in the wrong frame of mind to deal with this. Is John in? I need to ask if I can use his study for a couple of hours, maybe three. Just don't worry. Keep having fun.'

That last part, Orson knew, really didn't sound like his father, and it was like everyone who wasn't used to being around him knew it too.

They got halfway through Kung-Fu Panda 3. That was when Orson heard his parents' raised voices and a door banging. He never set a watch for these impending moments and didn't look at his phone for the time now; he just knew it had been an hour from the movie durations. That and it was *always* about an hour from one of them coming in like that. He pretended to go to the bathroom to go upstairs.

They couldn't even keep it out of someone else's house. They couldn't have the holiday they actually needed: one from their inability to go a fortnight without a day like this, and the equal inability to see it as a sign that carrying on together was pointless.

They do it for me, he thought again.

Natasha came onto the landing, listening for a moment the same way Orson was, unable to make out words as the voices had dropped but knowing what this was. The unmistakable lull in the storm before the winds picked back up again and the waves rose.

'I'm sorry,' Orson said, quietly.

'Don't be,' Natasha said, putting her hands on his shoulders. 'It's not your fault. Why don't we go to the rink and watch Ben's practice?'

'It's not a practice; it's a party he forgot about.'

'Oh,' she said. 'And he didn't invite you to go along? Well, that does it. Come on, let's find you some clothes and your coat.'

'I can't skate,' Orson said, certain he was going to end up wearing a pair anyway with Ben's whole team laughing while he tried to learn. Hearing his parents argue might just be better, because at least that was familiar ground.

'Neither can I,' Natasha said. 'But I know how to party. The rink has a bar and at least two good burger restaurants. I'm going to be driving, so how about we order one coke with a double rum and the other without and then switch who's having which when nobody's looking?'

Orson could already feel the welcome glow inside him. His tail lifted from the floor, where he didn't realise it had been.

Chapter Six

Natasha liked a slice of lime in her rum and coke, the same way Orson did. He hoped she wouldn't talk about his parents, and surprisingly she didn't. Her face carried all the questions she was resisting asking: was it always like this? How did he cope? Was he thinking of trying to move out and get away from it? As long as she didn't ask any of it like she was feeling sorry for him, Orson didn't care what else they talked about.

'Maybe I should try skating. Maybe I'll ask Ben to teach me. Can you hire a pair of skates here? When in New York with an athletic polar bear, right?'

'Absolutely,' Natasha said. 'I'll message him. He still hasn't seen us.'

Orson could see him from their window seat in the bar. Every time one of his team got the puck, it was like they were fighting to keep it and fighting their way forward all at once. When Ben got it, he was in charge. Orson couldn't have described the difference; he just felt it. Before Ben shot it at the keeper, there was just that little moment when he looked to see if his shot would have a chance. Everyone else seemed to waste that moment and just shoot, always without scoring. Ben had buried two before the game was up.

Ben saw them then. After the surprise, he waved like he'd been expecting them after all. The quick gathering of the team was him excusing himself from the next friendly. He changed out of his skates and came over carrying them. Orson knew it was because they looked and *were* too expensive to just put on a chair and walk away from. Ben looked like he should have been out of breath, but despite the sweat, he breathed and walked like nothing was taxing his body at all.

'I'm really sorry,' he said. 'I didn't think you'd want to come. Sit around watching this in a cold you're not used to when you could be watching TV under a duvet? I wish I could have just done that with you. I messed up; I forgot about this.'

'It's fine, Benjamin, don't worry,' Natasha said. 'Orson *was* going to stay with the kids, but there was a little tension with his parents going on, and I persuaded him to come here after all.'

'Tension?'

'They were arguing about something, and there's some news about a virus in London that might mean a lockdown. They might start telling people from England to come back from their holidays. Even if they don't, I might have to go back tonight.'

'What?' Ben said, sitting down. 'You only just got here!'

'It's okay,' Natasha said. 'The recall's not likely to happen. This is all hype in the news. Orson, just tell me one thing: if your parents tell you you're going back with them, do you want me to help you say no?'

Orson wriggled on his seat. 'Errr...'

'Because I can. I know how difficult it can be standing up to a parent, even when you're not a child anymore. I know it's not as simple as saying "grow a pair". Especially not when I know who your parents are. Always have been. I don't know why, but I expected some sort of change. It's only taken two days, and I know neither of them really have. Not much. But you have. You're grown up. So what do *you* want?'

'The night we got here, I wanted...' *to run away into New York and hide forever and never go home again? She doesn't need to hear that.* 'Ah, forget it. What I want today? I want...' He looked at Ben, wanting him to take his hand but knowing he wouldn't, and loving this moment all the more for how well Ben hid any thought of it, if he even had it.

What the hell *did* Ben want, exactly? Besides, Orson thought, to run from the house this morning as though he were really running from last night. That, he suddenly thought, was why Ben had forgotten the party. He'd gone to sleep with his head full of how he'd seduced an old friend after two days of barely getting to know him again and woken up with God only knew what. God was probably on Ben's mind too.

'I want to have my holiday,' Orson said, not sure how long he'd stayed silent for.

111

'Then you're going to,' Natasha said. 'Here's what I think's the easiest way to make sure of it: stay here with Ben for the rest of the afternoon. Let things calm down with your parents, then if they announce they're having to leave when you get back, it will be easier to tell them you'll come home when you planned to, because I've insisted you stay.' She got her phone out. 'Have lunch here. Have the skating lesson.' She looked at Ben. 'I'll send you some money right now.'

'I've got money, Mom.'

'Don't be silly,' she said. 'Save your money for when the new term starts; you're going to need it.'

She really doesn't know, Orson thought, and smiled. Ben probably got paid better for his modelling than most students got for washing dishes. However smart she was, it put a smile on his face to think that Natasha probably believed Ben *did* wash dishes. Ben was plenty smart enough to really have that job on the side as the perfect cover.

If Ben really *did* do that modelling, he realised, and felt even more certain he'd been more naïve than ever last night. In those pictures, where was Ben? It had all been about Ace. Did Ben even really know him?

'I'll go home and keep an eye on things,' Natasha said. 'I'll text.'

Orson put a hand in his phone pocket and found it empty. 'I left my phone in Ben's room.'

Natasha thought for a moment. 'Good. In fact, if Ben ignores his because you're having too much fun, then your parents will have to come down here if they want to leave and take you back with them. I don't expect they'll bother with that, will they? You could always go shopping too. So you're not here when they turn up.'

With Natasha gone, Orson was stuck not knowing what to say, realising he'd been drawing all his energy from her, and all the questions he wanted to ask Ben but couldn't in a public place (or maybe at all) came to him at once.

Ben nodded at Orson's glass. 'Scotch?'

'What? No way! If there's a place in hell reserved for people who waste good scotch, then it becomes a throne as soon as they do it using coke. *Rum,* Snowbear. Your mum bought it for me.' He sank the rest of it. 'Will you get me another one?'

'Sure, but if you want to try skating then perhaps we'd better do it afterwards. But if you're thirsty, you've got to try the milkshake bar over there. You've not been to the USA until you've seen how we do milkshakes. Is it still strawberry for you? They use fresh ones here. Wanna try mixing some M&M's in and putting a chocolate flake on the top?'

'Yeah, sure. Get me that.'

'Be right back.'

When Ben came back, the shake he had looked like vanilla with crunchy nut cornflakes mixed in and topped with revels. He'd gotten them both a huge raisin and sultana cookie each to go with it.

'You really do want to do today like it's our last, don't you?' Orson said.

'I don't think it will be,' Ben said. 'I looked at the news while I was waiting. The virus story sounds like it got over-hyped too quickly. Your friend's dad's doing a pretty good job of telling people not to panic right now.'

'Syd's not my friend, Benji. Syd was a right cunt about everything.'

Ben smiled. 'That's practically a term of endearment these days, where you come from.'

'It really isn't. You don't deny you gave consent for something just because things didn't turn out how you thought they would. You don't make your friends feel like they committed a crime, and a crime like that? I'm lucky people back home didn't believe it. They know I'm not that guy, but I still feel like I've got no friends anyway. That's what Syd did to me. I took responsibility for what I did, and then he said it was *all* my fault? Fuck him, and all the cunty newspapers who made him a victim too. Why are we talking about this anyway?'

'If he told you he realised he got it wrong and wanted to apologise, would you give him a chance?'

Orson hadn't thought about it. 'I don't know. Should I?'

'Yes. "For if you forgive your brother, so your heavenly father shall forgive you."'

Orson sighed. 'Benji, do you even believe in God, really?'

'Yes. Don't you?'

Oh boy. Ben looked as serious as he had the night he'd heard Orson's story in the car. The truth was bound to go into a conversation about whether he thought Orson would go to hell at the end of his life.

'I'm kidding. I don't mind that you don't.'

Orson rolled his eyes, the relief not coming to him so much as the dread that this was Ben's main kind of humour now. He hated it when people pretended to be serious. Syd's father was one of those guys, and being PM doubled it down. Tripled it. It took him back to the day he'd confronted Orson and said, 'I'm actually not joking this time.'

Orson told Ben about it. 'You know what I said to him? I told him how the fuck should I know when he's joking and when he isn't after he's always had such a dick sense of humour and it was all based on that? Then I told him to just get fucked along with his son. I said that to the British prime minister. I liked it. It felt good. It felt like the only thing worth knowing politicians for.'

'You always did have a fuse people could light. Especially with video games. I bet you're still a sore loser.'

'You know what I realised later, after everything? My stress level went down after I stopped gaming. I became a calmer person. I felt bad about times I'd talked to people like that. Apart from that one. And maybe one other. You know what I did not long after you left? I got suspended for three days for calling that dinner lady Mrs Taverner a slut. She wasn't actually one; I mean, who would go *there*? Eeeeeurgh. I just liked the word. *Slut*. And the look on her face. She couldn't believe even I said that.'

Ben smirked. 'You're a potty-mouthed, attention-seeking brat.'

'You'd better believe it.'

'I sure tamed you last night though, didn't I?'

Orson felt like his guts were full of two whole pints of that milkshake now, sloshing around. 'You...don't wanna talk about that stuff here, do you? Where your friends are?'

'Look,' Ben said, pointing at the rink. 'The team have all packed up and gone. There's nobody in here who knows me. New York's a big place. I bet nobody knows my family in here either, even if I do come here all the time. Who's gonna hear? Who'd care if they did? But if you're not comfortable then I'll be quiet.'

Orson looked around himself and realised he'd hunched up. He tried to relax. 'I thought you'd left this morning because you felt...y'know, guilty about it?'

'What was there to feel guilty about? Did you feel like that?'

'No! Okay yeah, maybe a little bit, but it's not *your* fault. I know it sounds dumb, but I thought you maybe woke up thinking you'd defiled your parents' house or something. The whole religion thing. Or maybe you didn't want me to think you wanted me to come on holiday here just so you could...y'know. Do stuff with me.'

'Do you think that?'

That face again. Orson wanted to be sick even though he knew he wasn't going to. 'No. Maybe. *Did* you think about that?'

'No, I didn't. I didn't crush on you since we were kids either. I never knew I was gay until I was eighteen, when I went to college. I don't think you ever crushed on me either. Even if our playground game maybe turned into a fantasy you never knew you had about a soldier doing it with his captain. Sounds like a video game side-story to me that you were disappointed you never got to play. Last night you told me you were thinking about fit shirtless bears. I thought you might enjoy some fun with one. I sure enjoyed it. Then I genuinely forgot I had an extra practice this morning.'

It was so matter-of-fact that Orson wished he could simply teleport out of the room and disappear somewhere. 'I'm sorry, Benji.'

'Don't be. I keep thinking maybe I moved too fast. If you got the wrong kind of idea then maybe it's my fault. I spent that whole meeting we went to wondering if I should have come out to you. I mean, on the first night I've seen you since we were kids? Who does that?'

'You did.'

'Yeah, I did. But it wasn't because I thought you'd do stuff with me. At least not until I left the bathroom door open for you to look at me if you wanted. That *was* kind of a flirt.'

'Yeah, and it worked.'

Ben stirred his milkshake. 'Mmm-hmm.'

'Benji, I don't know what's happening to me.'

'Really? You don't? It seems pretty obvious to me: you're discovering you might be gay. You kind of already felt curious, and now there's maybe more to it than "might be". Can I guess? Maybe you don't *want* to be gay because it's a straight man's world out there. Believe me, I know. I wasn't sure I wanted to be either. Until I let stuff happen. In a place where it was okay to feel what I felt like.'

'With Ace? The model?'

'That's how I knew, yeah. Look at me. I'm a fashion clothes horse. I was lucky; I had parents who could afford to buy me all the clothes I wanted, but you know why I wanted them? They looked cool on sporty bears. Like me. I'd see the ads online, on billboards, in the shop windows, and I wanted to look like that. It was "I want to be him." Then at college I *literally* wanted to be him; half the companies whose logo I ever wore were on campus scouting for models on the first day, part time work to help pay your way. So I signed up. Then I went to more and more shoots, and I finally admitted what was really happening. It wasn't "I want to be him." It was "I *want* him."'

'So you got him? It was that simple.'

'Not really. I couldn't do anything about it. I felt like it shouldn't be happening. But I kept going. Ace knew how to read it. The first time he came onto me, I told him I wasn't gay. He said, "sure you're not." When he rubbed my bottom and put his hand down my pants the first time, I said no. Like properly said it. He actually said "okay" and took it out and left me alone. That's how I knew maybe I'd be safe if something happened. So I got him alone again and told him to do what he did last week, and this time I'd let him. He was a junior. Totally

118

out. I think he liked breaking in a new boy who'd never done anything before. He liked a studious religious boy. Kinda quiet but confident. We were having sex most nights for most of my freshman year. Then just when I actually started to believe he was in love with me, he graduated, took a job all the way in Seattle and hardly ever called me. Until he said he'd moved on. I don't blame him. I never exactly called him my boyfriend. I don't think he really was. We just had fun.'

'You make it sound so easy.'

'Benefit of telling it like it's just a story. When I was living it? It was different.'

'How do I...I don't know, get where you are? How do I know?'

'You keep doing what you feel like doing. It'll come out in the wash.'

'Oh yeah, like who you want to fuck's just like doing laundry.'

'Do you feel like doing what we did last night again?'

Orson pretended to think about it. 'Yeah.'

'Okay then. We'll do it again tonight. Let's see if we can find out things you like. Or you could tell me if you already know.'

'I like having you talk clean to me. I don't know why. I don't know how you do it, but I like it.'

'Raised that way, I guess.'

Orson smiled. 'I still remember that last Christmas shopping trip where I came with you back in England. What your mum said. "Benjamin, I cannot simply poo out more money."'

'Oh, you remember that?'

'Yeah. You do too?'

'It was so embarrassing, realising everyone who heard it was now imagining my mom actually doing that.'

'Who *doesn't* wish their mum could shit money though? The way you're living now it's like both your parents can.'

'Yours aren't exactly poor either. Mayor of London's a pretty good salary. So's a virologist at a London college. Is it true they bought you an ironing board for your birthday?'

'How did you know about that? I never told you that.'

'Mom told me. She said that's kind of what they're like. Do you use it?'

'Fuck no, do I *look* like I use it? I'm a scruff-bag. Yeah okay, I use it in front of them back home, just so they know I'm taking more pride in my appearance, blah blah blah. It keeps them happy.'

'Right.'

What was that supposed to tell him? 'Why does nobody ever seem to like my parents? Why don't you? They're not bad people.'

'When did I say I didn't like them? They're different to mine. I don't judge though.'

'Oh come on. Stop doing the whole good Christian do-unto-others shit. Tell me what you actually think. People who never tell it like it is just annoy me.'

'I don't really think anything about it. Except one thing. Did they ever go to any of your meetings like I did?'

'Yeah, Dad did. Why are you asking?'

'Did he ever acknowledge that maybe he and your mom played a part in everything?'

'What do you mean?'

'When they let you do everything for yourself, saying it was teaching you how to be independent, did they really not know how you were spending your time? Did they never ask to have a talk with you where they said maybe you were spending too much time gaming and not enough time studying in school? Do you think they didn't know you started smoking and drinking when you were a teenager? That they didn't know you were eating junk food all the time? If that had been me, my mom and dad would have stopped all of that.'

'I'm glad they didn't. I never wanted the kind of parents everyone else had.'

'No. But it's like you've got them now. They're trying to do what they think they should have done when you were younger. It's too late for that. You're a grown-up now.'

'Urgh, not you as well. You're hoping they try to take me home later, aren't you? So you can see me stand up for myself and make a scene. You know what Ella said?' Orson showed him the text message.

'That's not quite how I would have put it,' Ben said.

'But the message is the same?'

'I don't think calling you rude names is the way to motivate you. Our coach is good at doing that because he doesn't curse at his players.'

Why did I get into this? Orson thought. 'Do you like it when I talk dirty and swear in front of you? With my "poo-poo mouth"?'

'Actually, I do,' Ben said. 'Even if I don't like hearing those words in my own voice. I like hearing you do it. That's you. Telling it like you think it is.'

'Good. Because I don't give a fuck what anybody thinks about me and my parents. I'm a better person because I let them help, and if they tell me we're going tonight then I'm going to have to go. So let's skate. Let's do that before they get here and tell me off for not having my phone on me.'

* * *

Orson decided to ask for the knee and elbow pads and helmet before Ben could insist he wore them. The only thing worse than going home tonight would be doing it with a concussion or a joint broken. An arm or a leg...there was an idea; what if he ended up in a hospital somewhere and they couldn't take him home? Would Ben stay with him to "keep him happy"?

'What are you grinning about?' Ben said.

'Thinking of you if you'd gone to medical school like your mum did instead of dentistry.'

'Oh, no thanks, totally not for me. About ninety-nine percent of dental patients leave the surgery alive. They also don't generally die from stuff *you've* done to them.'

'You'd better not kill me today then. Or let me fall and knock my teeth out.'

Ben took hold of the helmet Orson was wearing and pulled the mesh visor down. 'That's your teeth guard. It's not just to stop you getting smacked in the face with a hockey stick.'

'Aren't you going to wear yours?'

'For this kind of skating? I don't need one.'

'What if I grab hold of you to keep my balance and pull you over?'

'We're going to stick to the sides of the rink where the rails are. Grab that. I'll stay far enough away that you can't grab me.'

'I'd like to. You'd end up giving me a great big bear hug, and I'd squeak from how tight it was.'

Ben rolled his eyes. 'That's for later.' He wore a look right then that to Orson seemed like the moment a character in a cartoon has a lightbulb appear over their head. 'Actually, yeah. Good call.' Ben picked up his helmet and whomped it onto his head, not doing any of the fiddling about Orson had done with his. 'Let's go.'

'What changed your mind?'

'This.'

'Ooooooooohoho! Benji, that tickles! And my tail changed your mind?' Ben had run a hand down it, then back up again, getting close to where it joined Orson's butt, only his tracksuit bottoms stopping Ben's hand from playing with what was beyond the end.

'Otters are *lethal* ice-hockey players. One whip from that rudder tail and you're on your bottom seeing stars because the sting up your legs is that intense.'

'I've never seen an otter play ice hockey,' Orson said, thinking of winter Olympics he'd watched on TV.

'You mostly won't,' Ben said. 'They mostly can't do the right kind of tail control, so they always end up in trouble for fouls, so they get benched, so teams don't pick them. It's rare to find a pro-otter in ice hockey; they mostly steer clear of even learning it. But it's a shame, you know why?'

'I'm about to, aren't I?'

'Balance,' Ben said. 'You're not like cats, and you don't have a prehensile like rodents or apes sometimes do, but you guys have great natural weight distribution. Don't try and counterbalance by throwing your tail the other way. Let it go where it wants to and forget you've even got it. That's the key.'

Orson looked at Ben's tail and decided to tweak it. 'How would you know, stump-boy?'

'Because otters make amazing figure skaters.'

'Oh.'

'Yeah.

'Last time I watched figure skating, it was full of snow leopards winning everything. Like that one over there.'

'Her name's Jennifer. She comes here all the time; she's a show-off. She was like that in my high-school class as well. If you talk to her, she'll know everything about whatever you talk about.' Ben stepped through the door and out onto the ice.

'So people *do* know you here.'

'Come on, Otterpants. Take hold of the rail and put those skates on here where they're supposed to be.'

Orson managed it, feeling even less sure of his feet under him than he had on snow days back home with every pathway frozen. This was the limitless promise of broken bones with one false move.

'People do know me here, yeah. A few of them. They're going to watch me give a skating lesson. Lesson one, don't let this sag down.' He picked Orson's tail up with a hand under it. 'Keep it about there. Lesson two, don't hunch forward thinking it's going to save you. You're not going to roll into a ball like Sonic the Hedgehog.'

'Otters practically *can* roll up like that. Our spines let us.'

'Wrong technique for this. That flexible spine wants to flex back a little bit, like this.' Ben put one hand on the small of Orson's back and another on his chest and pushed in opposite directions until he stood up. 'That's it. Now let go of the rail slowly and don't move your feet.'

Orson did it.

'See? Balance.'

'So what happens if I move my...wuhhh!'

Ben caught him under his armpits. 'If you move your arms first, *that* happens. You lose your balance.'

He pulled Orson back up again. 'Start again and get to that stand without the rail. This time, raise your right foot by flexing your ankle until the skate's touching the ice with that jagged tip. That's how you push off. Push backwards and keep your left foot facing forward just like it is. See if you can glide to the rail.'

Orson managed it, twisting to avoid smacking into the wall cartoon style and going down again, controlled only by the one hand that grabbed the rail first. 'This was a shit idea.'

'No it wasn't. My first lesson, I couldn't even do the balancing on my own part. Hold on to the rail lightly with your right hand. Get a feel for pushing off with the right skate and just moving a little bit until you start to go.'

They circled the rink twice before Orson complained his feet ached, even if he was starting to get it. He didn't really think he was, he just wanted to hear Ben agree with him, and he did.

'These are *not* otter boots,' Orson said. 'I don't care if they've got a little rainbow-coloured otter on them, and by the way, he so gave us that design on purpose.'

'You want to know what skating really feels like before we go and get a burger each?'

'You are *not* whirling me round and flinging me out across the rink like that guy over there did with *his* friend.'

'That's why they're both going to get kicked out in a minute if they're not careful.' Ben moved in front of him with barely a movement of his feet. 'Hold on to my sides.'

'Won't I tickle you?'

'No. I'm not ticklish.'

Bullshit. Everyone's ticklish. Orson held on.

'Don't let go. Whatever your tail wants to do, let it. Just keep it up like I told you and this will work fine.'

'Woah, hold on, what are we...oooooh no! No no no no nooooo-ooooooookay, yeah, this works.' It was like riding a motorbike with nothing beneath you. Orson had ridden a real one a couple of times with someone at uni who had had one, whose name he now couldn't remember. He'd probably been too high. 'This as fast as you can go?'

'No, but speed skating isn't for a full rink covered in kids. Maybe a little bit more though.'

Orson nearly let go as they cornered this time, air rushing over his face. 'Fuuuuuuuck, Benji, I didn't say actually *do* it, you bear!'

Ben laughed. 'My species as an insult on its own? Cool, I've actually never been called it like that. Faster?'

'NO! Can you even *go* faster?'

Jennifer the snow leopard could, and backwards. 'Hello, boys. This the otter you told me about? He *is* cute. He can't skate though?'

'You had your first lesson once,' Ben said.

'I was a natural,' Jennifer said. 'Bye! Come get some coffee with me if you get him back to the door without him breaking something, I wanna hear his English accent.'

Ben did one more lap, and Orson was glad when they wound up on the other side of the rink to Jennifer.

'Okay,' he said. '*One*, you actually –'

'Relax, Otterpants. She wouldn't out me even if she knew. I said you were cute as in *she'd* like to date you.'

'Why? I "can't skate though".'

'Jennifer's good,' Ben said, taking his helmet off. 'I've got way more dirt on her than she'd ever get on me. She's secretly scared of red pandas.'

'Seriously? A snepper?'

'Yuh-huh. And she hates that word. Think you can last a cup of coffee without letting her push your buttons enough to use what you know?'

What's this supposed to be? A test of me with a reward? If I play nice, do I get to explode all over you later using the hard dick that's hidden under my 'otterpants'? 'Yeah, okay.'

Orson managed not to retch at Jennifer's decaf soya milk latte with extra foam and sugar-free chocolate sprinkles too. She wanted to hear his accent? Fine. 'Sure you don't want some tofu with that? Maybe some activated raisins? Some de-milked cashews? Or is it the sun-baked humous that's in at the moment?'

'Har har har, feesh-boy,' Jennifer said. 'Benjamin's *supposed* to have those kinds of layers around *his* stomach.'

'You should try me at skating on the Nintendo Wii sometime,' Orson said. 'I'm good with that kind of remote. You should see. And anyway, I thought soya was for red pandas. They eat healthy noms, right?'

'Eeeeeeuuugh.' Jennifer shuddered. 'He *is* English, isn't he?'

'Ben said you called me cute as in you might date me. Where would you like dinner? I hear McDonalds just brought out some kind of supreme widowmaker-burger or something. It's just brimming with cow lips and arse. And calories. Loads and loads of them.'

Jennifer laughed and held up a finger. 'Let me tell you about my boyfriend.'

Her boyfriend, Josh, another snepper (Orson resisted the word), was going to the next Olympics with her. Figure skating. He also owned a yacht. At twenty-five, he'd made his yacht money in pro-gaming and then seen the light and taken up a healthier lifestyle, remembering he could skate, because he'd met an amazing woman who'd shown him the way.

'A born-again *snow leopard*.' It was so passive-aggressive that Orson loved it.

'I've got to go. He's picking me up in his new Porsche.'

'Come to England sometime when you've got your gold medal,' Orson said. 'I'll take you out for feesh and chips; there's a great place I know down the road from my one-bedroom flat in Tower Hamlets. It's run by otters.'

Jennifer gave a five-star celebrity kind of wave.

'Go on, say it,' Ben said, head in hands, elbows on the table and looking with a smile right at Orson.

'Say what?' Orson said. '"What a bitch"? Forget it, Snowbear. I know what your game is. You're going to tell me some story about her that shows a side nobody could possibly think exists, and it's probably going to convince me.'

'Actually, yeah, you called it. She lost her parents in some kind of industrial accident before she could remember them. She was raised by two lions. Wealthy ones. Real estate. Millionaire kind of rich, except she doesn't care about their money. She only takes just what she needs to get by. She really *is* going to be an Olympic skater, most likely. After she spent what would have been her college years doing Christian aid work in some of the world's toughest places. *She's* pretty tough. It's just not the kind of tough you maybe thought she was.'

'Okay. So the boyfriend we just had to hear about. Does he really have a yacht and a pro-gamer profile out there? Does he even skate? Are they really going to the Olympics?'

'Yes, kind of, yes, and probably.'

'How can you be kind of a pro gamer?'

'He was one. She did get him to change his life. He sold the yacht. He didn't buy a Porsche either; he bought a Nissan Leaf and the kind of boat you can sail international waters in, but you've got to crew it. That's how they're going to Norway. Her foster parents could fly them there, but no.'

'What did Josh change his job to?

'He's a garbage truck driver. I think he does those new recycling ones.'

'A snep bin man. Who can skate like that. And a missionary who'd rather freeze her spotted arse off than take Mum and Dad's money.'

'Yep.'

'I kind of like her.'

'Thought you might.'

'Why the lie about the Porsche though?'

'She wanted you to hate her. Foam at the mouth a little bit. That's how she flirts with boys. Especially ones with your sort of banter. She likes that type. That *was* some banter, by the way. You're not bad with mean girls.'

'She'd cheat on saint-boy Josh the bin-snep with an otter? Guess I wouldn't smell like trash.'

'Probably not. But I think that's part of her game. She wants him to fear how she could get anyone she wanted. Just a little bit.'

'Yeah, but Benji, I would *never*. Apart from the healthy dose of narcissistic do-gooder, a species with retractable claws? Wuhhhh. Nobody calls me "feesh-boy" either. Do *not* get your family started on that one, like ever. I don't even like the fucking stuff that much. Fish and chips is a national disgrace, not a national dish. And I barfed a whole stomach full of the stuff out of a taxi window once after Syd got me to try absinthe for the first time. Besides.'

Ben waited. 'Besides what?'

'I think you were right.'

'Right about what?'

'I think I like boys. Who am I kidding about the whole thing? I *did* kinda like Syd. As in I kinda wanted to do something his oh-so-perfect father wouldn't have wanted us to do. I wanted to do to him what...well, y'know.'

'What I did to you?'

'I thought about it. I totally wanted to get into another boy's butt. I didn't want to use a wii-mote. I wanted something designed for it. Something he might have liked. That's how I've imagined it ever since, and no, I've never shared that at a meeting. Or that I think I'm gay.'

Ben smiled. 'How does it feel? Saying it for the first time?'

'Why are *you* asking? You've done it too.'

'I can't remember who I first said it to. I think it might have just been to myself in front of the mirror. How boring's that?'

'I'm glad I'm sitting down. My head's all swimmy.'

'Oh, now *that* I remember. More than once.'

'The first time you let Ace fuck you?'

'Yeah, then. I got it yesterday too, when I saw how Dad reacted to seeing that book. That's kind of what I really wanted to see. Not just what you looked like and how Ella handled it. She did what I knew she'd do. If I actually told her the truth? You like her, I know you do. But if she knew anything about who I really am, who you're just starting to make some sort of peace with being, you'd probably see something you didn't like half as much.'

132

'You're not planning a Christmas coming out to your whole family, are you?'

'No, Orson, most definitely not. You weren't a rehearsal. Telling you was a brave mistake that turned out not to be a mistake.'

'Then you took one hell of a chance with last night.'

'Yeah. Didn't I.' Ben drained his coffee. 'Don't think about tonight until tonight.'

There's not going to be a tonight. 'What do you wanna do before my parents fuck this whole thing up for both of us?'

'It's your holiday; what do you want to do?'

Don't pick shopping. Don't say you've got to see a proper USA mall like a tourist in some cringe-comedy movie who finds out it's really no different to all the crap England's got. 'Wasn't bowling invented in New York?'

'I don't know, was it? You want to go bowling?'

'Yeah. Would any of your friends come meet me? The team? I've done your snepper friend for you and only half-used the red panda thing. Think you can help me make some new friends without giving away how you've played with my dick already?'

'Yes,' Ben said, taking his phone out. 'I can do that.'

* * *

They got home just as the sky was black enough for the family to be drawing curtains. Ella waved to them from an upstairs window. She didn't look like she was having fun.

'Fuck,' Orson said. 'This is it.'

'You don't have to go,' Ben said. 'Don't try and handle this on your own. Let Mom do what she promised. If she hasn't already.'

'I feel sick,' Orson said.

'You'll be fine. Come on.'

'I can't do this, Benji. I don't know how to say no to them. It's pathetic, but I don't.'

'Then I'll make you a deal,' Ben said. 'And I mean this. I'll give you the best Christian promise I've got.' He made the cross sign. 'If you can do it, if you can stay here, then I'll wait a couple of days and pick a right time and I'll tell my family what I can't tell them.'

'Oooooooh no! Benji, that is a *bad* fucking deal! If I actually do it, what if you can't keep it? Don't guilt either of us into this.'

'Do you want to go home?'

'No fucking way.'

'Then it's be brave time. I can't expect you to do it if I can't. So this can be both our times. Want to see what we're really made of?'

Orson looked at the door, just like he had the other day, and felt like he was about to open a chasm to another world. No more *Home Alone*. This was like...what was that thing called with the monsters who said, 'The box. You opened it. We came' and then proceeded to tear the box-puzzler apart in the name of unholy S&M? It had an otter dyed white with pins all over him. That's what Orson felt like he was turning into, standing there.

'Can we hold hands?'

He barely knew he'd said it until he turned to Ben, who looked like he could fill up his pants.

Bearpants. How about that then. Still want to be brave?

Ben actually did take his hand. 'Maybe we'd better not when we go in though.'

Orson looked at the drawn curtains. 'Just so we're clear,' he said, knowing there was little for it if he destroyed this moment completely, 'I don't just want to stay so we can do last night again. I don't just want to get jerked off until I come. I want my holiday. With you.'

Ben squeezed his hand. 'I know. Ready?'

'Yeah. Here goes nothing.'

The door was open, left unlocked for them.

Ben's family were all in the kitchen. The cousins, Cliff and Holly were in the lounge, but somehow Orson could tell they were listening. Everybody was far too quiet. This felt like...

Okay, Orson thought. This felt like an intervention. He'd been through one before, only this one felt different. This felt like it wasn't about an addiction. It was about something that had to be talked about, and it could only be one thing.

Oh shit, Tasha. What the fuck did you say to them all?

She was the only one who could possibly know. The only one who had a hunch that that stupid pink bathrobe of Ben's might actually be –

'Your parents have gone,' Natasha said.

Orson felt a surge of something he didn't think he'd experienced even during a drunken, coke-fuelled gaming victory. He looked around himself and felt like the room was getting wider. 'What?'

'They've gone back to England,' Natasha said. 'They left you your ticket right here. They printed a copy for you. They said they both had to leave in a rush, but to tell you that there's not going to be a lockdown and they're not recalling people from overseas.'

That was probably his father's exact words, like this holiday was some sort of military service. 'They said that?'

'They would have liked to have talked to you before they went, but they didn't have time.'

'They just...' They'd *gone*? 'They said "I'm sure he'll behave" or something, right?'

'No,' John said. 'Nothing like that. They just left. It was rather sudden, but I guess there was nothing they could do about it.'

Ella sighed and looked at the ceiling. 'That dumb virus isn't even really doing anything.'

'Ella, be quiet,' John said.

Why was nobody talking now?

His parents had *left him here*? No goodbye? Not even a promise of good behaviour forced out of him? No arrangements to turn in his phone? No deal of any kind for him staying?

Why did he suddenly not like this at all?

'They left me here,' he said.

He *did* like it.

'Yes,' John said. 'For two whole weeks.'

'I'm still on holiday.'

'Yes, you are.'

He fucking *loved it*.

Everybody was watching him. That was what he hadn't liked. Not that they were doing it, but that they were all waiting to comfort him because he was supposed to realise his parents had simply abandoned him.

He wasn't giving them that. These people wanted him here. For the first time in far too long, people wanted him around on a massive scale. They weren't on the other end of a screen thousands of miles away this time.

'*Cool!*' Orson said, in little more than a whisper.

It had been *that* easy?

Ben wasn't going to have to keep his end of the deal. Orson hadn't *had* to fulfil his. Orson could have squeaked with joy.

Screamed.

'We're going to the cinema this evening,' Natasha said, hands on his shoulders again. 'But you don't have to. We're going to the latest *Miracle on 34th Street*. Perhaps not your thing or Benjamin's, and you've had a very long day out. With lots of healthy food already, I

137

imagine.' That smile of hers. What had she done to make this happen?

Don't ask. You don't really give a shit.

'I wouldn't blame you two if you just wanted a quiet snack and then bed this evening. Or perhaps a movie that's nothing to do with Christmas.'

*You have...*did *she have an idea?*

Orson didn't care about that either.

'Yes,' Ben said. 'That sounds good to me.'

Chapter Seven

Orson's decision-paralysis led to the longest shower he'd ever taken.

With the family departed, he and Ben had stared at each other in the living room as if trying to pick whereabouts in the house they wanted to do everything. They'd done nothing. They'd both stared at the TV, as if both were wishing the other would just suggest a film and make that all they ended up doing after all.

'Y'know,' Orson said, 'my feet still feel like someone stuffed ice down my boots at that skate rink. Can I just go take a shower? Maybe a long one?'

'Yeah,' Ben said, 'good idea. Use mine. I'll go use Mom and Dad's.'

Orson spent his overly hot shower repeating, *It's okay, you can do this,* to himself over and over until admitting that the more he thought it, the less he believed it. How was he supposed to be what he knew Ben wanted? He thought of Ben calling him the foul-mouthed attention-seeking brat. Good, he'd just be himself then.

Except it wouldn't be enough. What use was being a character that appealed to Ben when his last experience of anything to do with an arsehole led to someone bleeding from theirs in a public place? Not to mention disgrace in all the red-top tabloids that practically defined Crap Britain.

Cunty newspapers. He liked how he'd come up with that earlier, like it was a delayed-action thought from a year ago.

He was in New York now. Three thousand miles away from everything that bored him or disgusted him. He wanted to fuck *like* he was in New York, the land of endless promise and expense and actual snow at Christmas that the whole world didn't bitch about getting. Or *not* getting. The Americans at least made up their minds about what they liked and what they didn't. Ben like ice skating, God, and brat-otters.

Hey Benji, my parents aren't here anymore. Neither are yours. Are you ready to play a little game?

Yeah.

Yeah, why the hell not? Except it couldn't sound like *Saw.*

You wanna get Matthew's Gameboy? You wanna go all the way and get the PS5 hooked up? You wanna see what a deadeye shot I really am, coz I can blow you away.

That'd do it. That was him. That was what he was prepared to do.

Until he opened the bathroom door and there was Ben, lying on his front on the bed, knees bent and the soles of his feet pointing at the ceiling, completed naked.

'Woah,' Orson said.

'Yeah. See anything you like?'

'Errr...okay, yeah, I've totally been imagining this all day. Especially while we were skating.'

'Good ice-breaker?'

'What fucking movies have you seen, Benji? That is a terrible line.'

'I dunno, I just thought maybe what you wanted to see right now was some "bear butt".'

Before Orson could think of what to say, Ben was laughing at himself.

'Oh my God. Bears actually *do* use that. Does it ever work? Like on anyone? Just for that, I wanna *smack* your "bear butt".'

'Go on then. I dare you.'

Orson went over. He stared at Ben naked body for a moment. 'That *is* a butt big enough to crack ice. And it's all muscle, right? No polar fat. Not on you.' He touched it, rubbed it, and thought about sliding two fingers into Ben's crack.

'Oooooohohoooo!' Ben said. 'Somebody wants to get in there, huh?'

With the same fingers, Orson touched Ben's neck gently and ran them down his spine all the way to the base.

'Ooooooh! Tickles! Brrrr! Okay, you gave me the shivers right there. Do that again!'

Orson did it. Ben squirmed a little, laughed and sighed deeply. 'Nice. Gonna spank me then?'

Orson sighed, his stomach sinking and his limbs trembling slightly. 'I can't do it, Snowbear. I've...oh, come on, you know already. I've never done this to a guy. I don't know how to dominate. I've never been that sort of guy. So how do I do it and convince you I want to?'

'It's okay,' Ben said. 'Maybe you don't yet. Just run with this. You got an erection in those pants yet? From rubbing that bear bottom of mine?'

'Oh yeah.'

'Then you're doing great. Go back to that. Feel the fur. Stroke it where it wants to go.

Orson put both hands on Ben this time, stroked, and squeezed the big muscle, feeling Ben clench up under his hands. Ben arched his back and gave a soft, satisfied growl.

'Mmmmm, yeah, that's it. Nice. Dig in a little deeper. Urrrrrgh, yeah, that's what I needed.'

'I bet your hips are still stiff from that skating.' Orson slid his hands around to them and dug in again there, shoving forward slightly, then back, letting Ben relax and then arch up.

'Uhhh...uhhhhhhh! Oh yeah! Do that! Mmmmmm.'

What next? Orson flicked at Ben's stumpy tail, then took it between the ring and index finger of his right hand. 'Got your tail!' He pulled a little.

'Aaaaaaahhhh! Unfff, okay, nice! Not too hard though, Otterspotter, that's a very sensitive area on a bear. You might just wanna...oh...oooooohohoho yeah, that's it, you got it!' Orson was rubbing under Ben's tailbone, then above it, then both at once, remembering his left hand was doing nothing. Then it was sliding down into the top of Ben's crack again.

'Nice. Mmmm, is it warm down there? Wanna go further?'

'Yeah.'

'Like *further* further?'

'Yeah.'

'Okay. Let my tail go.'

Orson let it go. Ben rolled over. 'Want me to show you what you *should* have done with your friend Syd?'

'Benji, how many fucking times, Syd's *not* my...'

Ben bent his knees and spread his legs wider.

'Oh, *dude*, you showed me your butthole!' Orson looked away, stepping back from the bed.

Well duh, idiot, if you want to do butt-stuff with this bear then you're going to see it. What does it matter if you were on a climbing frame together once? Grow the fuck up, you stupid, gaming-addicted bag of shit.

'Gross, Snowbear.' Orson put on the best devil's smile he could come up with as he turned back to Ben, who looked like he didn't know what to do or say for once. Orson stood at the end of Ben's bed and put his hands on the end-board. 'Do it again.'

'Yeah?'

'Yeah.'

Ben spread his legs again. This time Orson looked, and kept looking.

'What's got four legs and an arsehole on the top?' Orson said.

'I dunno. Gonna tell me?'

'Yeah, Snowbear: the captain's seat in the cockpit!'

'Oh, is that so? Is that a little otter who belongs in the cannon-fodder gunner's seat questioning my authority?'

'What authority right now, *sir?* I'm staring right at your bear butthole. Which you totally cleaned in the shower because you wanted me to see. I bet you even douched, didn't you?'

'Oh, you know about that? Yes, I did that. Wanna do inspection? I've got a toy for that. Right here under my pillow.'

'Stay there.' Orson went for it himself, finding exactly what he expected. 'Oh nice. You even picked a red one. Can't possibly get lost in all that white fur, huh?' He looked at the butt-plug. 'Errr...I don't just stuff it in there, right? Do I put the lube on it or like...up you?'

Ben grinned 'I love the way you said that.'

'So give me an answer, dumbarse, or are we gonna sit here talking about sex all night instead of do...woah. Okay. Cool.' What had stopped Orson was that somehow, in all the staring at what Ben had revealed to him, he'd missed the obvious.

'Oh, you like my penis, huh?' Ben said. 'Yeah, nice, isn't it?'

He shouldn't have been staring like he was in some sort of science museum, but Orson couldn't help himself. 'You've got…'

'Yes, I still have a foreskin.' Ben's tip was poking out of it, an impressive size even though he wasn't hard yet. He wasn't even semi, Orson thought.

Holy shit.

'Go on,' Ben said. 'Touch it. Have a play.'

Orson sat on the bed, and with his left hand, he gently rolled Ben's sheath back and touched his tip. The blood rushed to Ben's cock straight away, and now he got the semi, a deep and satisfied rush of breath coming from him, his chest swelling up fully and his head relaxing back onto the pillow.

'That's the stuff,' Ben said. 'You totally *do* know what you're doing. You know what a tip does. Uhhhhhh, yeah! Make me hard!'

'How come you've still got a sheath?' Orson said, still trying to suspend his disbelief. 'I thought all American boys got snipped.'

'Yeah, but Orson, what does my mom do for a living? Who knows better that not only is the cleanliness thing a big load of nonsense but that when you snip someone, you risk making their tip less sensitive? My mom wanted me to *enjoy* sex one day, not just have it.'

'It makes your tip less sensitive?'

'Not always.'

'Oh. Damn. Coz they snipped me.'

'Really?' Ben said. 'In England?'

Orson rubbed Ben's cock on the underside, listening to him breathe deeply. He pinched his tip. Ben groaned with pleasure.

'How long before you come, bear-butt? You close already?'

Ben smirked. 'I need to see yours first. I've felt you hard already. Now I want to see it.'

'You just want proof I'm snipped. You don't believe me.'

'Yeah. Show it to me. Why does an English boy like you get circumcised?'

'Because he had that condition he can't remember the name of where your skin doesn't peel back over your tip and never knew that wasn't normal until he was like ten, so "Orson had dick surgery!" You've got *no* idea how fucking embarrassing school was for *weeks*. I dunno how anyone found out. I bet it was Syd being a wanker again.'

'You didn't know Syd back then. He never went to our school.'

'Oh yeah.'

'Well, *I* won't laugh. And I showed you mine. Gonna show me yours so I can get even harder?'

'Yeah, okay, keep your fur on. Let me drop my *otterpants*.' Orson dropped them to his ankles and slid his underpants down, liking how he actually was wearing the ones Ben had given him. 'There. Snipped otter.'

'Mmm, now *that's* what you call an erection, otter-boy.' Ben sat up on the edge of his bed. 'How about you stand there and stay hard and I do a little something?'

'Like...you're gonna...okay.'

'Yeah. I'm going to put your hard penis in my mouth. I bet you've never felt a bear's tongue either.'

'Or his teeth.'

'Don't be scared. I don't bite. I'm good at avoiding the teeth. Ace taught me. And just so you know, if you want to finish in my mouth, I would totally swallow for you.'

Before Orson could answer, Ben took him into his mouth, pressed his cock between his tongue and the roof of his mouth, and sucked hard. For a moment, Orson couldn't breathe, the pressure around the end of his tip and the pulling sensation that went all the way up his cock to his balls and crotch heavy and powerful. As Ben released him, he sighed out a breath he hadn't known he was holding, then heaved it down again as Ben sucked hard, then again, and again, and again.

'Benji, stop...I'm gonna come, and I can't do it in your mouth!'

Ben released him with a wet lick and a little nip at his tip. 'No? Okay, you wanna come *on* me?'

'No, I wanna rub dicks.' He didn't know why he'd thought of it, but Ben was straight there, standing up now and getting an underarm behind-grip on Orson's shoulders, nearly lifting him off the floor.

'Oh, cool, you mean like this?' Ben rubbed against him, keeping him on his tiptoes. Orson arched his back, breathing hard, rubbed back as Ben pulled him into a hug, and let go of the greatest squirt of his life. It went straight up past Ben's stomach and hit him underneath his chin.

'Good boy! Nice! *That's* a squirt.'

Remembering the house was completely empty, Orson let out the squeak he was trying to contain. The whole house would have heard it. He fell against Ben as Ben let him down back onto his pads and threw his arms around him in a hug of relief, the last few squirts still leaving him, this time going straight into Ben's warm, white fur.

'Nice, otter-boy. Shall we get a towel and clean me off? We've still got butt-stuff to do.'

'Oh yeah. *You.* Let's see if you go better and hit the ceiling. I'll get the towel.' Orson soaked half the towel from Ben's handrail in warm water and left the other half to dry him with. Rubbing him down was like cleaning a great big smooth rug.

'You know, I've never smelled an otter do that before,' Ben said, wiping his chin with his hand before Orson could get there and sniffing it afterwards. 'Mmmm.' He rubbed two fingers over Orson's nose in a quick stroke.

'You gross bear!' Orson wiped himself with the wet end of the towel. 'My own come on my nose? Get on that bed; I'm going to stuff your arsehole good for that!'

'Now you're talking.'

Ben got onto the bed, still as hard as he'd been before giving Orson head, and pulled his knees to his chest. 'Go on. Get it in there. You know how to do this.'

'Yeah.' He knew Syd had done the first part himself, because '*Nobody* is sticking their fingers up there for this', but he was going to do it to Ben. He coated his right index and middle finger in as much lube as they'd take without dripping. Keeping his eyes locked in with Ben's, he felt his way to Ben's hole instead of looking at it, rubbed around and pushed in.

'Ooooooh yeah...yeah...that's it...you can do deeper, get them right in!'

With his free left hand, Orson gripped under Ben's bent right knee and pushed back a little, easing his knee further towards Ben's chest. Ben pulled his left knee back himself, groaning with the effort of his flexibility being pushed to its limit. Orson twisted his fingers gently, pushing at all sides as he circled, before he slowly withdrew. Still holding Ben's right leg, he sniffed at his own right hand.

'Mmmm...totally clean. Good douche. If I'd done that with Syd, it would have knocked me the fuck out.' He picked the plug up. 'This thing feels cold.'

'Do it. Freeze me on the inside.'

'There's something I wanna do first. Roll over.' *I can do this. I can totally do this. He thinks I can't. He'll like it more.*

'Oh yeah?' Ben said, rolling over and looking over his shoulder. 'You wanna try and get that in there when I'm clenched tighteeeeeeeeeer! Unf!'

149

Orson had smacked him. The sound of it was beautiful, right before Ben's squeal, clenched teeth and the sound that would have woken any bear from hibernation.

'You spanked me!'

'Yeah. I did. Like this.' Orson did the other cheek, then back to the first. Ben was yelping by the time he'd counted to ten, more like a dog. Orson let him catch his breath for a moment. 'Can I grab your scruff?'

'Ooooooh yeah!'

'Good,' Orson said, taking a great handful of the muscle just below Ben's neck and bunching it inside his hand. 'Bad bear!' Smacking with his left hand this time, he lifted Ben up slightly when he arched up. 'You got any kind of muzzle? Ball gag?'

'Not here,' Ben said. 'Have you really never done this before?'

'I've imagined it. It's not so different. Tell me where something is I can give you to bite on. I wanna hear you do that.'

'Time out, otter. I've got to actually sit on that bottom later without my family wondering what I've done that makes me not wanna sit down. I'd rather not pretend I've got haemorrhoids.'

'Ooops. Yeah. And we never picked a safety word.'

'Oh yeah. Watermelon. That's what I always use.' Ben rolled back over, showing off his wet tip.

Orson picked up the plug again. 'You really want this cold? I'll go run it under the tap. The pipes in this place must be near frozen with this weather.' He did it until he could only just feel his own fingers holding it.

'Oooooohoho *man* that's cold! Freezing!' Ben couldn't talk after that; he was too busy making a sound halfway between laughing and panting as Orson slid the cold metal thing inside him and pushed as far as he dared. He switched hands with it, twisting with his left while he took hold of Ben's cock with his right and rubbed a thumb over his tip. 'Come, Snowbear. Hit that fucking ceiling.'

'Okay...okay...you're gonna have to take it out! Too cold! Oh man!'

'Uh-oh.' Orson managed not to pull it out too fast. 'You okay?'

'Yeah, I think so...uuuuurrgh man, that feels good to warm up in there again. Mmmmmmph!' Ben closed his eyes and put his head back on the pillow. 'Ooooohohoho *man*, that's a weird feeling!' He shook himself all over as if shuddering and throwing off water at the same time.

'You want me to keep going?' Orson tugged at Ben's cock again.

'Yeah.'

'Gonna come?' Orson rubbed harder, digging his thumb into the space where Ben's cock joined his balls this time. 'What *does* it take to make you squirt, bear? I'd be spent already if you'd done that to me. Hey, why *don't* you do it to me?'

The bravery he felt had come from nowhere, but it was here, and he hadn't even been drinking yet. The one

151

he was going to have if this turned out to be what he'd imagined all day was going to be the one he'd never match again.

'Oh,' Ben said, sitting up and picking up the plug from the bed. 'You want me to put this in you? Right after it's been in me? *Man*, you're naughty! You dirty little brat! You're as filthy as your mouth!'

'Yeah. At your service. Except I don't want that.' Orson pinched Ben's tip. 'I want *that*. Fuck me, Snowbear. Right up my aquatic otter butt.'

Ben's eyes danced. 'You sure? You wanna go straight to all the way?'

'Yeah. Do it. You see how hard I am still? I can totally come again. On that bed with *this* in me.'

'Aaaahh!' Ben said as Orson pinched him a little too tight. 'Okay, you *got* it, otter-boy.' Ben sat up. 'But listen. There's a catch. The catch is this.' He reached around and stroked Orson's tail. 'If I get behind you, that's gonna get in the way. Or you'll be really uncomfortable if we try to line it up your back. Or we'll break your tailbone.'

Orson shuddered. 'Shit, yeah...but only if we do it standing up, if we lie down...' He realised what was coming.

'We're gonna have to lie down, yeah.' Ben got up, put his hands on Orson's sides and slowly slid them down to his hips. 'But you know the best way to really get an otter's tail out of the way? He has to lie on his back. That means you'll be looking right at me.'

Orson's heart thudded so hard he thought it had burst even though it kept on going inside him, harder and faster with every second that passed.

'How about it?' Ben said, a devilish look on him as he turned Orson around and guided him down onto the bed into the warm space where he'd been lying. 'You might even get higher than my head this time.' He took Orson's legs under his left arm and pulled him round so he was crossways over the bed, his tail dropping over the edge of the mattress and lolling onto the floor. 'Put your legs around me. Yeah, like that. Now put your heels between *my* legs and lock on. Yeah, *that's* it.'

Orson locked himself around Ben and felt like he was pulling him in, even though he knew it was Ben moving. He felt Ben's tip tickle at his hole.

'Oh, wait, hold on,' Ben said.

'Don't,' Orson said, knowing what he was going for. 'It's okay. I took a test right after I got clean, and I've not had sex with anyone since. I've not had sex for nearly a year, Benji. I'm clean. I got away with nothing. Will you trust me?'

Ben looked at him for a moment. 'Yeah. Will you trust *me*? You wanna go bear-*back* now?'

'Oh, you'd better believe it. Bear-back me! Right now!'

'Okay, slowly does it. Nobody's been here before, and that means we're going to need plenty of this.' Ben reached for the lube and spread the rest of the tube on himself. 'Halfway should be enough for now. Then you can dream about what happens if we manage to go deeper next time. Okay, get ready, aqua-boy; this is going to make things *wet*.'

'What did you just call me? Okay, that's another new one, like I needed any more...' Orson felt the push, then the pressure, then everything felt like a bad case of needing to shit and not being able to run. 'Oh...uhhhh...Benji, is this supposed to...unf! Okay, maybe not so... I think I'm gonna –'

'Relax, don't clench. Breathe.'

'I *am* fucking breathing, or can you not hear me doing it?'

'You're not breathing, you're gasping. Relax. Think of my fingers feeling your jaw again.'

It helped, but not much. 'This isn't supposed to hurt, right?'

'It doesn't hurt. It's just unfamiliar. Don't panic, I'm not far in. Don't pant or you'll make yourself dizzy. Breathe slowly. Try holding it for three and letting it out. When you breathe out, tell yourself to relax your stomach, then your hips, then your bottom will follow.'

'What the fuck is this, yoga?'

'Actually, good thinking, it's not so different. Just try.'

Orson drew down a deep breath and tried the hold, only he wanted to keep holding. Ten seconds later, he let it out, wondering how otters were supposed to hold their breath for up to twenty minutes underwater when he couldn't have gone twenty seconds. His head swam. Everything else about him wanted to empty out. He tried not to clench. He tried the hold again. It was no use. He took a third deep breath. 'Benji, I don't think I can...' This time, when he let go, everything melted inside him. Ben pushed a little further in. Orson made the kind of sound he hadn't heard since Syd had done it, only Syd had sounded like he was in pain. What Orson felt was pleasure, not so different from taking a good solid shit but without actually doing it. How he hadn't he didn't know, just that Ben sliding deeper into him was making him hard, and no yoga class that had promised it during his rehab had ever induced this feeling.

'Halfway!' Ben said. 'There you go!'

Orson couldn't talk now. He was gasping again, but this time Ben wasn't telling him not to, and he wouldn't have heard anyway. When he came, he barely knew he was doing it, just that *something* had to empty out of him, and that was the place his body was letting him empty. It hurt, but it hurt *good*. There was a flowing warmth as Ben followed him, finishing unguarded inside him.

Ben stayed there for a while as Orson came down, still hard inside him, and when he did pull out, he moved quickly, grabbing something.

'Here, let me get this under you. We can wash a towel without suspicion, but bed covers are harder. These only got done four days ago.'

'Woah...holy *fuck*, Benji!'

'Enjoy it. They say there's no matching your first time. Even if we did only get halfway.'

155

'I don't think I've got space in me for all the way. Not with you. That's one *massive* fucking package you've got.'

'I'm only average at best. You should have seen Ace.'

'I'd have been terrified.' Orson was afraid of getting up as it was, lest his legs find they couldn't support him. 'You know what, I think I might need another shower.'

'So do I. Together?'

'Yeah. Let's.'

They turned it up as hot as they could both take. Ben faced Orson and put the shower gel on him, rubbing him down with it, then himself. With bubbles covering the shower floor and their ankles afterwards, Ben put his hands behind Orson's head and gently pulled him in and kissed him. Orson let him. Ben's kiss was as gentle and subtle as his fingers, his mouth covering the whole of Orson's and then a little of his face. Orson felt like he wanted to be inside Ben's entire mouth, until the reality brought him back.

'Mmmm...aaah aaann eeee!'

Ben released him and slid his tongue out of his mouth. 'Sorry, what?'

'Hellooooo, I can't breathe! You dummy!' Orson laughed.

'And you're an otter? You should definitely quit smoking.'

'Bite me. It's not that. It's that I always hated sports and you know I did. Remember how I always got picked last for every team? Nothing ever changed.'

'You said you tried running.'

'That was just to make a rehab counsellor think I was trying *something*.'

'I think skating might be your thing. You liked it today.'

'Yeah. Maybe.' Orson turned the shower off. 'I think we're clean enough.' He shook, splattering Ben in more water. 'You wanna go get a beer?'

'Yeah. I do. Mom and Dad have got some; they won't mind.'

I wasn't asking if they minded, Orson thought. Then Ben showered him in three times as much water with his own shake.

In the absence of a bathrobe of his own to put on over his pyjamas, Orson used his white Superdry hoody, usually reserved for any activity apart from eating or drinking. On Christmas Day he'd forgotten it. He thought he looked best in white. Ben's parents had loaded the fridge with Budweiser, which Orson never thought tasted of much, but tonight it tasted fresh and crisp. Obviously better in New York, just like Weissbier was better in Germany.

They clinked bottles. 'Good sex,' Ben said.

'Good hunting,' Orson said.

'Oh!' Ben said. 'I'd forgotten that. Yeah. Good hunting!' He clinked a second time, as if erasing his first.

It was something Orson had picked up from a sci-fi program with more gore in it than a kid that age should have been allowed to see, but he'd gotten into his parents' Netflix account long before they clocked onto

157

him. Years, in fact. They never used it. Ben hadn't wanted to watch that show, but they'd made 'Good hunting' their phrase whenever they'd pretended they were going into battle in a space ship. Of course, they'd never lost.

'You know,' Orson said, 'I sat up there on my own after you left. I wouldn't let anybody else take your place. I wanted someone to try, so I could tell them to fuck off, like I wanted someone to know how I felt, but nobody tried. I don't think anybody dared.'

'Oh,' Ben said, obviously imagining a lone Orson on the top of that climbing frame where there had once been two of them. 'Man. I'm sorry. I always figured you'd...wait, didn't we have a girl with us playing that as a three? Her name was Natalie, wasn't it?'

'She got bummed out when you left too. So she sat on the bottom of the frame with that other girl Amy. Know what I did?'

'What?'

'I climbed up to our spot and then went down a few rungs until I was right behind them. Then I jumped over their heads. You should have heard it, Benji. They fucking *screamed*. I can still hear it now. They were all like "Oh my God! He jumped over our *heads*! He could have kicked us and killed us!"'

'What did old Taverner do?'

'Oh, she didn't see. It was "last break". You remember that? We always had an extra fifteen minutes in the afternoon, and nobody really supervised it. I planned it for then. No way was anybody gonna pin that

158

on me if they squealed. Full plausible deniability. But y'know what? They didn't. I think they liked the adrenaline. I only managed to do it once though. The next few times, they caught me sneaking up. That became the game. They always won.'

'Plausible deniability, huh?' Ben leaned his elbows onto the kitchen table and put his head on them. 'What movie are we gonna say we watched?'

'*Home Alone*,' Orson said instantly. 'Let's actually watch it.'

Chapter Eight

The next day started with flailing arms and a feeling like he was drowning. Only when Orson was in the centre of the centre of the Barstows' living room with the sounds of laughing children surrounding him did he realise that not only was he wrapped in Ben's duvet, but they'd fallen asleep under it. Together.

Now someone had tipped water over his head. What was this, another otter joke?

Ben was worse off though. The hibernation thing was still kicking in, even though he was awake and bent half over like a zombie, but what was really cracking people up, including Matthew, who for once wasn't glued to the Gameboy in his hand but looking up and smirking, was that Ben had a boner.

Too late already, Orson wriggled out of the duvet that had wrapped him up so it was nearly a straitjacket and wrapped it around Ben, who didn't seem to notice he'd done it apart from to take two handfuls of it and then zombie his way to the bathroom while holding it up like a sack.

'That was totally your idea, wasn't it?' Orson said, noticing the Nespresso machine and capsules laid out as if done for him. 'You want a double?'

'Grooooooooss,' Matthew said without looking up. 'Make me mocha if you're going to.'

'I bet you're still pissing about like a noob trying to get the magic cape.'

Matthew flipped him the bird. 'I'm playing Mario.'

'The old-school green-screen version adapted for colour?'

'Yuh-huh.'

'Have you figured out how to warp from world two to world five yet?'

That opened Matthew's eyes and made him look up. 'You can do that?'

Orson looked around himself and decided all the voices were coming from upstairs. 'Give it to me.'

Matthew handed it to him as if expecting nothing. He was on level two already. Orson speed-ran the level and jumped in two places most people wouldn't think to, then ran along the top of the screen with Mario invisible to reach the three pipes. He handed the Gameboy back just as Holly was coming down the hallway with Tasha. 'You want the pipe on the right,' he whispered.

'What on earth's happening down here?' Natasha said, only half-pretending to be serious.

'I dunno,' Orson said. 'I just woke up and my head was all wet.'

Matthew sniggered. Holly sighed. 'I'm so sorry. I told them to leave you both alone.' Right on cue, in came Seth and Kevin. 'You two! Say sorry right now! That was a horrible thing to do.'

'Oh, don't sweat it,' Orson said after they both did, and made a show of pretending to be. 'I've never woken up so fresh in my life. What time is it?' He looked at the microwave. 'Seven-oh-three? Jeeeez, when I was a kid, early wasn't a word I even knew.'

Matthew looked to his right slightly as the music that said he'd beaten the boss kicked in. 'The espresso cup's overflowing.'

'Bollocks!' Orson said, flicking the switch. The switch did nothing. The machine started making a noise like it was grinding coffee instead of percolating. 'Shit! What did I do?'

'Oh, not again!' Natasha pulled the plug out of the wall. 'That's the second one this month. We took the first one back because it broke the same way. I *told* John we should have gone for Delonghi instead of Machtech.'

'Middle-class problems,' Matthew said.

'Be quiet,' Holly said. 'And give me that. What did we tell you about when not to use it? Get a cloth and help clean up.'

'No, I'll do it,' Natasha said, also getting out the cafetiere and the ready-ground coffee.

'You little pishers,' Ben said, coming into the kitchen still towelling his hair off. 'Which one of you was it?'

'Him!' Seth and Kevin said in unison, pointing at each other.

Matthew blew hair out of his eyes. 'What do you want for breakfast, boner-bear?'

'Enough,' Holly said. 'Or you can go *without* breakfast.'

'Oh, it's no big deal,' Ben said. 'He's a boy, and his turn will come. One day somebody's going to prank him so hard that he'll hear the laughter when he's falling asleep for a month. His whole personality totally invites it.'

'You hear that?' Holly said.

Ella was here now. 'At least Ben would know what to *do* with his,' she said.

'No shit,' Matthew said. 'What movie d'ya think they watched together under that duvet?'

Ella was middle-school bad-girl action now. 'Number one, you walking pee-hole for a mouth, Ben's got a girlfriend and you know it. Number two, if you knew anything about sex at all, you'd know that the canal has to be big enough for the boat.' She looked at Orson. 'No offence.'

'None taken.'

'That's enough, young lady,' John said as he came in wearing a turquoise dressing gown with silver roses that was even louder than Ben's pink one. 'We've tolerated your inappropriate Christmas presents already; we don't need this kind of talk entertained in this house. Why is the whole family piling into the kitchen?'

Matthew fished his Gameboy out of Holly's back pocket as he left. 'The lounge is off limits coz the otter farted.'

163

'Matthew!' Holly said again.

'I totally *can* clear a room that way,' Orson said, leaning on the kitchen surface as Natasha handed him his coffee. It smelled rocket-fuel strong.

'Yeah, he isn't joking,' Ben said. 'I'd know; I sat next to him at school. I don't even wanna know what he's like with a hangover.'

'Just wait till I try curing one with fish and chips,' Orson said.

'Fish and chips!' John said with a great big smile, his daughter's humour obviously forgotten in a second. 'Now there's something I've missed. With faggot gravy and mushy peas. I really liked British food.'

'You did *what*?' Orson said. 'The British don't know anything about food; they think Chinese food is British just because you don't get food like that from a Chinese restaurant in China. Same for Indian. Fish and chips is mostly a national disgrace, not a national dish, and I've eaten it in the prime minister's house; even his chefs can't cook it right. You know who does though? Harry Hausen's in Soho. It looks like a grease trap on the outside, but he gets five-star inspections from the EHO every year, and there's no beating how he cooks it. You know what his secret is? He's German.'

'I remember it well,' John said.

'Wait,' Orson said. 'Did I hear that? *You* remember a restaurant in Soho?'

'You'd be surprised who does business with a bank like mine,' John said.

164

I fucking wouldn't, Orson thought. *Nor would I be if I walked into Waikiki's and found you with a bikinied snow leopard on your lap.* 'The British couldn't cook a fillet steak if it told them how while it was still mooing,' Orson said, copying what the Spanish head chef at the place where he waited tables had once told him. 'There's only one thing worth knowing about from England: bread and butter pudding. You make the meanest version with panettones.' He looked at the several boxes of them that were lined up above the cupboard. 'Want me to show you how?'

'That's a fantastic idea,' John said. 'I've not eaten bread and butter pudding since we left. Tasha doesn't like it and never makes it, but I bet she'll like that version. Something new and different for the Barstow Holiday Barbecue.'

You could hear the capital letters the way he said that. 'Oh,' Orson said. 'You're having a barbecue later?'

'We're having a full house,' John said. 'Father Ebert's coming with his family, and the Hills from across the road come every year. So do the Rileys from number three round the corner. And this year we've got the in-laws too. And you.'

And not my parents. A party? This is going to take mega self-control to get through. I'd better not drink until after it.

While everybody had been talking, Ella had loaded up a plate of cake for breakfast from the fridge and emptied the coffee pot. 'If we have to play charades because we can't get the Playstation out, I will *diiiiiiiiie.*

165

Remember the Rileys' stigmatism grandma who thought me and Dad doing a teapot and a cup was a hooker giving a blowjob to someone in a wheelchair?'

'Of course, because you've never let us forget it,' Natasha said before John could say anything.

Orson couldn't help himself. 'What kind of teapot and cup looks like *that* even if you're half blind?'

'Well quite,' John said. 'We'll do Pictionary instead of charades.'

'Why don't you just get the Playstation out?' Orson said. 'I'd love to know what Stigmatism Grandma thinks a Pokémon battle is.'

'Her name was Deirdre,' John said, sounding not so different from Orson's father's Mayor of London on TV voice. 'She only passed away six weeks ago, so perhaps it's best if nobody mentions her unless the Rileys do first.'

He said that like it was to his family, Orson thought, and it was as if they all knew already.

'Don't worry about the Playstation either,' he said. 'Our children spend far too much time on it as it is. Except for Benjamin, who spends all his time playing hockey.'

Yeah, that's what he's doing every time he leaves the house, isn't it? Hockey practice seven nights a week. Except when he's posing in tight underwear in front of a different variation of Ace every time.

'Wait here,' Ben said, touching Orson's arm. 'I'm going to get something you'll like. We defrosted it yesterday ready for this. Sorry I forgot to tell you about

166

the house party too, but don't worry; it's not just going to be a house full of bears and one otter. The Eberts are porcupines and the Rileys are cheetahs.'

'Cool,' Orson said. 'Shredded furniture and the fastest pizza delivery boys in the west.'

Natasha burst out laughing, and Orson felt like it was more at her husband's grimace than his joke, even if she was putting a hand on his shoulder. 'I wish they could have been here! The Rileys are pushing their kids for Ivy League colleges already. They're eleven and thirteen. Apart from the one who's eighteen, but you won't see him and they don't talk about him.'

'He ran off to California to be a drummer in a rock band,' Seth said. 'He's awesome. When our insurance pays out, I'm getting a kit like his.'

'We'll *see*,' Holly said.

She's worried, Orson thought. *She thinks it might not pay at all.*

'A word of warning,' John said to Seth. 'Scott Riley probably *does* deliver pizza because his band make no money. But I'll give it to him: I *can* imagine him wanting to be the fastest delivery boy on the block. But he'd use a moped and probably come close to getting himself killed at least three times a night.'

'Oh, don't kill it for him, John,' Natasha said. 'Seth was getting good.'

'I'm not, I'm just saying. Oh, look what Ben's got.'

Ben had the biggest salmon Orson had ever seen. He was straight there, only half believing it was real. Until he sniffed it. *That* was real. He closed his eyes and moved his muzzle from the nose of it to the tail. It wasn't just real, it was genuine Scottish Highlands salmon, imported at the kinds of dollars Orson probably didn't make in an entire week.

And they're gonna fucking barbecue *this?*

Just try it. You might find it's insanely good after all.

'Well what do you know,' Ben said. 'The thing about fish being a magnet to otters is true too.'

'Yeah, you totally didn't get this because you're bears, and you've totally never been on a bear pilgrimage to a salmon run somewhere.' Orson mimed a bear flipping salmon out of the water and made a *fshhhhh* noise.

'Bears don't actually do that; they use a fishing rod,' Matthew said.

'Errr,' Ben said, 'we got it for you and your parents. None of us like salmon.'

'Oh,' Orson said, now staring at the salmon as if he were on an episode of *Creatures vs Food*. 'I hope your guests like fish then, because there's no way I can make up for Mum and Dad with that thing, otter or not.'

'Don't make him feel so awful with such nonsense, Benjamin,' Natasha said. She touched Orson's shoulder. 'We *all* like salmon, and we get one every Christmas for this.'

'Going to a salmon run actually *is* a bear rite of passage,' John said. 'And Benjamin still hasn't been. Every year there's some excuse.'

Oh I bet there is. He looked at Ben. 'Why not?'

'Urgh, can we not, Dad? It's not my thing. I don't like the smell of that much fish.'

Ella came in with her breakfast dishes. 'He doesn't want to wave Little Benji around in front of loads of other bears.'

'He can wear swimwear like I always do,' John said.

'Let's get the barbecue out and get started,' Natasha said. 'Or it'll be one o'clock before we know it and the food will be cold.'

Orson waited until everyone had filed out into the yard, pulling coats on. 'Little Benji?'

'I don't actually call my penis that. Did you really just believe a teenage girl when it comes to boy-stuff?'

'Only the part where you actually do call it something.'

'Of course I do,' he said. 'But it's a secret.' He smacked Orson's butt after sliding the fish plate onto the table.

'Oi! Next time I'll tell your cousins to pour the water on Little Benji instead.'

'Head's up, you know why our neighbours really like this party every year? It's because Mom's a total lightweight, and every year she gets too hot working the barbecue and doesn't realise how much wine goes back because of it.' Ben mimed throwing a drink back. 'By five p.m. she's usually said something outrageous and then tried to dig herself out of a hole. Until you and your parents were coming, she swore blind we weren't having a salmon this year. Know why?'

'I'm about to, aren't I?'

169

'Last year she told everyone about *her* first salmon run. She was sixteen. She *didn't* go with the swimwear. Most bears didn't back then. But she had a whole lot of fun with a guy who wasn't Dad. Okay, they hadn't met back then. But anyway, her guy turned out to be a girl.'

'Result!' Orson sang the 'I Kissed a Girl and I Liked It' song, then laughed at his awful singing voice. '*Did* she like it?'

'I don't know. That's where I stopped her talking because Dad had literally gone and hidden in the bathroom.' Ben took a large roll of tin foil from a cupboard. 'Salmon up! Want to help me wrap it?'

Orson helped. 'Y'know, I'd say it's a crime to barbecue something this good, but then again, you're not even going to fit it in that big range oven over there. This is a Schwarzenegger salmon, Benji, seriously. It was probably ripped as fuck on plankton steroids and ready to win that muscle contest and impress its bros. Then some bear swiped it out of the riptide on its way to the spawning love nest, and goodnight Vienna. Now its final resting place is a bear barbecue.'

'Who taught you English at secondary school? I had no idea you could be so eloquent.'

'Blow me. Oh wait.'

'Shhh! If you're tempted by that kind of joke already then please stay sober at this party, won't you?'

Orson felt for his pocket and realised he was still in pyjamas. 'Where are my cigarettes? I actually don't remember having one last night.'

170

'You didn't. They're where you left them: on the windowsill in the bathroom when you got undressed.' Ben paused for a second on his way to the door, holding the wrapped salmon. 'For the shower.'

Was he genuinely worried? Orson thought on his way upstairs. *Was waking up under a duvet with the TV still on with another guy under there really a red flag to this family?*

So he had a massive boner. We were both in dry pyjama bottoms. I've woken up with people in a worse state.

Orson shrugged, wondering if this kind of nonchalance really was Matthew Barstow's default setting. Then he saw the waste bin.

How were there two used condoms in Ben's bathroom waste? They hadn't used one all night. It was squirt, squirt, squirt, like it was a contest. For a moment, Orson thought of Ben's gentle fingers cleaning his butt out in the shower and his semi rubbed against his pants. Then he realised that if anybody saw this, regardless of how it must have been Ben jerking off the night before without wanting to make a mess, they weren't going to believe that Ben had acted alone. Not after all the jokes. He wondered if Ben emptied his own trash when nobody was looking. He thought of how obsessively tidy he'd seen John trying to be despite the house full of kids. He thought of John maybe having had a life-long licence to tidy the bedroom of his most doted-upon child at will, or Natasha making their beds for them, and the doubt was all there.

'You're catastrophising again,' he heard some therapist tell him.

No matter. It was easy enough to stop this unwanted thought. All he had to do was what he was doing: pocket the two condoms, put back inside their wrappers just for extra safety, and bin them downstairs.

Bad idea. Someone will see that. All it takes is one kid trying to get something back out of the bin. Or a team effort at taking out the trash that makes the bag burst.

I don't want to worry about this. I want to go downstairs looking forward to salmon.

Orson looked around himself, shut the bedroom door, then flushed them down the toilet.

* * *

Orson began to wonder if years of memorising rooms and maps in FPS games had given him a knack for real rooms. Not only was his unspoken job to keep John Barstow out of his own kitchen, but he was accomplishing it on little more than knowing where things were from the Christmas Day breakfast with Natasha. He taught her and Ella how to make the Panettoni bread and butter pudding, and not content with it, he found there was the right stuff to make gingerbread. The kitchen was smelling like Christmas, and it belonged to him. Natasha rattled off a barbecue list like she might have gone through medications and treatments with a junior doctor, and Orson remembered it all without phone notes.

It didn't get him out of playing charades though. Once the outdoors was in full swing, he teamed up with Ben and soon realised that what would get him through was making as much of a fool of himself as possible, and Ben soon followed suit. When Matthew decided to give them the chao garden from Sonic Adventure 2 to mime, Orson felt a chill of coincidence, and then only Ben knew why he was laughing.

Everyone laughed as Orson rolled forwards over and over and Ben pretended to control him with a joypad, then even more when they pulled each other's tails for Tails, then mimed hiking up a mountain for adventure, and then the best part: Ben got to be the chao, and Orson fed him the little coloured bricks and pretend animals. Ben even remembered how if you gave a chao a seed, it would plant a tree.

Turned out nobody knew what chao were. Ben explained it.

'My friend once had this bet,' Orson said. 'About clocking all the achievements in that game. Then he forgot the chao garden. That takes *days*.'

'What was the forfeit?' Father Ebert asked.

'I...' Orson looked at Ben. 'He had to eat a whole tin of dog food. I fed it to him with a spoon.'

'Did he finish it?'

'Nope.' Orson mimed bulging cheeks and made the puking sound. 'Do I smell the salmon being ready? Mmmm!' He did what he knew everyone wanted to see:

173

walked on tiptoes to the yard with his nose in the air, like a cartoon character following a visible scent.

From behind him, he heard what he realised he should have been waiting for: 'The otter seems a lot of fun,' Lois Riley said to Natasha, who had stepped back from barbecue duties to have another glass of wine in a cooler place. 'An English boy too. Where did you hire him?'

'Hire him?' Natasha said. 'Oh, right, the kitchen! Oh no, that's not it. He's an old friend of Benjamin's.'

'He's not the help?'

'Lois, I do enjoy your company, but really, what do *I* need hired help for? My family do these things for me because they want to.'

'Well obviously, but the otter isn't family. Is he?'

'His name's Orson. Why don't you go and say hello? He doesn't bite. I'd know, I once looked after him when he was sick and grouchy because he couldn't collect his Christmas present from the school party.'

Orson smiled. Lois Riley was moving her way to the other side of the yard to him by way of conversation and not taking her advice.

The priest had said hello, Orson thought. He liked Father Ebert, who not content with the glöög that was filling the kitchen with the scent of hot vodka and spices had helped himself to the open bottle near the stove and poured an extra shot in. Respect – the guy was still standing and on his fifth cup.

The salmon was the best Orson had ever tasted. All the better for not being served like a Michelin star dish, but in a heap, flaked off the bone and still a little bit rare, on a bed of potato salad with chives, pumpkin bread smothered in butter, spinach leaves with vinaigrette dressing and cherry tomatoes. Hell, it was the best Christmas meal he'd had full stop. It was all he could do to eat slowly and not scoff. There was enough dessert on the trolly (of course the Barstows actually had one) to fill a patisserie. Orson went for the sherry chocolate trifle and a side helping of peach tart. Surprisingly, they went together. The peaches had something like Amaretti in them, he thought.

Stuffed, feeling like he was on his break at work after dinner in the kitchen, he got himself a large scotch on the rocks and stepped away from the others to smoke. He realised he must be sleepy-tired, or the beer he'd already had had gone to his head, because it took him a moment to realise that the odd feeling he had was that he had company, and company had been there for a good few minutes, lurking like a stalking ghoul in a game of Silent Hill.

'Hi,' the cheetah dressed in leather about Orson's age said. 'I'm Scott.' He offered Orson a pack of Lucky Strikes. Orson took one. When had this guy come in? Had he even used the front door, let alone rung the bell? He smelt of gin, tonic, a hint of cheap cologne, and Orson would have sworn blind there was a hint of freebase smoke in the air had this guy not been so calm.

'For what we have just received,' Orson said, 'may Satan make us truly thankful.'

The cheetah laughed. 'Oh, you've met the Barstows then. Their religious shit bored me for years, but hey, good people.' He dragged enough smoke down to make most people cough their guts up, but he didn't. 'Oh, now I get it. That's what you've heard about me? That I'm in a Satan band? Or am I *actually* the devil himself now?'

'The second,' Orson decided.

'Fuck, I'm good. Just so you know what the game is, I'm not going to go talk to Mom and Dad; I'm timing how long it takes them to crack and come to me. I've been out here for an hour already. Nothing. But they'll bite. Just give it time. Do me a favour in a minute: see if you can get a couple of drinks down my mom. Spike her if you have to.'

'That's gonna be pretty difficult considering she won't come near me, let alone me go near her. Tell me something, did you ever have an otter nanny who maybe did something naughty? That how you got "corrupted"?'

Scott Riley laughed. 'I wish. Mom's just uncomfortable with strangers. You met any other otters here in New York yet?'

'Nope.'

'Let's just say Mom's used to otters being a lot less polite than you are.'

'That is a *scary* thought, cheetah-pants.'

Scott looked at him, surprised. 'I've been called a lot of things, but that's a new one.'

'Call it an in-joke here. Started on Christmas Day when Ben gave me "otterpants" and his uncle made a joke about which way round the big hole went.'

'That sounds like Cliff. Wait, you were here on Christmas Day? With the Barstows? Okay, now I've really gotta know: what's your story?'

Orson told him. The gaming, Syd Sheldon, the intervention, the thought of Christmas with Ben being his reward if he could turn his life back around.

'You ever feel guilty about Syd?' Scott said.

'All the time.'

'Don't. He deserved it for being that fucking stupid. The chao garden? Even I would have thought of that, and I'm not smart. Just smart enough to survive in Cali without much money and a bit of talent. I've got to meet the mayor of London though. There's a song in that, I'd bet money on it. Where's your old man?'

'Oh, my parents went home. Some political crisis.'

'You didn't go with them?'

'Why the fuck would I do that? You should go eat some of that salmon over there.'

'No, I mean you wouldn't by choice, but they didn't make you? After practically keeping an ankle bracelet on you for the last eighteen months, they just left you here? In New fucking York?'

'They didn't just leave me here, they...' Orson looked at everyone around the barbecue, drinking, laughing, and being families. Lois Riley looked like she had dared herself to have a spritzer or two, and that was all it had taken.

Mum and Dad really didn't say goodbye to me. They didn't even leave much of a message.

'Yeah,' Orson said. 'They left me here. But why wouldn't they? I've been on good behaviour.'

'That's overrated,' Scott said. 'You ever heard a song called 'Santa's Sleigh Ride'? It's about how everyone mistakes Santa for a burglar, and the last straw is when someone stabs him in the face with a biro. I dare you to find the laptop that's playing that Spotify Christmas crap and put that on there.

'Let me guess, that's your band.'

'We're called The Chainsaw Bears.'

'Even though the drummer's a cheetah.'

'Yep.'

'Is it true you guys are the fastest pizza delivery boys in the west?'

Scott shrugged. 'Gotta pay the rent somehow while your band tries to get a deal. I've got some free promo CDs I wrapped up for the Barstows' kids. I'm gonna go hand them out. By the way, just my two cents, that gaming addiction thing's a crock, and you should start again. You'd make more money as a pro gamer than you would waiting tables. You don't wanna be doing that forever any more than I want to keep being employee of the month at fucking Domino's.'

'Think I'll pass. But thanks.'

Scott turned around and gave him a sly smile. 'It wasn't a *gaming* problem you had, "Otterpants".' He flicked his cigarette into the snowy grass and walked up to the house with the same gunslinger stance he probably entered onto a stage with.

Orson took out another one to replace the one of Scott's that he hadn't really been smoking. Not because he wanted it really, but because he wanted an excuse to stand away from everyone and just look at them. His own home had never been like this. There were never more than three people in it at Christmas. He'd been dragged to various parties, sure, but none of them were fun. None of them had people like this who seemed happy to be there. His parents had never wanted a party in their home, or this sort of company.

Not once.

Orson decided he would live up to being the kitchen help and get started on the washing up. Not because it actually needed doing yet, but because the kitchen windows would give him a full view of how things went now that Lois Riley had decided to speak to her son and Mr Riley (whatever his name was – another non-introduction) had decided to join in. Public School Brats Riley #1 and #2 actually looked pleased to see big brother and were evidently failing in their efforts to hide the fact.

'Oh come on,' Natasha said. 'We've got a dishwasher for this!'

'I'm not really washing up,' Orson said. 'I'm watching *this* play out.'

'You wicked boy,' Natasha said, an invisible cloud of red wine scent all around her. 'Shit,' she whispered. 'Is that Scott?'

'He's been here for an hour already. Sportsman's bet? This gets explosive. Ready for bouncers Ben and Orson to step in and save your family home?'

'Let me do that if it happens,' John said, coming to the window now. 'Scott can be an absolute handful. Let's get away from the window before everyone else comes to it.'

'Can I keep washing up?'

'Yes, I suppose one person should watch them. Call me if you need to.'

Orson didn't. He'd washed up most of the guests' plates and all the cooking utensils by the time the waters had calmed, but he watched the Riley parents hug their eldest son and thought the only thing missing was Scott unexpectedly crying like his mom was. Brats #1 and #2 now looked like two kids who wanted one more rock and roll Christmas before their teenage robbed them of all the magic. Orson wondered if the younger one still did believe in Santa and had put his big brother coming home on a Christmas list.

'I know, right?' Ella said. 'I think I'm gonna throw up. It won't last. I'll give them two days before Scott and Eric have a Christmas punch-up.'

'Eric's daddy-chee, right?'

Before she could answer, panic came from down the hallway near the front door. 'Awwww no! No no no no no!' It was from behind a door, but everyone heard Sam Barstow, and the toilet still flushing after he'd opened it. 'Can someone help please? There's water everywhere, and it's leaking into the hall!'

The sound that followed was like a giant water bomb going off, then a great splattering, then a gush. Then Sam yelled, 'Oh *shit*! *Moooooom*! *Daaaad*!'

Orson got there first. Water and gunge was pouring out from over the rim of the toilet like thick soup. The front hall was already a paddling pool. At least Sam had got the door open.

'Okay, get towels,' Orson said. 'Get all the towels you can find; we need to bank this up like flood defences.' It was a miniature version of what he'd been part of in London when the River Thames had flooded and all hands were on deck on every street.

That had been a photo where he'd actually been glad to be snapped next to his father, actually doing something. Crisis management that wasn't about winning a round of something on a screen.

'Not you!' Ella said, stopping Sam before he could track shitty footprints all through the house. 'Everyone else. You three, get upstairs and get towels.'

'Please would be nice,' Matthew said.

'Just do it, fuckbrain,' Ella said. 'Or do you wanna be finding a motel tonight?'

'Oh good lord!' John said, after walking into the scene like he'd thought this would be little more than kid-generated Christmas overexcitement. 'What *happened* here?'

'I don't know, Dad!' Sam looked like he was about to start crying. 'I just went for a poo and flushed, and it just happened.'

181

'Alright, not your fault,' John said. 'I'll go and get the two mops from the kitchen; Ella, would you go out to the yard and get the big broom, please?'

Seth and Kevin had found towels, and Orson now knew the horror of what he'd accidentally set in motion as they threw them down on the floor and piled them up before he could say anything to stop them.

Natasha got there now. 'Oh my GOD! The towels! The cashmere towels Mom and Dad gave us last year! Oh...just...*fuck*! Who got *those* out?'

Seth and Kevin looked like *they* could shit now, just to add to the mess. Matthew no longer looked so stoic. He was trying to creep back up the stairs before his brothers could point out that he was the one tall enough to reach the towels.

'Don't worry, Tasha,' John said. 'We'll get new ones.'

'You *can't* get bloody new ones, John, they were a once-only design, and they cost fifty dollars each.'

'That's cheaper than replacing the entire downstairs floor and carpets, Tash. If it had got much further, it would have been in the dining room, then where would we eat for the rest of the holiday?'

Natasha Barstow sighed heavily, her hands to her mouth. 'Yes, you're right. I'm sorry, everyone. Let's just get on with cleaning it up.'

She stopped, looked around her, realising what Orson already knew: every guest at this party was now crowding around, despite the smell.

'Maybe it's time we were going home,' Father Ebert said, gathering his family with a spread of his arms. 'We'll use the side entrance, perhaps?'

'I'll go and open it for everyone,' Ben said. Orson hadn't noticed he was there, but now that he'd seen him and heard that voice come out of him, everything felt wrong.

He saw it a moment later and turned away just as quickly. On the bottom of the front door, snagged by the small amount of frame that sat proud on the floor, lolling onto the doormat, were two flushed condoms, tied at the top.

Chapter Nine

'Just a minute here.' John Barstow was picking up the sticky plastic mess from the doorway, looking a long way away from being the man who'd been looking forward to a family barbecue that morning. 'What is *this* doing in our toilet drainage?'

'It might not have come from ours, Dad,' Ben said.

John looked at his son with a staring, accusing frown. 'How exactly did you figure that out?'

Why did you speak? Orson thought. *Shit, Benji, why? It's always the guy who tries to cover it first. He knows it was me. He's gonna be pissed. If I'm not packing my bags by the end of tonight –*

'It's just basic plumbing, Dad. We don't have a tank, we're on the mains, and that means every toilet in the block feeds into it.'

'So this wasn't you? You swear to it?'

'I promise, Dad, this wasn't me.'

At least he's not lying about the flushing part, Orson thought, silently thanking Ben's father for using the wrong implied question.

'Boys!' John called out. 'Everyone in here now.'

'John, really,' Natasha said. 'Ben's right. Just don't react to this. It probably didn't cause the blockage anyway; it just came up. I've called the emergency plumber, and he'll be here in half an hour. Until he comes, there's an emergency bucket in the bathroom upstairs if anyone needs a wee. Why don't we all sit down and have another drink and...well, why don't we get the PlayStation out?'

'I want to hear this first,' John said. 'Myself.'

The boys were in a line. Even Ben, who'd already had his turn. John hadn't asked for it, but this was like a parade. Orson's own stomach swam. He didn't need to take a dump; he needed to be sick. He was going to be if this didn't end soon.

How could he possibly afford to repay the Barstows for the damage this had caused if he owned up? How could he *not* own up if John went crazy because none of the kids did?

'Samuel, was this you?'

'John, he's twelve,' Natasha said. 'Yes, I've had that talk with him already and believe me, this was not him.'

'No, Dad,' Sam said.

'Matthew?'

'No, Uncle John. I'm too young to masturbate.'

Ella couldn't hold it any longer. She laughed. 'Jesus, I bet he even believes that and thinks that's what condoms are for.'

'Was this *you*, young lady?'

'Dad, seriously, wake up. You see any boys around here I'm not related to? Okay, there's the otter, but he's a decent person, and I'm pretty sure he's gay anyway. So why the fuck would I *need* a condom, let alone flush one?'

'Don't you dare use language like that with me!' John snapped. 'Or say things like that about a guest in this house! Orson wouldn't dare behave like that in someone else's home and everyone here knows it.'

Orson's heart was thudding, just like it had when Ben had been naked on the bed. And taken Orson's clothes off him. And put lube inside his butthole and then his great big white un-snipped erect shaft.

Now Orson's panic was real, and nothing was happening to him in his pants except feeling like he might wet them. This was why Ben wouldn't come out to his family. This man would *murder* anyone who had done such things with his golden college boy.

'Orson,' John said. 'Please just tell me, that *is* true, isn't it?'

This is easy. All you have to do is look him in the eye and lie. You're good at that. Your father's the fucking mayor of London for god's sake; you learned from the elite.

'John.' Cliff was here now.

'What?'

'For God's sake, calm down. It was me. I flushed them.'

'*What*?' John said. 'You?'

'Yeah. Three kids is plenty for me, John. I never got snipped.'

'It's true,' Holly said, joining her husband and taking his hand. 'All of it, I mean. I'm sorry, John, but it's been a hell of a holiday season already with the house burning down and well...you know, we had to cheer up somehow just to stay sane.'

'Oh come on,' John said, now looking incredibly sheepish. 'You're a married couple; why would I judge that? You thought I wouldn't want you to do that because it's not your house?' He thought for a moment. 'Really? Did I make you think that, somehow?'

'Well, no,' Holly said. 'We just...'

'I was just lazy,' Cliff said. 'I often do it at home too. It's never totally blocked the drains before. I'm sorry, John. I should have just used the trash. I'll pay for the damage.'

'Don't be silly,' John said. 'It was probably just like Ben said anyway. They didn't cause the block.'

'Actually, Dad, Mom said that,' Ben said, still as cool as always. For once, Orson didn't like it.

John sighed. 'I'm sorry, everyone. I overreacted. Boys, I owe you all an apology. Ella, I shouldn't have accused you either. Or shouted. I'll do an extra penance in church next Sunday. Orson, I'm sorry I even asked you anything about it.'

'It's cool, Mr B,' Orson said. *I did not deserve that. Whether it was a guardian angel or sheer, dumb luck of coincidence, I just got away with more stupid shit that should have cost me.*

187

'Where's Sam?' Natasha said. Orson read it on her easily: she already knew, just like Ella did.

'He went upstairs crying about five minutes ago,' Ella said.

'Okay, I'll go,' John said. 'I'll sort this.'

'Take your shoes off before you go up there,' Natasha said.

How drunk is she? Orson thought. She might not be slurring speech or staggering, but there was the kind of edge to her that you didn't get from people like that when they were sober, and if you did then drink amplified it, just like this.

John sighed again. 'Uhhhh, too late. Sam already didn't.'

'I'll get the carpet washer out,' Natasha said. 'Let's get some more windows open; the place is starting to smell.'

Matthew took out his Gameboy again. Orson started to think it was a bit like him getting out a packet of cigarettes. 'Crowded house equals too many bears shitting in the woods.'

'Go to your room, Matthew!' Cliff and Holly both said in unison.

'Duh, my room's a pile of ash somewhere in Queens.' He went upstairs without resistance to whichever room he was in.

'I'll keep on mopping the hall out,' Orson said. 'We'll wash the floor with some bleach or something afterwards.'

'Use Flash,' Natasha called from the kitchen. 'It's here under the sink.'

Predictably, Ben helped. So did Cliff. They waited for the rest of the family to clean shoes and then get comfortable in the living room.

'You okay?' Ben said. 'I'm sorry about Dad. I think it's really the floor getting covered in sewage that made him as mad as that.'

'I fucked up, Benji. I'm an idiot.'

Now he felt like a bigger one, because Ben hadn't recognised his fear for what it really was, and he could have just said nothing.

'*You...*' Ben said. 'Not the...'

'Yeah. I saw them there and I panicked, and I just did it.'

Ben looked between Orson and Cliff in disbelief. 'You covered for us?'

'That's what family do, kid,' Cliff said. 'I knew it was him. It was written all over him. John was too mad to see it.'

'*Us?*' Orson said, remembering everything Cliff had told him about how he didn't have to become Ben's boyfriend. 'I was covering for *you*. You actually jerk off into condoms?'

Ben hunched up a little. 'I just like the feeling of them, that's all. Some people really don't like them, but I think they're...well...I just like wearing them.'

'Good,' Cliff said, patting Ben heavily on the shoulder. 'Means you're bein' careful.' He winked at both of them.

189

'Could you thank Holly for me too?' Orson said.

'She wasn't playing along, Otterpants,' Ben said. 'The only part Cliff invented was the flushing.'

'Oh.'

Cliff grinned. 'Three kids is definitely enough.'

'Hey Cliff,' Orson said. 'Can I just tell you something? I just...there's something I was wondering if I can help *you* with.'

'Sure. What's on your mind?'

* * *

The plumber, Orson thought, was almost like a dog version of Ben. His tail wagged at everything, like an exaggerated version of service-with-a-smile, and even though it was still with concentration as he stuck tools down the drain and tried some simple unclogging methods, he still said, 'Yep, it's properly bunged up down there!' with the same enthusiasm a rocket engineer might have given to a big, NASA-scale challenge. 'We're gonna have to bring the snake in.'

At least it wasn't really that I flushed two bear-sized condoms, Orson thought. He wasn't going to get to see the snake in action though, however it worked, because Ben had brought Matthew downstairs.

'What am I down here for?' Matthew said.

'Your dad and Orson want to talk to you.'

'The otter? What for?'

'Stop calling him that,' Cliff said. 'You know his proper name, so use it. There's some advice he wants to give you, and I want you to listen. Let's go in the yard.'

'It's cold out there.'

'So put your goddamn coat on,' Cliff said, in the kind of voice Orson knew meant 'stop talking'.

He'd lost count of how many times he'd wrapped himself up for the snowy outdoors lately, but Orson was starting to think he'd miss the comfort of this many layers when back in England. They sat on the garden chairs near the now closed-up barbecue.

'I'm not especially smart,' Orson said. 'But I gather you are. Let me tell you how dense I can be. When you went upstairs, I realised all along, there's a question I just never thought of. If your entire house and everything in it burned down, how come you've still got your Gameboy?'

'My friend borrowed it.'

Orson already knew it, because Cliff had told him ten minutes ago.

'It's the only thing you've got left, right? Apart from the comic books you rescued. Then you donated one as a Christmas present for a complete stranger. Was there much else you managed to get out of the place that wasn't completely wrecked?'

Matthew looked up, and this time Orson knew he wasn't going to say anything. His eyes really could say more than he often let them.

'I wanted to tell you,' Orson said, 'that it's okay to be upset, and that maybe you should talk to your dad about how you're feeling lately. Because he's good at talking like that. He did it for me too, even though he's kind of a stranger to me. He's done it for Ben as well. Your parents are supposed to be totally uncool just when you're about to be a teenager, but hey, yours are here for you. I made a mistake once. When I felt kinda like I think you do, I didn't talk to mine, and...well, I'm not exactly sure they *were* there for me. So I know what it's like to feel like you're all alone even when surrounded by people. I played on whatever I could get my hands on all the time too, and I was sarcastic and cynical to everyone, and I didn't talk much, and everything except gaming was lame. I didn't behave well in school either, and I didn't care how much trouble I got in. Because the best things I'd had were gone.'

It had the effect sooner than he'd expected, and Orson felt so disarmed, he knew he was going to have to walk away and let Cliff handle it. Matthew had his hands to his face, trying to hide his crying.

'It's okay,' Cliff said. 'Come give me a hug. I'm sorry we didn't talk about this sooner.'

'I'll go inside and play games with the others,' Orson said.

'No. Don't.' It was Matthew who said it. 'Your house burned down too? Tell me about it.'

'No, my house didn't burn down. I still had my room with all my things. I felt like my house might as *well* have burned down. I was so mad at everything that I actually felt like setting the place on fire. What I lost was my best friend. When Ben moved away, I felt like I'd lost my *only* friend even though it wasn't true. I didn't want anyone else to try and take his place. So I shut myself off from people. All I wanted to do was gaming, gaming, gaming. I know you're not addicted to that Gameboy, but I just wanted to tell you, people like you and they want to help you not feel so shit about everything. I didn't let anyone help me back then. It didn't lead to anything good. So yeah, be Bernard from Megamind if it helps. I know it actually *is* your favourite movie because your dad just told me. But y'know that part where there's a different Bernard who "has feelings"? Don't let that not be you.'

Matthew smiled and wiped his face. 'I'm not allowed to insult otters directly.'

'Then give me a hug too.'

'Won't you be slippery?'

Cliff sighed. 'Matthew, we've talked about offensive stereotypes.'

'I'm hugging him, aren't I?' Matthew said. 'It was a joke, Dad. How could he be slippery with this many jackets on?' Matthew wiped his face again and this time brushed the hair away from his eyes so it stayed away from them. 'I'm sorry I kept calling you the otter though.'

'Oh, don't be. I've always been Orson the Otter. Parents think it's cute when you're a kid, but you know what I've realised mine really hated?' He'd only thought of it now, but he knew it was true. 'My parents hated how I *never* stopped finding it cute. I always *did* want to be an *otter* otter: we're playful, we're squeaky, we

193

always want to be in water, we like feeeesh, and we're called Olly or Oscar or Orville. Or Orson. My parents hated people nicknaming me Double-Oh. Who did they have to blame for it but themselves?'

'Yeah,' Matthew said. 'At least I wasn't Benjamin Bear like my cousin.'

'My parents hated that pants thing on Christmas Day too. That's why I loved it. Ben started actually *calling* me Otterpants. I like it. You know why? Because I'm a big kid. Pants are funny. Especially if they've got a big hole in them. So are fart jokes and pee jokes and dick jokes. I've loved being a kid with this family. I used to be that kid. Then after Ben left...'

'After Ben left what?'

'I don't think I had much of a childhood. I... I don't think I really...' Orson decided it was time to stop. He didn't want to say it.

'Hey Orson. Was Ella right about you?'

'Right how?'

'*Are* you gay?'

Cliff put his hands on his son's shoulders. 'That's too personal a thing to ask, Matthew. Even if we are talking about serious stuff. Who someone likes is their own business. You know that. Why did you ask Orson that?'

'Because I think I am.'

Jesus, Orson thought. *Of course. Why else? Cliff missed that? Now I've really got no clue what I'm doing.*

'What?' Matthew said, his slouch gone and now standing up straight. '*He's* proud of what he is. Why

194

shouldn't I be? Mom said the same thing when I told her this. So did the school counsellor when I told her.'

'Errr...liking the species you are isn't exactly the same thing as...urgh, shit, what am I meant to say right now, Cliff?'

'Boy,' Cliff said to his son, 'you really pick your moments for surprise, don't you?'

'You don't mind though, do you?'

'That you think you might be gay? Of course I don't,' Cliff said.

Matthew looked like he'd known it all along. 'You're not like Uncle John and Aunt Tasha. Or Ella. Or Ben. Or Sam. They're all weird about it with the whole church thing. They don't like me anyway. I heard Ben call me a "little stinker".'

'Okay,' Cliff said, obviously trying to smile his way out of bewilderment. 'Well done for suggesting a heart-to-heart with my kid, otter-boy. Come on, *stinker*. We're going for a walk round the block to talk about a few things. Starting with how Ben called you that with love and affection.'

'Yeah, right.'

'Definitely charades time for me,' Orson said, making his way back into the house. He decided he'd tell Ben that the pep-talk had gone well. Until he saw Ben in the corridor, looking horrified.

'Matthew thinks I don't like him?'

'It's not really like that.'

'Then why did he say that?'

Oh boy. 'Ben, how much of that whole thing did you hear?'

'Just the end of it. I was coming out to ask you if you wanted another drink and see how it was going.' Ben looked tired. 'When did he hear me say that? I said it to Ella, and she agreed because...oh, come on. You remember me in school, how you used to be jealous because I was good at so much? Well, I know how you felt. Matty just *does* everything as soon as he picks it up. Drawing, story writing, music; he's creative. Like I wish I could be, and it takes him no effort. And he can skate. He's a fat little bear, but he could practically skate backwards while still playing that Gameboy. He got it within weeks when it took me months. That *is* a little stinker.'

'Totally, Snowbear.'

'I *did* say it with love and affection. He thinks I *don't* love him?'

No point in sugar coating, Orson decided. 'He said he thought you didn't *like* him. You can have a talk with him later too. Believe me, I think he'll be open to it.'

'Oh?'

'That walk they've gone for might last a while.'

'Come upstairs with me for a few minutes. I want to show you something.'

Orson thought he could do with lying down for a while. Maybe after whatever Ben showed him, he'd be able to. Hopefully Ben just wanted to show him his dick and have some quick fun to celebrate getting away with the condom flushing.

'Here,' Ben said after shutting the door and taking out a black plastic box. 'Take a look.'

Orson opened it. Ben was in every photo, in all his glory, a different brand on the underwear in each one. In several of them, he was posing with the bear Orson knew was Ace, but from an unusual front-pose for the two of them.

'I know you didn't believe me,' Ben said. 'So there they are.'

'I *did* believe you,' Orson said.

'They didn't end up in a magazine or on a billboard because they weren't deemed to be good enough,' Ben said. 'They still paid me for the shoot. But I'm not who they wanted to actually sell their stuff. I didn't...have the appeal. I didn't show these to you because they remind me of that sometimes. They make me feel bad about myself.'

'Really? Benji, you look absolutely *smoking* hot in these!'

'When I look at them, I don't feel it. Can we put them away now, please?'

Orson sealed them shut again. 'Somebody's in a bad mood then.'

'Don't, Orson.'

It sounded like too much of a warning for Orson's liking. 'Oooookay, so...you brought me up here to show me those. Sure I can't do something to cheer you up? Just quick and quiet? Or do you wanna do me?'

'You can't do what I need when I feel like this. I want to lie down for a bit. Can you go play a game or something? Why don't you show Matthew how to get the magic cape? You seem to get on well with him.'

'Benji, don't be a dick, okay? So your cousin hurt your feelings. Boo hoo, that's what kids do without meaning to. I did it to my parents plenty, and loads of other people, and sometimes I feel bad for it, but it wasn't really my fault. I was just being a kid.'

'Go be a kid with my family then. You're good at that.'

'You know what?' Orson said, his hackles rising on his back. 'Just fuck off then. I *did* believe you when you said you were a model. I *do* mean it when I say you should have got picked. It's not just because I'm always horny when I think about your naked body, after *you* sprang a full naked show on me when I wasn't expecting it. Right down to showing me your arsehole. If you're going to act like one, fine. Do it on your own. I *will* go be with your family.'

Ben sat up, with a look Orson didn't like. 'Actually, I was wrong. Maybe you *do* have it. Talk to me like that again.'

'Now you want to get off after pissing me off? Forget it. I'm serious. I'm not playing around, and this isn't an act.'

'You know what I once got Ace to do to me? I got him to spank me until I started crying. He thought I'd safety before I got there. I didn't. I kept crying. So he got cold feet and asked me what the whole idea of this was. I told him just keep going and I'd tell him when to stop. So he did. Until I told him to comfort me. That's when I really let go. Right to the point where afterwards he sat me down and asked if I needed *real* therapy. I don't care about what Matty said. *That* was hurt feelings.'

'For asking if you needed help? Seriously?'

'He was supposed to get why that routine worked for me. I loved it. Then he ruined it. All my life I've been this nice, good person who's everything the world says he should be. I just wanted to be like you. Bad, not caring, doing what he wanted. I wanted your life. I wanted *your* parents. I wanted Ace to make me feel like I'd had all that and punish me for it *and* I wanted to know I was being bad all at once just by doing it.'

'Ben, that's all fantasy and play. You don't really want that, and believe me, you do *not* want my life. You're going to be a dentist. The world actually needs you. I'm going to be waiting tables for rich assholes until I retire to whatever dump I can afford.'

'Jerk me off. I need the release. Put your hands down my pants.'

'No.'

'Please?' Ben said. 'Come on, please don't make me beg. I've been horny all day since I woke up with that erection they all laughed at. I've been adjusting my pants all day when nobody was looking, trying not to go into the bathroom and play with myself. I failed twice. *You* found the evidence. Was my semen still warm when you flushed those condoms? Did you take a sniff?'

'Okay, yes, they were, and yes, I did.' Maybe that would do enough for Ben that he could jerk off again on his own. Then Orson decided better. 'Fine. Here you go, you needy little brat-bear. Your shitty behaviour sucks, so if what you need's to come and go to sleep with your pants still full of it, it gets you off my back.'

Orson played it rough. Ben seemed to like it, even though he insisted on no noise. Hard himself, he got nowhere near a climax as Ben reached his, his head back and looking at the ceiling rather than at Orson, with no sign of affection, or even telling Orson he liked the tip thing. This time, he just seemed to expect it.

'Thanks,' Ben said. 'That's better. Unnnnf, okay.' Before Orson could think of cleaning himself up, Ben pulled his hand out, went into the bathroom and locked himself in.

What the hell had just happened?

Orson cleaned himself up with tissues, a brief moment of humour at thinking that at least when he flushed these they wouldn't block the drain this time. He hoped the dog with the snake rod had finished unclogging when Ben flushed the toilet. Then Ben didn't come out. Orson heard him groaning like he was hurting himself somehow, then found that so impossible he had to wonder what was going on.

When Ben came out, he looked defeated. 'Orson, I'm sorry. I don't quite know what came over me. My head's just been in not quite the right place since this morning. It's kind of...okay, it *is*. It's...' Ben sighed. 'Everything I just did was selfish and rude, right down to not letting you clean up first. I'm sorry.'

'Ben, tell me what's wrong. Seriously.'

'I can't stop thinking about how at the end of all this you're going to have to go home. I'm going to miss you all over again. I'm going to know you're missing me too and feel even worse when I think like that. I can't shake it off. Because it's different this time. We're not kids anymore. We aged our whole space captain game up because *we* aged up. So now this feels different. It feels worse. It was bad enough we had to go through it in the first place. And that I couldn't call you or text or go online with you because...it all just felt too painful. Because...'

Orson put his hands on Ben's shoulders. 'Because what, Benji? Tell me.'

'Because Mom and Dad sat me down to talk to me about it. Kind of like you did with Cliff and Matthew. A how-are-you-really-feeling kind of talk. Except I think you got yours right. Dad...told me I had to just move on. Dad told me...'

'Go on.'

Ben sighed. 'Orson, I really don't think you want to hear this.'

'I think you need to say it, Benji. Whatever it is.'

'Dad told me I could make better friends. He told me he didn't like you because you didn't behave well at school and you weren't a Christian. He told me you had poor values and behaviours and it already showed. He didn't want you passing it on to me. He said it was better that we were moving away because New York was a better place for me to grow up than London. And I...'

Orson kept himself steady, unsurprised even if everything inside him was rising up. 'Just say it, Benji.'

'I decided he was right.'

'It's okay,' Orson said, hands still on Ben's shoulders as his friend looked at the floor. 'I don't have to ask if you still believe it. Not after you let me come here.' As soon as he'd said it, he smiled and waited, and sure enough, Ben lifted his head a little.

'Orson. That is *terrible*.'

'I know. But seriously, Benji, if that's what your dad felt like about me then why did he let any of this holiday happen at all?'

'I don't know. I was amazed when he told me you and your parents were coming. I figured it had to be a holiday *they* needed and not you and that maybe they'd had to promise you being on your best behaviour. Something like that.'

'They certainly did that. Have I been on it?'

'The *very* best. I'm sorry I haven't. Okay, I was doing well enough until just now. I'd never have hurt you, okay? I'm sorry if me being in a bad mood was a little bit scary.'

'Only because I've never been able to imagine it. Finally I actually get to see that you *can* be in one.'

'Dad would never hurt you either.'

Orson rubbed down Ben's sides now, his arms beginning to get pins and needles from being on his shoulders for too long. 'What makes you say that?'

'Are you kidding? I saw you downstairs when he was mad about the flood. You were about ready to run.'

'Only because I'm the one who really flushed the condoms.'

'Who gets like that about something like that?' Ben said, tensing up all over again.

'Forget about it,' Orson said. 'It's over. It's not like I've never been in trouble before. Or gotten out of it. The stakes were just a bit higher this time. Like that's a call I *really* don't want your dad to make to mine, telling him I did that. He would have done it, wouldn't he?'

'Definitely. But don't you think it's just totally wrong that he blames his own family, but a guest can't possibly have done that? It's almost always the guest when things get embarrassingly wrong at a party.'

'I know. That was weird.'

'I don't want you to go,' Ben said. 'At the end of this. I want you to stay. I want to go to my parents and ask them to have you here for longer until your visa runs out, and that might give us enough time to figure out how you could get a work permit. I liked your idea about you running away from home into New York. But why do it there? I want you to live here. But I can't ask for that. I already know what Dad will say. And he can't know why. You saw how he reacted when Ella even suggested you might be gay.'

'I think she actually knows.'

'So do I. We both know why she's keeping her mouth shut.'

Orson wasn't sure but decided he could work it out later, when his head wasn't so full of what Ben had just said. 'You'd really want that? For me to live here? Like...as your secret boyfriend or something?'

'*Will* you be my boyfriend?'

'You mean like...long distance?'

'Yes.'

'You want to be in a relationship with me? From like...four thousand miles away?'

'That's how I know this is real. It doesn't matter how many miles there are between us. I don't want anyone else who's only *half* a mile away. I want to be with you. Even if I can't physically be with you.'

Orson felt light all over. 'Ben, are you saying what I think you are?'

Ben nodded. 'I'm in love with you. Why else do you think I ran out of the house late for practice? I forgot to set the alarm. I fell asleep a lot later than you thought. I listened to you being a naughty boy because I was awake contemplating how you're so much more than just that. Everything about getting to know who grown-up you is since you came into the house that evening has got my head all over the place. So yeah, Otterpants. I'm in love. It's with you. Love's scary. It's why I've not been myself all evening. I'm scared. But I'm so happy. So how about it? Can we have a relationship? Could you learn to love me back?'

Orson felt a tremble pass all the way through him. 'I *do* love you. I always have. It's just a little bit different now. It's not boyhood friendship love anymore. It's... I'm a little bit scared too. I find out I'm gay and I fall in love with the guy who made it happen all at once? It's like I'm trying to mix in with your family just to distract myself.'

The release of saying it spurred him on. It made him forget everything he'd been thinking all afternoon since the conversation with Scott, all through the one with Matthew, all to the point where he was dreading leaving the Barstows' house as much as Ben was dreading being left without him too.

'No,' Orson said. 'I don't want to go long distance. I want to stay here. Let's make it happen. Let's do what you said. Let's be brave.'

'I can't,' Ben said. 'I'm sorry. No matter how much I love you, I just can't do that. I can't risk it. I don't want *you* to risk it. You want to do us always together? Okay. I'm ready for that. We leave it a couple of weeks and then I get on a flight to England.'

Orson started. 'And forget about your college? Your career? Everything? Leave your family behind?'

'Hello, is Orson home?' Ben tapped his head. 'How do you think I know I'm in love with you? None of that matters like you do. Not anymore.'

'Benji, I think we both need a time out,' Orson said. 'Step back. That's what they call it in rehab. Let's take one. Before both of us get so caught up in love that we do something so totally stupid we regret it for years. You know I'm right.'

Ben looked at his eyes for a moment. 'Okay,' he said.

'We'll work this out. Maybe I go home and then come back. I can work with that plan. I'll get another holiday by working on Mum and Dad again. More good behaviour.' *Yeah right. That'll never fucking work and you know it. One reward is all you're getting, and the rest is expected from now on, because that was the deal.* 'Or I'll just save up. I'll get a proper green card somehow. I'll think of something. Maybe I'll...' Orson laughed. 'Maybe I'll be a pro gamer. For you. I'll do the one thing I'm any good at that could also ruin my life. To make money to be with my boyfriend.'

'*Now* who's crazy-in-love?' Ben said.

'You'll be a dentist. You'll have plenty of money too. We'll have our own house like this together, and it won't matter anymore who in each of our families likes what.'

'Yeah.' Ben smiled, and a moment later Orson knew he didn't believe it. 'But it's complicated. It's a conflict. No offence, but it's one I don't think you know. You're good at telling your parents you'll just do what you want and that's it.'

'You wanna bet? Lately, I'm totally not.'

'You're still miles ahead of me.' Ben took Orson's hands and took them off himself. 'I *want* Dad and my whole family to support my choices. To like that. I'm just wired to please them because family's always been everything to me. It meant so much. Then I went to college and things just...changed. I worked so much out and kept it to myself. I realised things. Orson, it's not just love that can drive someone crazy.'

Now Orson understood. He still didn't count himself as smart, but he understood this, and why this whole evening had put that look on Ben, brought that behaviour he was now ashamed of out in him. He felt like it was a mad thing to do, but he had to get Ben to say it. One release and then another. 'Then what is it?'

'Hate,' Ben said. 'I hate my dad. I actually do. The way he raised me was a lie. It wasn't about being a good person. It was about being his idea of one. His idea of one is not being what I've always known I was. I've crushed on boys since we were at school together. It wasn't you. I didn't lie about that. It was Lando. You remember Lando?'

'Orlando Sanderson?' It made sense. He was another polar bear. Another bear who just added another layer of complication.

Ben nodded. 'Don't worry. I know he died. I know it was tragic. I couldn't go to the funeral, but I sent his family a letter saying how much his friendship once meant to me. Without saying what it *really* meant. That's when I knew life was too short not to be who I was. It still took me years to actually do anything about it. Because of Dad. Because do you know what he said when I tried to ask him what he thought about it? Without making it about me?'

Orson felt cold. That Ben would be better off dead? Ben couldn't hate anyone for much less. Orson found it so hard to think Ben could hate anyone at all, but it seemed too real.

'He said there are places bears who feel like that go. Where they get made better so they can go back and be a part of their families and their churches again.'

'Oh man,' Orson said. 'You mean like that conversion therapy thing?'

207

'That's where he'd put me.'

'You're twenty-one years old,' Orson said. 'He can't put you anywhere.'

'That's why he'd try convincing me to go on my own,' Ben said. 'I'm scared of him succeeding. Because I hate him. All I want to do is love him again. I want him to keep loving me. That's how he'd do it. I tell myself not to hate people. I believe in God, I believe in the Christian faith; it's a good way to guide yourself through life. Except about that. The path Dad chose is wrong. It always has been. Except when I sometimes think it's not.'

'Benji, listen to me,' Orson said, afraid now, 'and listen good: there is nothing wrong with you. You do *not* need that shit, okay? Say it to me.'

'I know.'

'So say it back to me.'

'There's nothing wrong with me. Except that I hate my dad. He's a jerk. He's a...total penis. He's a moron.'

'Atta boy. Let it all go. Parents suck. Believe me, I know.'

'He's an...an...Orson, my dad's an *asshole*.' Ben put his hands to his mouth. 'Oh,' he said, through them, then he sighed, then sighed again, his whole body tensed up and heaving with it. 'Oh my.'

'There you go! Say it again. Call him something worse.'

Ben started to breathe fast. 'Asshole!' he said, his voice full of anger and his fists clenched. 'My Dad's

208

an...an...an asshole! A dirty, stinking, un-douched asshole!'

'You go, bear! We're getting there! Give me the rest of it! Let go! See how good it feels! Talk like you're gonna smack him one!'

Ben couldn't say anything. Ben was hardly breathing at all now. Then he started again, and it was like he'd just been drowning. His breath got faster, then faster still, and even without having his hands on the right part of Ben's chest, he felt everything. 'Holy shit, Benji, your heart's racing! Sit down. Come on. Sit down right here.'

'I'm fine. Just give me a minute.'

Ben clearly wasn't. He was leaning against the wall and panting. Then when his head was obviously too light to keep standing, he dumped himself onto the bed so hard he almost bounced off it, and shifted back to the wall as if trying to escape and finding only a corner to huddle in.

'Oh fuck,' Orson whispered. He went for the door, thinking one clear thought: at least Ben's mother was a doctor. 'Tasha! Can you help me in here?'

Holly came out. 'Tasha's in the shower trying to make herself feel less drunk,' she said. 'Anything I can do?'

'I...need some help here.'

Holly saw whatever was in his eyes. She ran. Not only that, but she was prepared. 'Okay, we've got this,' she said. 'Can you shut the door?'

Orson shut it, and Holly sat next to Ben. 'Okay, big guy, count to one hundred with me and try and keep your breathing slow.' She put her hands on Ben's back. 'One, two, three...'

Ben's lips moved, but he wasn't talking, just concentrating, trying.

'Nine, ten...that's good, keep counting. Orson, would you go downstairs to the cupboard under the sink and get one of those plastic bags that we use in the little food waste bin? Anyone asks just say...you're picking up all the candy wrappers in Ben's room.'

Orson pretended he was in a game, a stealth mission. Everyone was in the living room watching cartoons. The front door opened, and Cliff came back in with Matthew. Orson was trying to slink out of the kitchen when they saw him. 'Candy bar wrappers. Ben's got a sweet tooth. I can't stand such a mess. You guys okay?'

'Everything's cool,' Cliff said. 'Little talk helped.'

Orson took the bag upstairs and gave it to Holly, who now at least had Ben counting out loud and probably wouldn't need it. 'Shall I get Tasha if she's out of the shower?'

'No,' Holly said. 'Don't. She doesn't know this happens to him. You got lucky. I know, and I know why.'

'Shall I go for a bit?'

'No,' Ben said. 'Stay.'

Orson sat down next to him.

Ben took his hand. 'Thanks.'

'Okay, bear.' Orson put his other hand on Ben's back. 'That's it. Nice deep breaths, nice and slow. Just like you told me to do on the first night here.'

'I'm sorry,' Ben said. 'It's been nine months. I thought all this was over.'

'Shh,' Orson said. 'You don't have to explain. Just breathe.'

It took a few minutes, but Ben eventually got to his feet. 'Thanks,' he said. 'Both of you. I think we just got lucky. I'm fine. Can I just lie down for a bit on my own?'

'Give me a hug,' Holly said. 'There we go. There's our calm boy back. Alright, lie down. We'll just say you're taking a nap.'

'Holly.'

'Yeah?'

Ben looked at Orson, then at Holly and then went with what Orson had a feeling was coming. 'I love this otter right here. I love Orson. So I just told him so. We talked about how it might work and...yeah. Everything.'

Holly nodded. 'I had a feeling. When you say everything...eighteen months ago?'

'No. Not that. Can you tell him?'

'Yes. Put your head down and nap.' Holly gave Orson a warm smile. 'Come on. Mine and Cliff's room. I gather he's out walking the block having a talk with Matthew.'

'Yeah,' Orson said. 'I kinda feel like I interfered a bit. He cried because of stuff I said. That's not what I meant to do.'

211

'Perfectly healthy and good for him,' Holly said. 'Don't worry about a thing. You know Cliff drives a cab. Anyone told you what I do?'

Orson was ashamed to admit it, but he didn't know, so he admitted it, and Holly just kept smiling.

'I'm a nurse,' she said. 'I met Cliff because I met Tasha first when we worked in the same practice.' She shut the door. 'You're a good person. So please don't take what I'm about to say personally, but you need to be careful with what's going on here. This needs to stay hidden at the moment.'

'No shit,' Orson said. 'Wanna tell me something I don't know?'

'Yes,' Holly said. 'Eighteen months ago. Sit down with me.'

There was a sofa in the guest room. Of course there was. Everything about this place had money and luxury written on it. Whatever Natasha earned was good, but Orson had long since realised that the disposable income that went above and beyond most other people's was from John's investment banking. Now he was more acutely aware of it for some reason he couldn't quite place.

'This is a more complicated family than you see on the surface,' Holly said. 'My husband's brother isn't a bad person, but there are certain ideas I'm not sure if he's ever going to fully come around to. My sister-in-law's tried her best, but completely changing a man is sometimes impossible even for the most educated of people. Natasha's never heard anything from Ben himself, but I think she mostly knows. I also think she'd rather not face the problem. Ben doesn't want her to have to either.'

'So what happened eighteen months ago?'

'Be careful if you get into this with Ben,' Holly said. 'I think he wants you to know, but I don't think he wants to talk about it. That's why I'm doing this. The reason I know about this at all is because eighteen months ago, Ben nearly took his own life. He didn't do it because he called Cliff instead and told him everything.'

For a moment, Orson couldn't speak. '*Ben* nearly did that?'

'Exactly what most people would say if they ever knew,' Holly said. 'Ben didn't make an attempt, but he sat there trying to think of a reason not to. I know you had a talk with him the first night you were here. I expect this is all making sense. I don't believe Ben really hates John, but the reasons he has the problems he does are obvious. He wants to sort this all out, but he doesn't want this to explode. Especially not now. If our insurance doesn't pay, my family are going to be homeless. John and Tasha have already said we can live here as long as we need to. The last thing Ben would ever want is to create a massive family problem when his parents are helping *another* family. He wouldn't want to feel that responsible.'

Orson took a deep breath. 'Fuck. Holly, tell me something honest here: should I just go home early? Before we risk making this whole thing explode?'

'Of course not. You heard what he said in there. I imagine before he panicked, he was even more honest with you about his feelings for you, and you with him. You can't run from this, Orson. You'd regret it forever. You need to be careful, but you need to stay for each other. Then after you go home, you need to stay for each other however you can. For as long as it lasts. Do you love him back?'

'Yes.'

'Then you know you can't go home yet. Stay.'

'Okay.'

'I haven't seen Ben so happy before,' Holly said. 'I wasn't expecting him to fall for a friend he'd not seen in years, but I had a feeling he had when I saw how he's been all Christmas. When he came home from college, he looked worn out and trying to keep his chin up. When you came, he managed it.'

'Really?'

'Yes. He really is a nice boy. Nothing you've seen was an act just because you've seen how vulnerable he really is underneath. He's polite and caring and puts others before himself. He's also smart. He'll be a brilliant dentist. If he doesn't try out for the college draft into the NHL. We've told him not to put pressure on himself, but that's like...well, actually, it's about as effective as telling his father the same thing. If you ever get to meet John's parents, you'd see a pretty rich and clear picture of how this passes down.'

'Parents. Who needs them?'

'Yeah. They fuck you up, Mom and Dad.'

'Hey, you know that poem too? I found that one in a book at school. I liked it because it started with that. I think it was by someone called Lark or something.'

'Well, whoever they were, they had it right,' Holly said. 'Come on. Let's go get a drink together. It's not just my husband who occasionally sneaks a cigarette either. Can I have one of yours?'

Orson went for his pocket, where he found two Camels left in their softpack. 'Sure. Maybe after this I should try not buying any more. I don't think Ben likes kissing a smoker much.'

'If he loves you so much that he worked himself up to a panic attack then I doubt he cares much about your vices. Now.' She held her hand on the doorhandle. 'Anyone asks what we were talking about, we'll say it was my son.' She opened it. 'What exactly did he say to start that long walk around the block off?'

'Errr...maybe you'd better –'

Ella appeared at the top of the stairs. 'Hey, you two have *got* to come downstairs for this. Mom got straight out of the shower and onto the whisky. She's trying to get the PS5 out. Dad's trying to stop her.'

Orson sighed. He wasn't going to get involved. 'Let's just go for that cigarette,' he said.

At the top of the stairs, he heard the raised voices.

'John, just stop trying to get in my way, will you? It's my house too, for God's sake. Orson's upstairs with Ben, and I want to play video games with our children on my own television like a *normal* family does.'

'Oooooh boy,' Orson said to himself. 'Holly, could I nap on the couch in your room?'

Ella's head turned sharply. 'Why don't you just use your own bed in Ben's room? Aaaaaahaha, did you two fall out?' She grinned wickedly. 'I knew it! It totally *was* you who flushed the condoms! How mad is he?'

'It's nothing like that,' Orson said, squirming.

Ella laughed again. 'I bet you had one each and had a race. Who came first?'

'Don't be silly, Ella,' Holly said. 'It was my husband who flushed them. Ben's alone in his room right now because he's not feeling well. Something from the barbecue disagreed with him, and he doesn't want the embarrassment of using his bathroom with a guest right next d–'

Something made a heavy, glass-smashing noise.

'Oh, I don't give a fuck, John!' Tasha shouted from downstairs. 'Just let me deal with it. I'm perfectly capable!'

'Woah!' Ella said. 'Go Mom! I'm taking that as a total call for backup.' She took off down the stairs with Holly following.

Reluctantly, Orson followed himself.

Chapter Ten

Orson might not have been on familiar ground watching Ben have an unexpected panic attack, but arguing parents was a ship he could sail, and if it sank, he'd always fancied he could swim. Someone else's parents in someone else's house suddenly didn't seem too different when it was a familiar scene of broken glass and simmering tempers.

'Guys,' he said, 'come on. If this is about me, I'm right here. I don't mind if someone wants to get a games console out. That was a rule my parents made, and they're not here.'

'You see, John?' Tasha said, dumping broken glass from the dustpan into the bin with a deftness that said she could still hold a room no matter what her head felt like. 'I'm setting it up.'

'Tasha, *please* don't,' John said. 'Orson, your parents didn't make that rule. We did. Our kids spend too much time gaming, and this holiday, we wanted it to be gaming free. It wasn't just because you were coming. Your whole situation just woke us up to how it would be better to reduce certain things.'

'It's ridiculous, John,' Natasha said. 'Just say the real truth: you're afraid of our children *and* your brother's children turning into Orson because of video games. They won't. It won't be because you banned gaming for the holidays. It'll be because neither of us are Orson's shit parents.'

'Woah!' Ella said, staring at Tasha and then at Orson. 'Mom, that's kind of...'

That's kind of she just swapped sides, Orson thought, as Natasha's words stung him. 'Errr...right,' he said.

John raised his hands and physically took a step backwards. 'Tasha. Please.'

'Don't Tasha me, John. I am *so* sick of that already. You saying my name like it can make me come round to whatever you want. I'm setting up that console, and my kids are going to play with me if they want to. You want to stop me? Try.'

'Tasha,' John said, keeping the same distance as his wife pulled the TV forward in a way Orson thought meant she was certain to break it before this was over. 'We have a guest in our house who has an addiction problem with gaming.'

'John, it's okay,' Orson said. 'It's like I said, I'm fine with it.'

'Orson, I respect your efforts to be diplomatic, but I want the rules I made to stand.'

'Oh, you made this rule yourself now, did you?' Tasha said, banging the console down next to the TV. 'Well I make the rules in this house too, John, in case you hadn't noticed. A guest in our house with a gaming problem? Your brother's an alcoholic. Who have you stopped from drinking this holiday?'

'Well certainly not you,' John said, his hands now on the back of the sofa. 'Tasha, nobody wants to see you be like this. You think the children are going to play on that with you? Where are they? All hiding from this.'

'That one isn't.' Tasha pointed at Ella.

'That one's had enough of this bullshit already,' Ella said. 'You're drunk, Mom. Why don't you just go to bed?'

'You mean the bed where my husband never touches me anymore, let alone does anything else? At least Cliff and Holly *could* flush used condoms down the goddamn toilet.'

'Mom, Jesus Christ, just go already. You're ruining this evening for everybody right now. Dad's right. Nobody wants to play on that thing with you.'

'Fine!' Tasha shouted, ripping the cables out.

'Woah!' Orson said, rushing forward to grab the TV as it tipped. He made it in time.

Natasha Barstow, now storming to the kitchen, opened the lid of the bin and slammed the PS5 into the trash. 'That's just fine! We'll just do that with it and then we never have to worry about a guest in our house having a relapse. Or corrupting our kids.' She pointed at Orson. 'Why did you let him come here, John? You don't even like him.'

'Moooom!' Ella said, her hands now at her face. 'What the actual hell!'

John looked at Orson with a pained, embarrassed grimace. 'I'm sorry,' he said. 'Tasha, that is not what I said when we discussed Orson coming here. You know it isn't. I said I thought he was a badly behaved child once, but now that he's an adult and he's been dealing with his problems, we should give him a chance to have a nice holiday with us. That's the Christian thing to do.'

'Oh, don't start with God right now, John. You want another truth? I've not believed in God for years. I only started in the first place because I was in love with you once.'

Boom. That wasn't just a shotgun blast, it was a double from both sides, the one thing Orson had secretly hoped one of his parents might do to the other to spell the end of their marriage and somehow always been relieved they hadn't done. Now Tasha was doing it? Like she loathed John Barstow as much as Ben had said he did?

'Natasha,' John said, taking his wife's arms gently. 'We *still* love each other. You've just had too much to drink and you're tired. If you're really feeling this way about us right now, why don't we talk about it tomorrow? In private, away from our children and our guest. Who's most likely seen enough of parents fighting lately.'

Tasha glared at her husband for a moment, simmering down, then she removed his hands from her. 'You're right, John. This is what I've been saying all along.' She looked at Orson. 'That poor boy doesn't have a gaming problem. That whole thing's nonsense. He has a *parent* problem. You're right. Let's keep our rules. At least we make them.'

'Now isn't the time or place, Tash. Come on, let's go up to bed. Cliff and Holly will stay up with the kids.'

'It's *never* the time, John, is it? I'm just going to say it.'

'Tasha, Orson is not our child, and it's not our place to say these things.'

'But you know they're true, John. So stop pretending you don't. He isn't Richard and Julia's child either. They were never parents to him. They don't give a shit about him. I wish I'd never met Julia. She's a self-absorbed egomaniac, and her husband's no better. She won't forgive her husband for *one* affair that went public? You should have seen how many people she slept with at the same time when we were at college. She couldn't stick medical school because she was too obsessed with wanting people to love her all the time. She only married Richard because he's a status symbol. They never wanted a child, then they think they're such brilliant parents for letting him do everything for himself because it "makes him independent". It made him neglected. *I* looked after him when Julia and her cretin husband couldn't be bothered, and they knew it. When we left England, what did he have? I was glad when they left our house. I still couldn't stand them from the minute they walked in. I only let them come here because I felt so sorry for *him*.'

The room fell silent. Ella had her left hand on Orson's shoulder. She'd had it there right from the start of her mother's speech, as if realising Orson had come into this ready for familiar territory and now getting to a stage where he couldn't say anything.

Now she was in action. She walked up to her mother.

'Mom, seriously, shut the fuck up. Look at this room right now. Do you actually not realise what you're doing? You're drunk, you're talking crap and you're *totally* humiliating Orson.'

'No, she isn't.'

Everyone stood silent again after Orson had said it. For a moment, he didn't want to say anything else. The weight of the world was already lifting. He wasn't going to panic like Ben had, but he needed the same moment. He'd needed it since what Scott Riley had said. Since before that, when he'd skated with Ben, when he'd talked with Tasha about how they might talk to his parents. From before the holiday even started.

'Everything she said's true.'

'Oh come on now,' John said. 'This has been a long day and a long party and everyone's tired. This isn't a good time to decide what's true and what isn't. These are all just unhelpful thoughts. Why don't we *all* go to bed?'

'Because it's only seven thirty,' Orson said. 'And I want to get that PlayStation out of the bin and use it.

Because Tasha's right. I don't have a gaming addiction problem. I let my parents convince me I did. I went to rehab because I was told to. I sat in those circles, and I accepted I was responsible for my own actions. But it's like everyone but me knew it, and now Tasha's finally the one who said it: my parents were never responsible for me.'

Tasha looked completely disarmed now. Her own daughter swearing at her had gone over her head, but this hadn't. Had she just wanted a good old-fashioned row and then wanted Orson to walk away hating her, for some reason? Now that the clouds were finally parting inside Orson's head, she looked mortified, as though any minute she'd start taking it all back. She opened her mouth and got up off the barstool she'd been sitting on.

'No,' John said gently, holding a hand out to stop her. 'Let him talk.'

You want me to talk? Orson thought. *Okay then.*

'My parents are arseholes.' He thought of how Ben had said the word and then lost it. He wasn't going to lose it. He was the OtterSpotter. He was going to destroy whatever he wanted and be standing after it. 'You know how long I've defended them for? It was all bullshit. I thought they were the coolest for just letting me do what I wanted. You know what I see when I look at kids who are like I was now? I feel sorry for them. I'm not a gaming addict. I'm a big kid who never learned self-control because the two people who should have taught me what it was couldn't be bothered. All I ever did was surround myself with people who didn't tell me

223

when to stop. Or I didn't listen, because if my family were fine with it then who else's business was it?'

Orson fished the PlayStation out of the bin and put it on the bar top, not caring that it was covered in the gunge from the barbecue leftovers. 'It'll clean up, right?' He didn't look at anyone when he said it. 'You know why my dad paid to put me through rehab? Because it looked good. Because it was public. He cared about wanting to look like a responsible parent. Well too late, Dad. You never did it when it mattered. Nor did Mum. You two should never have been married in the first place, let alone actually had me. Living with you two and your pathetic, petty little problems with each other was often enough to make me wish you hadn't. Who *wouldn't* just want to hide and play video games in that house? Now you actually want to be my parents? When I'm a grown-up? You want to tell me I can't drink a beer in someone's house when it's eighteen to drink where I come from? You wanna tell me I don't even drink? You want to buy me a holiday on the condition that I behave? Because it's good for your public relations? If you'd ever been my parents in the first place, none of this shit would ever have happened!'

He came back to the room, remembering to breathe, and heard himself doing it almost like Ben had been. He realised his parents weren't there, that he'd been talking to them anyway, and now he was in a room full of bears who in the space of a week had been more of a family to him than he'd ever had in his life.

Good behaviour? He wasn't well behaved. He never would be. They might as well see it.

'Fuck,' Orson declared to the entire room. '*Fuck* my parents. *Fuck* their selfish, pretentious lifestyles. Fuck their delusion that either of them make the world any better just because they're in government. Fuck them using this holiday in somebody else's house to emotionally blackmail me. They left me here without even saying goodbye, for Christ's sake! Well fuck that too! They think I'm going home to them? To that? Letting them control my life? When I go to that airport, I'm changing my ticket and I'm getting on a plane to any-fucking-where but there.'

The room was deathly silent.

'I'll just...yeah, I'll go pack my stuff. I'll be out of here in less than an hour.'

'Orson,' John said.

'What?'

'Come here.' Before he could do anything, or think anything else, John Barstow was hugging him.

'Errrr...okay, I really didn't...I don't...'

'It's alright. I bet you feel ten times better already. Tasha was right, and I'm sorry I tried to stop all this when it was obviously so needed.' John released him. '*Do* you feel better?'

'About a *hundred* goddamn times. Oh yeah, and sorry about all that.'

'We *all* use such language sometimes,' John said. 'You're quite forgiven already. If you needed to rant and swear to let go, you could have talked to any of us at any time. I'm sorry we made you feel like you had to behave like a guest all the time. We should have just let you be a person. Especially after your parents left.'

Before Orson could take it in, Tasha was there, another hug coming his way. 'I'm so sorry,' she said. 'For saying such awful things. I *am* drunk. I should have sat you down on a sober day if I wanted to say all that. I just...it's all pent-up feelings. My patients aren't the only ones who do it.'

Ella hugged him next, with a massive grin. He was glad to see it back on her. 'Told you you didn't have to be a whiny fucking pussy.'

'Excuse me, young lady,' John said, only sounding vaguely authoritative now, 'but Orson getting a free pass does not mean you do. Did you actually say that to him at some point?'

'Yeah, Dad, and I think we can stop pretending this family's so perfect and never says a curse word or has a rant now, can't we? I'll just do extra penance in church or something. Maybe Mom can take me so she can renew her faith. But sorry, we're not doing Mom right now. We're doing the otter. Who just kicked *butt*.'

Natasha Barstow looked relieved that her daughter had moved that subject on so quickly. She meant what she said, Orson thought. Every word of it. That was a conversation he hoped the family *did* have after he'd left.

'What are you lot all hiding in the den for?' Ella said. 'Get out here and give him a hug?'

Orson put his hands to his cheeks as the rest of the family came out. '*Everyone* heard all that? Oh my *God*, I'm dead. I'm dead I'm dead I'm dead I *died*!'

Matthew was the first to get his hug in, and he whispered, 'No you fucking didn't.'

'Matthew!' Holly said yet again. 'You are terrible at whispering.'

Everyone else took their turn, and Orson said, 'What is this? An endurance test of how many bear hugs someone can take? Lord have mercy, if I survive it with my ribcage intact, *I* might just take up Christianity.'

'You don't "take up Christianity", otterbrain,' Ella said with her characteristic eyeroll. Orson thought of how someone had told her not to be so rude when she'd used that term for him before, but now everyone was smiling. 'You actually have to go to church and read the bible, and y'know, *believe* in God maybe?'

'You'd always be welcome at any Christian church anywhere in the world, Orson,' John said. 'But it's entirely your choice. And no, we in this family don't believe that non-believers go straight to Hell. There's a lot you might be surprised to learn. But this is the land of freedom, and freedom means your choice.'

'He gets it, Dad,' Ella said. 'He's not dumb.'

'For an otter,' Matthew muttered, still grinning.

'You'll apologise for that at once because it's not funny,' Holly said. 'At all.'

'Whaaat, Mom? He knows I'm not serious! Okay, fine, I'm sooo-ryyyyy!' Matthew looked at Orson. 'I got bullied at school for a year about my weight by otters.

But you're a good one. And if you really can clear a room when you fart then it *would* be cool to have you in church with us. I'm going this Sunday.'

'*You?*' Ella said. 'Since when did *you* believe in anything, comic boy?'

'Matthew's always believed,' Cliff said. 'He just finds it a bummer getting out of bed on a school day, let alone at the weekend. Actually, now's a good time. Matthew has something he wants to say to everyone.'

Oh fuck, Orson thought. *We're doing this now? Please no. Please, after everything that's happened today already, can we just not have this one?*

'Yeah,' Matthew said. 'I want to tell everyone... "We're closing in ten minutes."'

'Don't be silly, boy,' Cliff said. 'The family need to know this, and it will sound better coming from you.'

'Alriiiight, Dad, be frosty. What I was supposed to say is that while we were out for a walk, the insurance company called Dad and said everything's gone through and they're going to pay for our new house.'

The whole room made celebration noises. Orson was glad: it masked his deep sigh of relief. He *was* pleased for them.

'Thank the lord for that,' John said. 'I'm so happy for you.'

'Clifford,' Holly said. 'You got this news an hour ago and you waited to tell me?'

'You were...' Cliff cleared his throat. '*Busy*, Hol.'

'Oh. Yes. So I was.'

'Busy with what?' Ella said.

'Private stuff, maybe?' Sam said. 'Y'know, people do that without you having to ask all the time.'

Orson decided he had a better way of deflecting this. 'Holly caught me scratching myself in an awkward place when I thought nobody was looking. It was bad. I couldn't get to the bathroom, so I just did it in the upstairs hall. Why didn't anybody tell me she's a nurse? She actually *did* offer to take a look at my rash. Then we had a long talk about...a bit of good health advice for me.'

Despite obviously knowing the truth, Cliff laughed. 'Boy, what *have* you been doing since you got to New York?'

'Living with bears,' Orson said.

The whole room made the 'Oooooooooh!' sound of liking a risky joke.

'Drinks for everyone except me?' Tasha said. She already had a glass of iced water. 'Orson, guests first. Whisky on the rocks?'

'Actually, that'd be nice,' Orson said. 'Thanks. Think I need some fresh air, too.' He took his cigarettes out. 'Does anyone else secretly smoke?'

'Hey Aunt Tasha,' Matthew said. 'Dad thinks I might have that hibernation thing Ben's got and thinks I should ask you for a check-up.'

'Sure,' Tasha said. 'When I'm a lot more sober and a *lot* less embarrassed with myself, we'll book you in. No problem.' She stopped, about to pour Orson's drink. 'Guys. Guys!' Everyone turned to her, hearing the urgency that had changed the room again.

'What is it, Tash?' Holly said.

'Guys, where's Benjamin?'

Everyone looked around themselves, and a moment later all looked sheepish. Family gathering without the one everyone had come to as soon as he walked into the room that first night? Natasha looked like forgetting her eldest son existed was worse than anything she'd said.

'He was tired about an hour ago,' Orson said. 'I think he's probably hibernating.'

'Well, you got that wrong, Otterpants.' Ben's voice came from out in the hall. 'Because he's been out here listening to this whole show for the last ten minutes.'

What happened next amazed Orson beyond words. Ben stepped into the room, and gone was any sign of what Orson had seen barely an hour ago. If Ben had napped at all, there was no sign of the hibernation syndrome either. Just a bright-eyed bear who looked like he'd showered, put a little fur-gel on his head, styled up, sprayed cologne and come down because the party had only been getting started when he left it.

'So...you heard everything?'

'My turn.' Ben spread his arms wide and gave Orson the most heart-stopping hug he'd ever had. One hand on the small of his back as Ben buried him in his body, and the other on the back of his head, rubbing it as Ben's face rubbed the side of Orson's.

Oh dear God. Ben was going to do something crazy. Orson just knew it. He wasn't going to be able to hide the trembling inside him as soon as Ben let him go.

When that happened, Ben put his hands on Orson's shoulders. 'Nice rant, poo-poo mouth. We were such a clean-living, uneventful family, and then you had to come along and otter the place up.'

'Benji, I love you to bits,' Orson said. 'But if you make one more otter joke, I swear to God I'm going to personally book you a salmon run holiday this summer and come along myself. So that I can take pictures of your "bear butt" for your mom to pin to that fridge over there.' He smacked Ben on the left buttcheek.

'Yeow!'

'That's for the otterpants gift under the tree.'

'I've got to *sit* on that "bear bottom" you just smacked, Otterpants. But hey.' He smacked his own on the left, with his right hand. 'Mom can actually pin my naked bottom on that fridge any day of the week.'

'Benjamin, are you okay?' John said. 'You're dressed for going out. *Are* you going out?'

'No, Dad. I just wanted to look good. Mom, Dad, everyone, I've got something I want to talk about.'

Orson thought he might pass out.

'Okay,' John said. 'This isn't *quite* a family meeting as we've always known it, but fine. Let's talk. Does everyone need to be here?'

'Yes,' Ben said. 'Guys, I've realised something this holiday. It might have been a long time, and we're quite different, but...well, this otter right here is still my best friend. We were talking about some things and, well, he wondered how he might come and live over here in the USA, so we can see each other all the time like we used to. He doesn't have much money of his own, but we do. So can we help him out? Is there anything we can do?'

Orson felt light-headed. 'I'm just going to sit down right here.' He got to the couch, just about.

'Yes,' John said. 'There is. We can talk about this tomorrow. Whatever that talk was, Benjamin, I'm not sure your best friend was expecting you to do this right now, was he? Too many big things can't happen in one night, and I think we need to let things settle down a bit after the one we've all had. We've got Cliff and Holly's new house to celebrate, and I think your best friend needs some space.'

The others, Orson realised, were mercifully withdrawing from this and getting on with having party drinks.

'Whatever you think is right, Dad. It's your money we're asking for, after all.'

'This is what I mean, Benjamin. It's money *you're* asking for. Orson didn't ask for any such thing, and he doesn't look like he wanted you to. This talk of yours did not go as far as this moment, did it?'

'No,' Orson said. 'Ben, thanks, but this wasn't what I meant for you to do.'

'I'm sorry then,' Ben said. 'I misunderstood.'

You're playing a game, Orson thought. *You wouldn't look so happy about this otherwise. You came downstairs with it all planned out, and the only thing that changed was that I had a rant that your drunk mum brought on.*

'While you're both here,' John said, 'I think an apology is in order. From me. I did say those things Tasha said I did. Benjamin can testify to that. I told him to move on and make better friends. I was very wrong to do that. Instead of thinking I didn't like you, Orson, I should have thought about how being friends with Benjamin might have made you better, not corrupted him. He's proven himself pretty uncorruptible, and you're...well, far more aware of your issues than I ever thought. I shouldn't have encouraged your separation as friends when you were children. It was wrong and I'm sorry.'

'Thanks, Dad. I respect that,' Ben said.

'Yeah, thanks, Mr B. Apology accepted.'

'Mr B. I like that. It makes me think of "Mr Bubbles", the bodyguard machine on Bioshock.'

'*You've* played that?' Orson said.

'You might be quite surprised by the things I enjoy,' John said. 'Why don't I go and make peace with my wife, and we'll see if that PlayStation still works? If it doesn't then I'll go out and get another one tomorrow. You don't have to game if you don't want to. No pressure. You can always go upstairs and talk more about your life plan with Benjamin. He'll give you good advice.' John patted Ben's knee as if to wish him good luck.

I'll get him back for asking millionaire-daddy for money on my fucking behalf, Orson thought. He checked how close the nearest family member was and knew it was far enough. He beckoned Ben in and whispered in his ear: 'I want to put my "poo-poo mouth" around your unsnipped cock right now and suck you off until you come down my throat, Snowbear.'

Ben grinned. 'I bet you'd be a dead-eye shot with your penis when it comes to my poo-poo hole too, OtterSpotter. You still haven't done *me* yet. Have you got an erection right now? Are those otter-sized pants wet already?'

Orson's turn to whisper: 'Your family are going to figure out what we're doing even though you're not touching me.'

'I know. But just you wait till we're in my bed later.' Ben sat back and took a deep, satisfied breath. Orson thought this wasn't just a smile, it was a full-on smirk. An unmistakable kind.

'What are you playing at, Benji?' he said quietly, without being close to Ben's ear this time. 'I'm not mad at you, but that was a stunt just now. Why did you pull it?'

'I'm testing the water,' Ben said.

'For what? If you're planning on doing what I think you are, *please* just don't do it tonight.'

'Relax, otter. I'm not going to do it tonight. But maybe things I said were wrong too. I'm surprised by what just happened right here with Dad. I need to know if maybe other things have changed as well. It's going to take time, and the right place.'

Orson sighed with relief. 'Thank you.'

'I've never said that word I said upstairs in my entire life,' Ben said. 'Thanks. For getting me to try.'

'I'm not exactly sure I did you any good after all, Benji. You've really never said it? Never in your life?'

Ben shook his head. 'I've got some hang-ups too, otter.'

'Being polite is *not* a hang-up, Benji. I'm not proud of having a dirty mouth. I should take a lesson from you and try cleaning it up.'

'Please don't.'

Orson looked at him and didn't doubt his sincerity. 'We're going to be such an odd couple. Of friends, that is.'

'Yes. We certainly are. Poo-poo mouth otter.'

Orson went for the whisper again. 'Ass-invading butt-stuffer bear.' He licked the inside of Ben's ear. It made Ben twitch.

'Ooooo!' he said, shaking himself off. 'That dirty tongue!' Ben's eyes danced. '*Do* you wanna go upstairs? Watch some TV?'

'Actually, no,' Orson said, watching John and Tasha hug each other now. 'That PS5 will work. Trust me, I once threw one out of a window and it still worked. Have your family got Galactic Sky Gunner?'

'It's never in its box,' Ben said. 'Lately none of the other games seem to come out of theirs.'

'Good. Let's sort out one of *my* hang-ups. Game on, polar bear. You up for it?'

Chapter Eleven

'I'll only ask this once and then I promise I'll let the decision be yours,' John said. 'Are you sure this is a good idea?'

Orson took out his phone, glowing inside from the realisation that he hadn't been surrendering it for three days and simply hadn't thought of it. 'I'm setting a three-hour limit. I doubt I'll make it to two. They're going to wear me out.'

'Come on,' Ben said. 'Once they see how good you are, they're not going to *want* a turn, let alone get one.'

'Relax, bear. I'll share.'

'Rap music!' Ben said, and straight away Orson knew why: John's nose and mouth wrinkled in upturned disapproval.

'Oh,' he said. 'Are you into that?'

'No,' Orson said. 'I don't really like it. I like clubbing music. House, drum and bass, trance, something to make a floor of people move their tails. Except the bears. They've got little stumpy ones like Benji's, so they move *butt*.'

'Ugh.' John put his hands to his head and forced a smile. 'Your dad always liked female country and western singers. You should ask him about his CD collection.'

'He bored me to tears with it on the one occasion he could be bothered to help me with my homework. Music. I hated music at school, and no offence, but I don't like country. Besides, I'm not talking to that arsehole again.' Orson smiled. 'Hey, you kids, is it ready?'

'Ella can't plug it in,' Sam said.

'Swivel,' Ella said, holding up a finger as she wrestled with the wires behind the TV.

'Gonna let me do it yet?' Matthew said.

'Orson, you do it,' Ella said.

'Benjamin, could we have a quick word outside for a minute?' John said. 'Before you "get down with the kids"?'

Relax, Orson told himself. *It's no good jumping every time someone wants to talk to Ben alone.* What was that phrase he always liked from the cartoon with the green hare who ran a space crew? *Let's croak some toads.* Or something like that.

He plugged the wires in, surprised how quickly it all came back to him. 'Y'all ready to blow some shit up?'

They turned it on. If the Barstows got any genuine spiritual high from a good church service then Orson felt like he understood it. Hearing the PS5 loading screen sound did the same to him. So did the tune of EA Games as their logo came up. The sound of Galactic Space Conquest's music was like being saved from the rapture.

'Here,' Matthew said. 'This should keep things fair.'

'Did a twelve-year-old kid just pour me a scotch on the rocks?' Orson said as he took it, and everyone else looked either amazed or awkward.

'Matthew Barstow, *what* did I say about this?' Holly said, coming back into the room, presumably to take on her role of babysitter.

'What? It wasn't for me. I think it's gross. It's like drinking burning vomit.'

'Oh what the hell,' Holly said. 'Go get me one too. It's not like I'm often in a house where it's available.'

'He's all buzzed up because now he doesn't have to worry about how he burned their house down,' Ella said.

Holly sighed. 'Alright. Let's have it now. Before anyone does any gaming.' She took her drink from her son. 'Matthew was not responsible for the house burning down. He *felt* like he was, but it was me and Cliff who really made it happen.'

'Mooooom,' Matthew said. 'Really? Now?'

'Come on,' Cliff said. 'We talked about this on our walk, didn't we? Let your mother explain it. Unless *you* want to.'

'Laaaame,' Matthew said. 'Gonna *die* right here.'

Holly looked like she was going to enjoy this, Orson thought.

'Matthew felt responsible because what started the house fire was the iron being left on. The safety cut-out for when it got too hot didn't work. By some miracle, the insurance company accepted that explanation, and it was true. That model *should* have cut out after two minutes of non-use standing up. The reason we never thought they'd accept the claim is that Matthew couldn't bring himself to lie and let us tell them that the last person who used it was an adult. We never thought they'd accept that a twelve-year-old boy should have been learning how to iron. Or that both his parents were teaching him, and they should have checked it was turned off.'

Ella was staring at her cousin pie-eyed. '*You* were ironing. *You* were doing a house chore. *You* asked if you could do that. Your mom and dad actually gave you a lesson in how to iron because you wanted it?'

'Tell any of my friends and there'll be a rumour going round your church that you're secretly an atheist,' Matthew said.

'I don't know any of your friends, you future McDonalds employee. But could you iron Orson's otterpants later? I don't think he's ever seen an iron.'

'Actually,' Orson said, 'I ironed my own school uniform since I was about his age. Soon as I got out of school though, I dumped the iron in the bin like your mum did with that PlayStation.'

'Are we playing this or what?' Ella said.

'My turn first,' Matthew said.

'Dream on, ironing boy. What were you ironing anyway, a dress?' Ella picked up the number one controller.

Orson nearly squeaked: it was a transparent collector's edition. He decided he *would* squeak, remembering how his mother had asked what that awful noise was when Ben had grabbed his tail on Christmas Day.

That's the sound of an otter having FUN, Mum. Actual fun. When was the last time you had it? Was it awful for you?

'We'd better get playing before the otter shoots something in his p–'

'Ella!' Ben and Holly said together.

'Where's the second controller?' Ben said. 'I'm going first too. I'm captain.'

'Before you do,' Cliff said, 'any chance you could help me and Matty with something? Just for a few minutes?'

'Yeah, of course. Am I getting my coat on?'

'Yup.' Cliff looked at his watch. 'Actually, would you come for a drive with us somewhere? Maybe for an hour?'

'Dad,' Matthew said. 'He doesn't want to miss out on gaming with Orson.'

'Oh, don't worry,' Orson said. 'Go. We'll still be gaming when you get back.'

Ben looked torn. 'Guys, is this something urgent or could it...well, maybe wait until later?'

'Benji.' Orson touched his arm. '*Go*. Family first. Before gaming. Trust someone who didn't say that to himself enough before.'

Ben looked like he'd be glowing red if it wasn't for the white fur. 'Sure. Of course. Sorry. I wasn't thinking.'

'Awwwwww!' Ella said. 'Isn't it practically a Christmas movie?' She sarcastically pinched her own cheeks. 'Guess I'm playing with Orson first then.'

Without turning his head to her, Matthew held up his middle finger as he walked past his cousin and said in his laconic monotone, 'It wasn't a stupid goddamn dress. I don't want to wear a dress.'

'Matthew,' Ben said. 'I think you and I need to have a little talk about naughty language first. Believe me, I'm going to be having it with my BFF later too.'

That'll last about as long as it takes me to make you 'squirt' with the filthiest talk I can whisper under that way-too-thick-for-a-polar-bear duvet. 'Game on!' Orson said. 'We doing hard mode?'

* * *

An hour later, Orson's whisky-fuelled enthusiasm made him forget one thing: as soon as he logged in to his old PlayStation account, a bunch of ghosts from the past were going to get notifications that he was back online.

They flooded him with messages. Several were asking how true it was that he Wii-moted the PM's son. In graphic detail.

Orson looked at Ben, not knowing which of several cover stories that flashed through his head would sound better or worse. Ben just shrugged, obviously knowing what Orson did: if Ben explained it for him then it was obviously a cover.

'It was a dare gone wrong,' Orson told them all, after realising that he could have escaped from a couple of messages, but instead the flood had given the kids enough detail that they were already building a picture. 'Syd Sheldon basically did that to himself, but I was there, and completely grossed out. And drunk. The kind of drunk you never want to see. There's "Mom kills the room" drunk like earlier, and then there's what I got. I think I might have helped Syd get that thing up his butt, but I don't really remember much. That's why people like to remember for me.' He looked at one message. 'No, I didn't make Syd c–'

'I think they get it, otter.' Ben put his hands on Orson's shoulders. 'College boys having fun, and it got a little out of hand. Guys, don't think less of Orson. He got punished enough for what happened, and he doesn't do that kind of thing anymore.'

'No, of course he doesn't,' Matthew said.

'Private stuff is private stuff, Matty,' Ben said, as if reminding them of whatever talk they'd just had.

Orson knew he'd have to wait for details, if he got them at all. Perhaps it was better if he didn't and Ben took everything to do with his cousin from here.

'Here we go,' Orson said. 'Let's kill some womp-rats.'

Maybe I should have thought more about becoming a real astronaut, Orson thought, wondering if he would have had the grades to unlock that next step if only he'd applied himself more in school. *Forget it, though. The only route in is through the air force, and the military is the one place worse than the houses of parliament for teaching people to be conformists. Being an officer only really amounts to 'Do as you're told' with a bit more licence regarding* how *you do it. Pretend space captains on a screen or a climbing frame are limitless.*

'Man, is he in a zone or what?' one of the kids said.

'Here, you take it,' Orson said, thereby finding out it was Kevin who'd said it. Matthew had taken out his Gameboy again but wasn't playing, and Orson knew what he was waiting for.

'You were right about the magic cape. I still can't get it.'

Orson grinned and winked. 'Gimme that fucker,' he mouthed, with a slight whisper. 'Okay. Stock take time. Let's warp you back to Hyrule or whatever the village is called in this one.' Orson found the warp like he'd only played this yesterday and not a good ten years ago when Ben was still around at school, watching him do it. 'Hold on, you've got the Pegasus boots and the Roc's feather but you haven't got the ocarina yet? Uuuuurgh! Right, let's sort this out. Only three secret seashells too?'

'I just want the cape, butt-stuffer.'

'Matthew,' Cliff said. 'Be nice.'

243

'That the worst he's got?' Orson said. 'Well, here's the worst *I've* got: you don't get the magic cape in this game. That's on the Snes Zelda. That's your real punishment for bringing a Gameboy you weren't supposed to bring. I wanted to see how long you searched for it before going on GameFAQs. You've actually lasted nearly a week.'

Matthew stared for a minute, all traces of the Bernard persona gone. Cliff didn't keep a straight face for long and neither did Ben. Thankfully, Matthew rolled his eyes and smiled. 'Okay. I just got totally owned.'

'Yeah,' Orson said. 'By an otter too. And now you're getting the ocarina, unless you want to get caught by the glitch in this game where you can miss getting one of the songs and then spend hours getting to the end only to find you can't finish without it. Here you go, you talk to Marin right here and she gives you a hint about where the ocarina is. Spoiler: it's in the dream shrine.' Orson clicked the B button and moments later was staring at the screen, then smiling, then laughing, and so was Matthew.

'What's funny now?' Cliff said. 'Do I even want to ask?'

'I'm just a big kid, Cliff,' Orson said. 'How did I never think of doing this? You ever played this?'

'Me? Please, I can't even play snakes and ladders right.'

'Every time you talk to someone in this game, the name you pick for yourself comes up at the start. So

Matthew called his player OhShit. "OhShit, have you tried looking under the rocks by the hut at the top of Hyrule? OhShit, Madam Meow-Meow's dog has been kidnapped. OhShit, if you wake the wind-fish, the island might die.'

'Boys,' Cliff said.

Once Matthew got the ocarina, Orson got pulled back into the PS5, where all hope was lost for whatever the kids had named their ship, and they had reverted to Crash Bandicoot.

Hey OtterSpotter, are you ignoring us or what, bitch? came a message from someone he hadn't blocked yet.

Here he came then. Orson decided to switch voice on for this one, and a moment later Ben came into the room with his phone on and a WhatsApp call waiting. 'It's for you. Guess who. You're on video call, so look smart. You might as well be on parade.'

'Yeah, yeah, Barstow, just put the otter on already.' Kingsley's voice hadn't changed, no matter what a year of air force training might have changed about the rest of him.

Orson took it from him and hit pause on the TV. 'Hey, tree-head.'

Kingsley actually looked surprised that Orson had remembered the old schoolyard taunt. 'Even the forces can't use that one as an insult now. Offensive to people with antlers.'

'Boo hoo, wolf-food.'

Kingsley smiled, and Orson realised he'd missed that dry, discerning smile and never realised it until now. 'Good answer. Although when I'm training, you should see the wolves behind me, puffing like they've got asthma. So you're at Barstow's? Why didn't that butthead bear tell me? Where does he live now anyway?'

'New York. I'm playing Crash with...' Orson realised he had to count. 'Four kids, one teenager and my...BFF. So quit it with the poo-poo mouth, will you? *You're* the one on parade right now.'

'Seriously, Brookfield, what happened to you? There's dropping out of Sussex, then there's wiping all your social media and going off the grid. I was worried.'

'Chill out already, antler-boy. I'm still alive, aren't I? It's not like you being in a military boot camp for the last nine months meant I could call you much, was it?'

Kingsley shrugged. 'Fair.'

'We'll catch up in the new year, okay? I'm sorry you were worried about me. I'll explain later. Quite a lot's happened. Good things. You might not even recognise me apart from my face.'

'This does *not* sound like you, Brookfield. What happened, you get religion or something?'

'Something. Call you when I get back to London. I've gotta go. Gaming to catch up on.'

'Hold on, there's something I need to tell you. Can you go somewhere quiet for five? Or call me back later on your own phone? Seriously, you blocked *me*?

Orson muted him for a second. 'Public school boy who couldn't get into Cambridge. Stag. You get the idea.' He looked at Ben. 'Should I take this?'

'Yeah,' Ben said. 'I would.'

A little unease crept in. Orson felt sure Ben had already heard what he was about to, and it was going to bring the mood down.

'Sounds like a total butt,' Seth said.

'Yeah, but he's *my* kind of butt,' Orson said. 'I ditched all my friends back home, but maybe I should have kept him. I'll be right back.' He took Kingsley off mute. 'Hold on. I'm gonna go to the bathroom.' Orson locked himself in the one downstairs that still smelt like the snake had been all the way down the pipes and right into the sewers. It was freezing from the open window, but he didn't dare shut it. Somehow it still smelt of the half can of jasmine air freshener someone had tried to cover the smell with. He went back to the hall, got his parka off the hook, pulled himself into it and locked the door. He put the toilet seat down and sat on it. 'I hope this is good. I'm in a freezing cold bathroom that flooded with shitty water earlier.'

'Just hear me out, whatever you feel like when I start this,' Kingsley said. 'The thing is, we're all worried about Syd.'

'Oooooooooh no. No no no. Not my fucking problem.'

Kingsley stayed quiet for a moment, and Orson didn't like it. He was obviously too prepared. 'I'm not gonna pretend he wasn't a shithead, Brookfield. I know why you're still fuming about it. But listen, me and the guys, we all told the truth about what happened, because we knew you weren't the bad guy. I'm not calling in a favour exactly, but can I tell you what's been happening?'

Orson thought of Ben telling him he should take this. 'Okay. I'm listening.'

'Syd tried to join up with me last year. He got this sudden revelation that he wanted to be in the service.'

'You're kidding me. Syd?'

'I know. My two cents, I think he was desperate to stay around me. I didn't think it was for him at all, but he was so certain that there was no telling him. Then he actually passed the test for pilot. I couldn't believe it. That's when I just said good luck to him. I was lucky to get engineering. Not gonna lie, it burned. I really wanted to fly, even if I did get a first in engineering from Sussex. But oh well. Life. But thank God Syd did it. It was the entrance medical when they discovered he was sick.'

'Sick? With what?'

'Testicular cancer.'

Orson clutched his coat around him a little tighter. 'Ooooooh boy. How bad?'

'Stage three. It was aggressive. Syd even told the doctor he thought the lump was just an infection he'd had in the same place before, and he got it from too much rough wanking. As if. They took him straight from Cranwell to the hospital to get a blood test and a scan. While I went through initial officer training for nine months, Syd went through hell.'

Orson sighed slowly and quietly to himself. 'Did the treatment work?'

'Yeah, but it was nasty. Syd couldn't quite believe it when they told him he'd actually got to remission. He's gotta go for a yearly check-up for pretty much the rest of his life, whatever type of cancer this thing was. But here's the thing. There was this one point where he decided he didn't want the next course of treatment. He'd rather be dead than live with what he thought he'd be like if he had it. Think about it for a second.'

Orson thought about it, then thought about everything he'd just come to know about himself, to enjoy with Ben, and he felt sick. 'Did he lose both of them?'

'No, thank God. Just one. It was the only reason I was able to talk him into having the surgery. They granted me a special weekend's leave from IOT so I could go see him and talk to him. Reading between the lines, that was Daddy calling favours in. Before you ask, yes, he still can. Just like I promised and hoped to hell I was right and so were the doctors. But it's fucked with his head, Brookfield. The whole thing. He's not the same. We think he's got a drug problem and he's trying to hide it. He didn't go back and try to join up again. He says he wants to travel the world first, and then next minute he says he's too scared to go.'

Orson sat back against the tank. 'So what do you want me to do about this, stag? He hates my guts.'

'I don't think that's true. He said he wished you'd talk to him.'

'He said what? I got publicly humiliated because he gave my name to the press. He said I made him do it. You were there. He was a fucking liar, Kingsley. I'm sorry he went through what he did, but would *you* be the one to reach out to him if you were me?'

'I'd think of it like this, otter: if one of you talks to the other and you manage to keep talking, eventually it won't matter who broke the ice. It's like I said, what happened changed him. I know he doesn't see a lot of his past the same way. I think if you talk to him, you'll get the apology you deserve.'

'You *think*.'

'Imagine you were him, just for a second. If you don't get surgery to lose one of your balls, you'll die. You don't want to die, but you don't want to live knowing you might not enjoy sex ever again if everyone's wrong about one ball being enough. Then while you're figuring it out, you remember that you named a friend to the press and said something you knew wasn't true, just to try and make your own humiliation seem a bit less bad. When you're already low, and you're scared, that's when you start thinking maybe you *deserve* to die.'

Orson couldn't speak for a moment. 'Did that happen? He told you all that? That that's what he was thinking?'

'I promised him what we said to each other would never leave that room. So it hasn't. But sometimes, Brookfield, you know what people are thinking even if they don't say it in exact words.'

250

Orson wanted him off the line. He wanted to go back to everything that was happening in the Barstows' house this evening and have the rest of his Christmas after that without thinking about this, least of all that Kingsley might actually be right. John Barstow had apologised this evening, admitted he was wrong. Would Orson have much to lose if he said that regardless of blame, he was sorry to have been the only one in that room who was prepared to carry the forfeit out? There was one way to get out of thinking about this.

'I'll think about this,' Orson said. 'But if I do it, it's once only. I reach out and he throws it in my face? That's the end.'

'Thank you,' Kingsley said. 'Just so you know, Syd doesn't like me much either right now. He tried to come and see me yesterday. The guards wouldn't let him on base because he was drunk. At least he called me rather than make a scene. So I went down to the gates. I told him he needed to sober up for at least a couple of weeks and make a promise he'd get off whatever else he's been doing that he won't admit to. Otherwise I don't want him around my family. It was harsh, but I had to.'

'Fair play,' Orson said. 'Wait, hold on, your family?'

Kingsley smiled. 'Yeah.'

'You're a father?'

'Right before I was about to start IOT, Verity tells me she's pregnant. Yeah, wasn't expecting that. Two days before graduation, I've got a son. I nearly missed my parade, but you know Verity, she's a stubborn woman.'

'You'd have regretted it for the rest of your life!' came a voice in the background. 'If you'd not collected your best recruit award from the chief of defence, our son would have had to hear about it one day.'

'Best recruit *and* a dad in the same week?'

'Don't be jealous, Brookfield. It's exhausting keeping *both* going.'

'What's your son called?'

'Emory.' Right on cue, the noise began. 'Yeah, that's him saying hi right there. I've gotta go. If you do talk to Syd, you can make sobriety a condition before you actually meet him. The rest of us are starting to do that.'

Perhaps, Orson thought, *it would be better if I didn't.* His own sobriety hadn't mattered much this evening, even though he was far from drunk. He went back into the living room, found the scotch on the rocks that had diluted a fair amount from the ice, and went to the kitchen to top it up.

'Kingsley tell you about Syd?' he asked Ben, who was there as if waiting.

'Yeah. Poor guy.'

'What do I do?'

'Whatever you think the right thing is.'

'I think the right thing right now is gaming.' Orson went back in to find they'd actually waited to start playing Crash Bandicoot, the title screen still on but muted, and instead were crowding around Matthew, watching him try to beat the level five boss on Zelda.

'What did your stag friend want?' Ella said.

Orson forced a smile, thinking about what Kingsley said about not using exact words. 'To know if I was still his friend. We Crashing?'

* * *

The real crash happened just before Orson's three hours were up. He was glad. He did want to play more, if only to get back to the list of names he'd guiltily blocked, thinking how odd it was that he'd never done it before and simply disconnected from his account altogether. If he'd really wanted to wipe the slate clean, he would have deleted it.

Hadn't he told his parents that he had done that ages ago?

I lied to them right from the start, he thought. *A lie that came back to hand me my life back instead of haunt me.*

A text came through from Kingsley: *'Forgot to mention: I asked Verity to marry me on Christmas Day and she said yes. You've got a wedding to go to next year. I'll send you dates once we have them.'*

There was only one response to that: *'When are we having your stag party?'*

'Har har har, rudder-butt.'

He still couldn't stop thinking about Syd, right down to finding his social media pages and staring at them, wondering about hitting 'unblock'. He needed a distraction. Ben coming out of his en-suite bathroom wearing just his underpants wasn't quite enough.

'Hey boyfriend,' he said quietly. 'You're not sleeping down there tonight, are you?'

'Hell no,' Orson said. 'But do you think we can keep this quiet? What we did before would get the entire house running in here thinking you were killing me or something. How do we keep your family from finding you bollocks deep in me?'

'Simple,' Ben said, running a hand down Orson's back. 'You top me instead.'

'Aside from how I'd squeak like hell as soon as I came in you, I don't think you'd actually feel much on your end. I don't think my dick's actually big enough to get very far inside that great big white butt.'

'Sure it is. It's all about position. We'll find one that works for us. Why don't we google bears on otters and see how the pros do it? By the way, you know why gaming's good for you? You forgot to go for that cigarette.'

'Yeah,' Orson said. 'I actually did.' He took the pack out and found he still had two left. He put them away again. 'Want to try slightly more smoke-free otter?'

'My pleasure.' Ben brushed Orson's face on both sides, then his neck, then gently pulled him closer and kissed him, his tongue touching Orson's a little. Orson didn't do much besides stand there and put his hands on Ben's back, just above his butt. Ben's breath tasted of alcohol behind the overpowering mint toothpaste, but Orson could have sworn there was a hint of green tea behind it from the mug Ben had drunk while they'd played Crash.

'Am I doing this right?' he said.

'Stop worrying about getting everything right. It's enough that it's you. Kissing you's different. I cover your mouth with mine so much I have to remember you need to breathe. But you breathing through your nose on me's hot.'

'Can I say something that's going to sound totally dumb?'

'You know I'll find it cute.'

'Will you show me how to brush my teeth properly?'

'Sure. Did your dentist back home never show you that?'

'He's a Chinese chee, and I have real trouble with his accent. I don't actually have any fillings or anything yet, and I guess he took it for granted that I know how to brush.'

'You probably do.'

'Show me anyway.'

'Ah,' Ben said, a mischievous grin on his face. 'You liked it when I checked your teeth. You want my hands feeling underneath your jaw like that again.' He placed his fingers lightly under Orson's jawbone. Orson lifted his chin up and sighed with pleasure as Ben did the routine again.

'Why's this hot to me?'

'I don't know. Maybe we're college roommates and I'm studying for a test and practicing on you. Wanna go in the bathroom and help me study for that exam on otter teeth? There actually *is* an exam like that. One for every species out there. You come under mustelids

255

along with weasels, stoats, ferrets and mink. Gonna show me some mustelid teeth?'

'You bet. Ooooh, what's this?'

Ben's had gripped his tail at the top. 'I'm walking you to the mirror.'

'Okay, this is weird...you know my tail's half my balance, right?' Orson managed to walk anyway, but the room around him seemed weird, like he could tilt one way and go over, then the other. 'That was funny,' he said to their reflections in the mirror.

'Yeah,' Ben said. 'Take your pants and shirt off.'

'You practicing dentistry or medicine?' Orson said, taking them off. 'Your patients will always be *in* clothes.'

'Not this one,' Ben said. 'Okay, open wide, let me show you. There are your incisors, there are your molars, there are your fangs, like you didn't know that one. You guys don't have wisdom teeth. Be thankful for that, by the way; I had to have all mine taken out right before college. They knocked me right out for that.' Ben opened his own mouth to show Orson the rows of perfectly lined, powerful big teeth. He tried to talk and say where the wisdoms would have been with a finger in his mouth.

'You dumb bear,' Orson said. 'Hold on, I'm getting my phone for the light.' He grabbed it from the bed. 'Open wide again; let me take a look. Those are impressive, Snowbear. Perfect for tearing apart salmon. Mmm. Bite together for me. Cool.' Orson set his phone down and copied the jaw check Ben had done on him.

'Am I good there?' Ben said.

'I guess so. I wouldn't know, would I? I'm just playing like a big kid.'

'You *are* a big kid. That's why I love you. I needed you to come here to remind *me* how to be like that. Everything's been so serious for so long. This is the first Christmas in ages where I've really had any fun. Ice hockey might look like fun, but it can get to your head when it's about trying to win. Knowing you were watching me play, it made me feel like I could play it like a kid again instead of having to be some kind of star.'

'You didn't know I was watching.'

'I imagined you were. Then when I found you really were? I actually felt joy. That's when I knew I was in love with you. Except it didn't hit me just like that. It trickled in. Having hot sex with you felt like such a release, except it *didn't* release everything. Playing dentist with you like big kids? That kinda does it, except I've still got feelings inside that don't seem to release. That's what I think loving someone is. When nothing takes it out of you.'

'Yeah. It's cool,' Orson said, wondering how he could make anyone feel like that. 'But I can't be a kid forever, Benji. I need to grow up. I've been the defiant brat for too long. And the guy who nothing serious matters to because it's all about having fun. Yeah, I kept to my three-hour limit tonight. But I've got to live in the real world now. You wouldn't want to be with someone who only ever wanted to play games. Or never got a day job that actually pays a wage you can live off.'

'There's plenty of time to work out how to do that,' Ben said. 'When you go home, sit and have some time with yourself and come up with some ideas. Your computer science degree wouldn't have been a bad start. Why don't you pick it back up?'

Orson thought for a moment, deciding it would kill the mood if all he did was come up with reasons why not, until one came to him he had to voice. 'You know how I think we're the same?' he said. 'Do you think we're both just two people trying to convince our parents that we're who we're supposed to be? I talked a hard game about defying mine tonight, but we both know how difficult it's going to make everything if I actually do that. That's your world too, right?'

'Why don't we go to bed and put off thinking about serious things until tomorrow? Or maybe the day after that. Or maybe forever?'

'Yeah, I'd like that.'

Before getting into bed, Ben locked his bedroom door. 'I'm not supposed to do that, grown up or not. Dad's biggest fear is his whole family dying in a fire because he couldn't wake them up to get them out of the house. Ever since he had this dream where it happened. The whole religion thing means a lot to him, but do *not* get into a discussion with him about dreams. Definitely don't tell him any of yours either.'

'As if. I dream about fucking fit shirtless bears, remember? Bears like this one.' He smacked Ben's backside as he climbed onto the bed.

'Unf!' Ben said. 'Yeah, there we go!' He kneeled on all fours over Orson. 'Do that again.'

Orson slapped him on the other cheek now, feeling the rush of Ben's breath on his face. It only took a few slaps before the tent in Ben's pants was poking out hard.

'Won't they hear the noise of that and wonder what we're doing?' Orson whispered.

'Oh yeah. Didn't think of that. They'll be asleep though probably. One more for the road?'

Orson gave him two, and then Ben nipped at his nose and rolled over onto his back. 'Gonna play with that hard erect penis that's in those pants right now?'

'You like designer brands for pants so you can think about how you just put a come stain in something expensive, don't you?' Orson put his hand in Ben's pants and felt how hard he was. Ben was fully out of his sheath and his tip so sensitive that he arched up at only a small, brushing touch. Ben breathed as quietly as he could, and this time his breathing quickened to panting in hardly any time. Orson stroked the underside of Ben's cock near the tip, and his breath became louder. Orson listened intently to the house around him behind it, waiting for footsteps on the landing that would mean having to put a pillow over Ben's head or something. Would Ben like that? Orson didn't think so. Suffocation play was risky. He thought about asking and then realised Ben's ultra-control from before had gone, and he was going to come.

'Hey...otter! Hold up! Not yet...I want to come when you top me.'

'Okay.' Orson stopped, taking his hand out of Ben's pants but leaving the other on the back of his neck. 'What do I do? How do I get far enough in you?'

'Me on my back and you on your knees. Let's...uh oh...oh boy! Too late...I'm gonna...' Ben panted hard, trying to hold it.

'Woah, nice! You're gonna come hands-free? Go on, bear. Come in those designer pants. Come hard. Let it go!'

Ben released with Orson stroking the top of his head, helplessly panting, and arched up as if still trying to hold even when his pants were already wet and he was still squirting. His chest heaved in and out while inside Orson's half-hug, his head back and nose pointed to the ceiling, gasping in the relief of having released.

'Oh boy...oh *God*, that never happens!' Ben said.

'Yeah? Well I *made* it happen,' Orson said. 'Lift your butt up, naughty bear!' He took Ben's pants off him, thought about using the dry part of them to clean Ben up, but instead took a deep sniff of them and said, 'You want me to clean you up with that mouth you inspected a minute ago?'

'That's filthy, otter.' Ben could only hold the seriousness for a few seconds. 'Do it. Lick me clean. Taste it.'

Orson put Ben's cock in his mouth, rolled his tongue around it, swallowed, then realising he was still holding Ben's pants, he dropped them onto the floor and released Ben from his mouth with a wet sucking sound. 'I am *so* hard for you right now. Let's get in that butt.' He licked both his hands and slickened himself up. 'Did you lube up tonight while getting ready for bed?'

'You bet I did,' Ben said. 'All yours. Just don't stuff it too hard. Gently. Like I did for you.' Ben bent his knees, showing Orson the pads of his feet and lifting his butt off the bed by rolling back slightly, arching his surprisingly flexible back.

Orson could only just contain himself. Ben was so tight, he had to ease in inch by inch. Ben was breathing deeply with satisfaction at every little push, his cock still hard and wet on the tip again.

'Can you come a second time in five minutes?'

'I don't think so,' Ben said. 'I really want to, but I'm spent. I'm just hard. You like it?'

'Yeah. I could fuck you looking at that hard cock all night, Snowbear.'

'Good boy, keep it coming. You can push deeper, I've got room. Uuuuuuunf, yeah, like that.'

Orson felt a rush to his head as the blood surged to his own cock, halfway deep inside Ben and harder than he ever thought he'd been. He opened his mouth and tipped his head back.

'Don't!' Ben said. 'No squeaking! That's an order! You wanna wake the whole place up?'

Orson only just held it, trying to concentrate on the feel of Ben's leg gripped by his arms and the tightness around him. It only made him need to squeak more, so he gasped.

'That's it!' Ben said. 'Pant, otter! Pant hard. Huff and puff like a great big bear.'

That was the order that did it. Orson held it for a few more seconds and then came, obeying the first command of not squeaking and instead panting for his life, imagining he really was as big as Ben and had the lungs to match, and everything else. He *felt* big, emptying himself into Ben's limitless hole.

'Oh...oh man...yeah, that did it! I'm a top now!'

'You did great,' Ben said.

'Did you come?'

'A little bit. It stung. I kinda feel like I need to pee. Okay, I think I *do* need to pee.' With Orson already out of him, he got off the bed, leaving Orson to collapse on it. After a moment, Orson realised Ben had been in the bathroom for a while and yet he hadn't heard any sound of water.

He got up. 'You okay, Benji?'

'I'm fine, don't worry. I've had this before. I think I'm a little bit sore from what we did yesterday still.'

'Shall I shut the door?'

'No, it's okay. I'm not embarrassed. Ace saw me like this too.'

Orson went to him and put a hand on his shoulder while Ben stood there pointing his dick over the toilet. 'You sure you're okay?'

'I'm all good. Sex with you *and* masturbating into condoms because I was aroused all the time was a bit too much. This whole feeling joy at Christmas again has made me a little bit hypersexual. Would you mind doing something though? Everything you just filled me with's dribbling out. Would you clean my bottom for me and the top of my right leg?'

'You got it, bear. Towel or toilet paper?'

Ben laughed. 'Wet towel, otter. *Warm* wet towel. Toilet paper makes a mess. Besides, you're not wiping my...' Ben laughed.

'Hah! You were actually gonna say arse! Go on, bear. Say it. Say I wasn't gonna wipe your arse.'

Ben stood up a little too straight for Orson to get too far in with the towel he'd put under the hot tap. 'You weren't gonna wipe my...my...'

'Go on, Benji. Say it!'

'You weren't gonna wipe my *ass*, otter.'

'Atta boy.' He took hold of Ben's cock. 'Now, what's this? Or is one little push enough for one night?'

'That? Oh, that's just my unsnipped penis, and it needs a bit of a break before you play with it any more. I never answered your question from before though, did I? I don't call it Little Benji. I call it Destroyer.'

'Yeah right. You just made that up. Fair play about the rest thing though. I'll give *Destroyer* here a rest and let it go right after you've told me it's also your big bear dick. Go on. Say something naughty.'

'Well...I can try, but I don't really want to feel bad about myself after such a good time. You not wiping my bottom was kinda funny, that gave me a little tingle. But...okay. Here goes then.'

'It's alright,' Orson said. 'Don't. Sorry.'

'It's cool. Frosty.'

'*I* can still call it your big bear dick and it's hot, right?'

'Totally. But can we let it go floppy now and just snuggle up?'

'You got it. I'm a little bit worn out too.'

They got back into bed, and Ben pulled the covers over. It was going to be like a sauna in under five minutes, Orson thought. 'Oh yeah, not asking for details or anything, but how was your little talk with Matthew?'

'Oh. He told me everything he told you. And then some.'

'Did you, like...tell him anything back?'

'No. I don't think I needed to. I think Cliff picking me for that whole thing made it fall into place in his head. I said sorry about the little stinker thing, and he said he didn't really care about that. He didn't think I liked him because he thought I already knew he was different, but he realised he judged it wrong. Then he told me just *how* different.'

'You think it helped him?'

'I don't know,' Ben said, rolling onto his back. '*Can* I tell you something he said? He said he wouldn't mind if I did.'

'Yeah, sure, although I don't know what help I'll be. I can still only half believe we've been doing college boy stuff since I got here and that I've somehow accepted I'm gay within a week. Or at least I think I have. But sure, shoot.'

'When he told you he thought he was gay, what he really meant to say was that he thought he was queer.

264

The difference just depends on who you're talking to, but here's the thing. You noticed how he reacted to Ella's dress joke, right? Well, he told me he wished he had a sister like I did, so that he could have had girls' toys in the house when he was growing up, and things like dresses to try apart from his mom's stuff. He told me he likes guys but he kind of wants guys to treat him a bit like a girl sometimes.'

'So he thinks he might be trans?'

'Kind of but not exactly. He said he didn't identify as a girl even if he sometimes wants to feel like one, but he doesn't exactly feel that it matters that he was born a guy either. He said it's like he doesn't care, because why be one or the other? He feels like the world tells him he's a boy, but he doesn't really get what it is.'

'Oh,' Orson said. 'So he's a nonbinary person?' *Do I know more about this than I thought? Where did I pick it up from? It wasn't a big part of school or anything else in my life. Gamers are whatever they want when they're behind a screen, and we're often more concerned with a score or a kill count than what we are.*

'He called it "enby",' Ben said. 'That's when I didn't know what to think.'

'How come?'

'Matthew's a "cool kid" at school. Like I was, only he's attitude cool where I was jock-cool. Smart-cool too, but with the attitude it's all about trends. The way he said the word, that's when I felt like saying what you're never supposed to. It's like he's maybe following a trend. Except what if he isn't? So I couldn't say it. But that's why I told him to go see Mom about it. The whole hibernation syndrome thing was a cover; I don't think he's got it, he just doesn't like getting his lazy bottom out of bed on a school day. All part of the attitude again. Mom's the one who can work out if this stuff is real or not. Or at least give it the time. I didn't really know what to say. I don't know what this feels like. I *do* identify with being a guy.'

'Sounds like you handled it right. If being an enby is part of the cool thing then it will wear off. Maybe he'll identify like that for a while and then realise it was the wrong thing to do just to be what he thought trendy was. Or maybe he won't and that's actually who he is. Or does he want to use they-them now?'

'Oh, he wants to do it all. He wants to come out about it at school and try to get everyone on board with him. It's brave. It might also be crazy. Too much too fast. But this is what I mean: I'm still in a closet because I couldn't do all that with who I am, but why should I tell someone else it's the wrong thing to do? So I didn't. I told him he needs more thinking time. Maybe getting him to talk to Mom will help.'

'Even though you think she's secretly still kind of homophobic?'

'It's different when it's not your own kid. When you're doing a job, you do the job. Even if it's family. She can always refer him to somebody who doesn't have her buried hang-ups. Except I wonder if she really does have them. Maybe *I* judged somebody wrong.'

'I think you handled it right. Maybe wherever it goes from here is another tomorrow thing.'

Ben rolled over onto his side. 'Thanks, otter.'

'No problem.' *I just gave someone life advice that was good? Me?*

The two of them cuddled up and turned the light down to low, and within a few minutes Orson was proven right. 'Benji, I don't think I can sleep with you like this. I'm sweating already.'

'Are you?' Ben said, brushing a hand down Orson's back. 'Wow, you *are* starting to sweat. Sorry, I guess you don't need such a thick duvet.'

'It's not the duvet, it's the massive amount of heat pouring out of your hot furry body even when you're not literally hot for me. And your big bear heartbeat's thudding all through me when we're cuddled up; it's like being in an earthquake simulator.'

'Oh,' Ben said, putting a hand on his chest. 'Yeah, it's a pretty strong engine alright. Sorry I can't switch it off.'

'It's kind of exciting,' Orson said, putting his hand on Ben's chest and feeling his heart go *thump-thump* against it. 'But I can't be excited if I'm going to sleep. How do I learn to sleep with you without everything about you turning me on?'

'I could ask the same question,' Ben said. 'Let's use the duvet from your bed though.'

'You'll be too cold.'

'Maybe you'll balance it out.'

They tried it.

'It feels wrong,' Ben said, after squirming about, trying to feel comfortable. 'I need the other one back. Why don't I wrap up in it and you lie on top and put yours over you. That might dull my heartbeat down for you too.'

They tried it. The other duvet wouldn't stay on the bed unless it added an extra layer to Ben's side, which was then too hot.

'I'm wiped out, Benji. I'm gonna have to sleep down there tonight. We'll figure this one out tomorrow too.'

'Okay, yeah, I give up,' Ben said. 'Happy dreams. Let me get to sleep first though. You snore like a train. I was dreading trying to get to sleep if you dropped off first.'

'Oh, do I?'

'Otters always do. They're the worst roomies at summer camp. People think it's always the bears who'd be like that, but we're always quiet. You guys and the sneps keep whole camps awake.'

What an odd thought. Otters snored like that? Orson realised he wouldn't know. He'd never been to summer camp, and on all the school trips he'd ever been on, he couldn't remember rooming with other otters.

Now he had a boyfriend he couldn't sleep with. Just his luck.

'Hey,' Ben said. 'You still awake?'

'Well yeah, otherwise I'd be snoring and driving you nuts, right?'

'I think I should come out to my mom.'

Orson turned the bedside light back on. 'Really?'

'Yeah. I'll never manage Dad if she doesn't already know, and if I ever do that, it'll be better if she's prepared. If Matty can be that brave then it's time I at least took a step. I want to tell her. I'm going to ask her to get breakfast with me somewhere and tell her there's something I need to talk about. See where it goes.'

'Okay. Good idea then. Tomorrow?'

'Maybe.'

Orson didn't turn off the light. He knew what was coming, and he knew he'd never sleep now.

'Will you help me do it?' Ben said. 'Will you come out to her with me too?'

Chapter Twelve

<u>Three Days Later</u>

Orson thought Waffle House was a good place for this. He thought the 'We're Never Closed' promise should include 'But we are quiet sometimes', because he and Ben had fortunately picked a morning where they weren't going to be surrounded by commuters or anyone on holiday. Schools had gone back, John had gone back to work, and Dr Natasha Barstow worked part time these days and had a day off in the week. This was it, and Ben looked ready to make her spend the rest of it taking a very long walk.

Until breakfast was over.

Ben had primed his mother with the suggestion that what he needed to talk about should wait until their waffles were finished. Orson was the last to finish, with Ben keeping him talking until the ice cream had almost melted over the peanut butter and chocolate sauce he'd picked for his waffle, and Orson realised it was deliberate – a delay he was supposed to pick up on and then not be surprised when Ben bottled it and said maybe this should wait for another day. Another day would mean Orson was already flying home.

'The thing is, Mom,' Ben said after the waiter had cleared their plates, leaving them with just a topped-up coffee cup each, 'I think you've probably already guessed this.'

'I guess a lot of things about you, Benjamin, but after I've done it, I remember they *are* just guesses and I'm not a mind reader.'

'Bet your job would be easier if you were.'

'You'd be surprised. If I actually could hear what was inside a patient's head, it would probably give me a lot more than I'd ever be able to process. Too much information can mean more than just "I didn't need to know that".'

'Yeah. Tell me about it.'

Natasha smiled. 'Come on. Tell me what you need to tell me that's too risky to say at home. You've been looking around you since we got here making sure nobody we know's in here. If I'm going to be knocked off my feet, then I've been prepared for that for at least the last half an hour.'

'I've been...hiding a lot since I went to college, Mom. There's a lot I discovered that I didn't want to talk about until now.' He looked away from her. Orson thought he was trying to get up the courage to keep looking at her eyes.

'Go on,' she said.

'Come on, Mom. You know, don't you?'

271

'This will always be the moment where you'll wish you'd been the one to say it if you don't,' Natasha said. 'Don't make me say it for you.'

'I'm gay, Mom.'

'There. That wasn't so hard in the end, was it?' She took Ben's hand over the table. 'It's okay. I'm glad you could finally tell me.'

'Not so hard? I feel like I'm going to faint. And I know what you're going to say next. It's not so different from how I used to get this kind of adrenaline every time I got an injection at the dentist. Now here I am trying to become one.'

'I hadn't thought of that,' Natasha said. 'But yes, you're not wrong. Except this *is* different and we all know it. You never asked your friend to come with you to that, for one thing.'

'Well, there's the thing, Mom.'

'What thing?'

Natasha looked less sure of herself now, Orson thought.

'You know why I couldn't say this at home, right? Even with Dad at work. I couldn't do it in *any* place connected to him. It's not like I think he's got the place bugged or anything, but...you get it, don't you?'

'Of course I get it,' she said. 'Let me guess: is part of the reason you kept this secret for so long that you didn't want me to have the burden of keeping it from him too? Knowing what he might say if I told him?'

'Yeah.'

'You needn't worry about that. I have more secrets from him than you realise. Some are actually far bigger than the sexuality of his son would be.'

'Like what?'

Natasha visibly thought for a moment, her eyes scanning the room slowly, a less obvious version of what Orson too had noticed Ben doing since they got here. 'You're old enough to know the truth now,' she said. 'This would be a good time, if your concern is about what secrets my conscience will let me keep. But with no offence to Orson, you might be better off talking to me about this part alone, later on.'

'Family only stuff?'

'Yes.'

'If you're going to drop a bombshell on me, Mom, I'm going to end up telling Orson anyway. Before I tell anyone else.'

'Alright then,' Natasha said. 'But first I think I'd better tell you how I first guessed you might be gay, because I doubt it's what you thought.'

So it's not the pink dressing gown. Orson smiled.

'Yeah,' Ben said. 'What gave it away that Dad didn't see but you did?'

'Your girlfriend,' Natasha said. 'Your father saw exactly what he wanted to: you in a straight relationship. I saw you in a relationship with a young woman who was obviously gay herself. Her body language, her style, the way she talked, I couldn't have missed all that. I've seen it so many times before: two people really can love each other and have a

273

relationship, but really it's a cover for how one of them is gay and they both know it. I started to guess you might both have acknowledged it. Or perhaps you did on her side, and she knows nothing of yours.'

Ben sighed. 'She knows, Mom. She's one of the few people who does. I know I'm saying the obvious when I say Orson is as well, but here's the thing: I told him on his first night here with us.'

Now she was surprised. 'Did you?'

'Yeah.'

'You came out to an old friend you'd not seen in years who probably seemed like little more than a stranger now? On the first night of your reunion?'

'Yeah. Talk about a way to get to know each other again. I went to that meeting. I heard a whole world of personal stuff in that meeting I went to with him. It made me brave.'

Orson wondered if Ben had genuinely mixed his own memories up to make that night say what he wanted it to. He'd come out before the meeting. If anything, that mentality had worked the other way round, making Orson spill more than he'd really wanted to, turning that meeting into a genuine one and not just a place where he wanted to get phone numbers to pick up a gaming pal who'd help him run away into New York forever.

'That's how Ella's guessed it too then,' Ben said. 'She wouldn't have missed that about Edie either.'

'Oh, I'm not so sure,' Natasha said. 'I think she sees what she wants to too. But never mind her right now.

Are you still sure you want my truth too, right here right now?'

I want it more, Orson thought, reflecting on how bad that sounded even in his head but refusing to deny he was going to enjoy this. He had the luxury of getting on a flight in two days time and whatever Natasha said not affecting him.

'Yes,' Ben said. 'If you think you can shock me, I doubt it. Let's have it.'

'I *do* love your father, and he loves me too,' Natasha said. 'But neither of us have ever pretended we were saints. He tried to give up certain parts of his life when he married me, but men don't change who they are just with one promise to someone. He ended up confessing a lot to me after a few years. By then we had you and Ella, and Sam was on the way. So I couldn't tear the family apart over it. I said I forgave him. Then I started doing the same thing he'd done.'

'What thing?'

'Affairs,' Natasha said. 'With other people. It's all part of the lifestyle of your father's high-flying business. Trips away, drinking, gambling, throwing money at the world like it will never run out, probably some cocaine in the mix as well, and women. That's who your father's always been. The Christian side of him isn't a fraud; he believes in it all, but he believes more in "love your God and do as you will" than the family thinks. Because he's made sure of it. The side you all see of him is the one that never lets on about what goes on outside of the family home. I think he's come to like it. A double life appealed to him before he knew it. His conscience wouldn't let him keep the truth from me forever. He believes we have a stay-together-for-the-kids marriage. What he'd never expect is that deep down, I'm the same as he is.'

Orson couldn't help but smile. 'Well shit,' he said quietly. Ben, he thought, looked like he'd just discovered the last Jedi.

If that was a good analogy, Orson thought, then a better one was that Cliff was Yoda – Cliff knew everything. Orson thought about when Cliff had told him that his brother and sister-in-law weren't everything they appeared to be, and he couldn't help but smile.

Natasha sat back, and a smile played on her own lips. 'I have sex with other men because it feels good, Benjamin. Your father's never known about it. It's enough for him to think that I allow him to have our marriage with a caveat that away from home he can do what he likes within reason. He's a selfish man who I love. *I* enjoy the side of him I see when he's at home. I stay with him partly because he's a good provider. He's rich. I'm not badly paid either. It's a good family. But can I keep from him that his son's gay for the rest of our lives together if that's what's necessary? You're goddamn right I can.'

Ben stared at her. '*Wow*, Mom. Holy...would you have ever told me this if I hadn't told you my secrets first?'

'Yes,' Natasha said. 'I didn't want to feel like I was forcing you to come out to me by asking certain questions, but I did start to think that if I was right in what I'd seen then perhaps sharing some secrets with you might make you feel like you could do it more easily. It was going to be an icebreaker, eventually.'

Before Ben could say anything, Natasha half held a hand up and looked at Orson.

'I'm sorry I said such awful things the other night even though I meant them,' she said. 'I'm glad you arrived at the truth about your parents yourself after it. It needed to happen somehow. It would have been better if I hadn't been drunk and done it the way I did it, but I was going to have a talk with you too otherwise. But here's the truth about why I did it: my husband was pissing me off so much that day that I was ready to *really* dump some truth on him. Me saying all that about your family was a way of releasing that stress without having to talk about my own. That sounds awful too, and I'm sorry, but I am who I am.'

'It's cool,' Orson said. 'I totally get it. It was good it happened like it did. I never really wanted some boring, soul-searching talk. I've not been to a party where shit went down in far too long. I needed that.'

Ben didn't look like he was going to faint now. Whether the release had lifted his spirits or having more dirt on the father he sometimes thought he hated had, Ben looked like he was enjoying himself.

'Come on,' he said, just like his mother had to him. 'You've got to tell her.'

Orson could only just believe it: it seemed so easy. Ben was the one who'd had to be brave. He could do this with complete impunity now. 'I'm gay too, Tasha,' he said. 'After all the jokes, all the fun at that book Ella gave me, which by the way Ben told her to –'

'I thought as much,' Tasha said. 'Very clever, young man. Use your sister so you don't give yourself away, and yet I still think she doesn't know. She probably believes Orson is and that you're just a good friend supporting him. Besides, there's a good Christian wolf in that book who she likes.'

'Ella likes Austin?' Orson said. 'Wait a minute, she's *read it*? Have you?'

'We both have. Contraband books appeal to just about any teenager regardless of how virtuous they believe themselves to be. I think Ella wanted to understand it. Todd and Colton aren't a bad introduction to why some guys like other guys. Before too long you'll be able to tell her too.' This looking at Ben.

'I do *not* think so, Mom. You're not surprised that Orson's gay?'

'Of course not, and it's nothing to do with the prime minister's son episode at all. I simply made no assumptions about who he might be.'

Ben nodded. 'Tell her the rest.'

'The rest?' Natasha said.

This didn't feel so easy.

'Well, it's...kind of like this,' Orson said. 'Ben and I...we got to know each other pretty fast. That meeting on the first night, I kind of wish I hadn't gone to it, except I'm glad I went, I just maybe...taking my supportive friend was kind of...not a mistake exactly but...there were things that I said that maybe...' He remembered Ben's hands on his shoulders that first night, telling him to breathe for calm. He took a deep breath and slowly sighed it out. 'Ben and I...did stuff. Together. Stuff just happened. Then we realised we *liked* stuff...okay, yeah, we knew we liked it while we were doing it, it wasn't like you "realise" that after you've done it. I'm such a dumbarse. So the thing is...yeah.' He took Ben's hand. 'Ben and I are into each other. Like we've spent two weeks getting *really* into each other.'

'Oh God, otter,' Ben said, rolling his eyes. 'You totally planned that line, didn't you?'

'Planned what line? What are you...*no*! No, I didn't plan that! Oh for fuck's sake.' He closed his eyes. Mostly so he didn't have to keep looking at Natasha's face.

Dr Natasha Barstow, with all her years of everything under the sun walking into her clinic and doing its show, was dumbstruck.

'Ben asked me to be his long-distance boyfriend,' Orson said, looking at Ben instead once he'd forced his eyes open. 'I said yes. We said we'd both try and figure out a way to see each other more often eventually. I don't know how it's going to work; I really hope it even *can* work. But I said yes. Because I love him.'

Ben squeezed Orson's hand tighter. 'I love him too, Mom.'

'Good lord above,' Natasha said, slouching back in her chair like a worn-out parent, looking up at the ceiling. 'Talk about a Christmas reunion nobody expected. Nobody expected *that* kind of union. Okay. I'm not shocked, honestly. There's nothing wrong here. I'm just...'

'You wonder how you didn't see it?' Ben said.

'I know exactly how I didn't see it,' Natasha said. 'I never once in your lifetime imagined you might be the kind of boy who went for interspecies romance. That's real life boys like Todd and Colton; that's what I see when I meet patients like that, and people outside of work like that too. I simply never would have thought it. So many of your friends are bears. All the girls who you've been a magnet for your whole teenage were bears.'

Orson was having all the fun Ben had enjoyed just minutes ago now. 'Sorry Dr B, he really goes for an otter dressed in space-gunner gear who never misses a shot.'

'Orson, if you want to write an adult movie, could you not do it out loud in front of my mom?' Ben hunched up like he was glowing under his fur. 'Mom's already thinking of enough questions while she plays the last two weeks through in her head wondering how we ever got this past her, and you're about to get hit with it all. Buckle up, *Otterpants*. You're about to fly by the seat of them.'

'Actually, I just have one,' Natasha said, her composure seemingly fully back. She leaned in, did the looking around thing they'd all been doing, and said quietly: 'How did you two manage to have sex with each other so quietly for the last two weeks?'

'Who's to say we had sex?' Orson said, wearing a great big smirk that threatened to make his face ache if it lasted too much longer. 'Maybe we just gave each other a stiffy and said, "This is nice, wanna turn BFF into *boyfriends* forever?"'

'Yes, of course, that's what you did every night.' Natasha sat back. 'I've examined *many* otters, Orson Brookfield. Take it from me that when you have to do certain things to them, they make noise. I've actually wished I'd put earplugs in my ears on several occasions like that. You made enough noise at Christmas breakfast with a simple tail pull. So, I believe I may have answered my own question in what I've just deduced, but let's not go TMI in a Waffle House on a Saturday morning. How do you kids put it now? Let's keep it SFW.'

'You mean that I obviously wasn't the bottom?' Orson said. 'Guess again.'

'Orson, my friend,' Ben said. 'You're telling my *mom* what we do in bed together.'

'So what?' Orson said. 'She's a doctor; she's heard it all. She can take my otterpants off and examine me like that any day.'

A waitress whose badge said Brandine, an otter who looked to be in her forties-ish, was there to refill their coffee. Nobody had noticed her approach.

'Sounds like a fun little family,' she said.

'You know,' Natasha said, 'I've never thought of it before, but if doctors and waitresses share one thing about their jobs, it's that they *have* pretty well heard it all from the people who come through their door at work. Right?'

'And then some,' Brandine said. 'You folks let me know if there's anything else you need.'

'How about a shot of propofol?' Ben said. 'So I can wake up on my bed later and this will all have been a dream.'

Natasha shook her head. 'This will be a fond memory soon enough,' she said. 'But we have to talk seriously for a few minutes. Starting with another question: who else knows about this? Anyone in the family?'

Orson almost answered and then closed his mouth at the last minute. He looked at Ben, tagging him in.

'Holly and Cliff know,' Ben said. 'I came out to them about a year and a half ago. I had to tell someone. I was struggling, Mom. Like...mental health struggling. Thoughts I didn't want. But we can talk about that some other time. I was fine after I told them. In a phone call. Because I couldn't wait for face to face.'

Natasha took it all in. 'Right,' she said, putting her hand on Ben's left, while his right still held Orson's. 'Well done. No surprise there either. You don't *have* to talk to me about anything if it's better that you talk to someone else. Did you go to the campus doctor? A therapy session?'

282

Ben looked like he was thinking about answering, then just settled for, 'I'm okay, Mom. I did what I needed to do. There was some medication for eight months, but I managed to come off it. Okay, I...I'm glad I could, because it was ruining things downtown.' He looked around again. 'I couldn't get an erection without a *lot* of work, Mom. I'm twenty-one years old and at college. Depression meds did *that* to me?'

'Age and side effects aren't always as linked as you might think,' Natasha said. 'Everyone's different while they're on antidepressants. But good. You came off and things have been better. So let's talk about what none of us want to for a minute. Your father. I'm going to suggest you don't be this brave with him yet. Maybe not for a *while* yet.'

'Yeah, I thought so too, Mom,' Ben said. 'But I keep thinking, why should I have to wait to tell the world who I really am? The way this feels like it's going, he's going to know sooner or later. Maybe it's better that he gets it from me and we just let him do the whole thing about trying to talk me into conversion therapy and get it over with. Because I'm not going, Mom. I'm prepared to tell him. I don't care how many times I have to do it. You told him you don't believe in God anymore. I do, and I'll tell him I know that's not what God wants. God wants me to be with Orson. Why else did I get a Christmas reunion like this?'

Natasha nodded through all of it. 'You're a brave boy, Benjamin. You don't have to prove that to me.'

'It's not about proving anything, Mom.'

283

'I know. All I'm saying right now is that bravery perhaps doesn't have to take the path you're talking about. Before you say anything else, just listen. Your brother and sister would be quite surprised by this, but I think they could deal with it. I don't think they'd stop loving you just because it turned out you were different in one big way all along. What I don't think they could handle is living in our home with your father if *he* handles it badly. I think this would be better said and done when Sam and Ella are older and have moved out, or at least gone to college. I know it sounds selfish of me to ask this of you, but peace in my own home is something I need. I think the family needs it.'

'So Dad's breaking his marriage vows but he couldn't handle his son having the life that makes *him* happy?' Ben said. 'What a...what an *asshole*, Mom.'

You go, bear, Orson thought. *Tell it like it is. The cunty newspapers are waiting for both of us.*

'I know,' Natasha said. 'But I love that asshole, mostly. He still loves me, for all his flaws. That's how I know I can work on this. There are ways he could come to it on his own terms. Let me see what I can do. It doesn't have to give any hint at you. We both know we've got a little marriage fixing to do after the things I said the other night. He'll try to get me back on board with my faith. I'll have very little of it. I'll suggest marriage counselling; I know some good people for that. We'll have discussions; I'll come up with how it's never sat well with me that he isn't a progressive man. Homosexuality will come up. I'll talk about how I've

284

learned to think of it as part of being a doctor. You get it? This needs to be handled in a way that's less direct than what you two just did with me. I'm the one that approach works with. The man I married simply isn't.'

Ben took it all in for a moment, his coffee untouched and getting cold. 'Alright,' he said. 'It's not like I was looking forward to telling him anyway. Maybe we just never tell him. Maybe he goes to his grave one day never knowing. But Mom, look, I'd *like* to go on a salmon run with him one day and not wear speedos. I'd *like* to know I don't have to worry if I get an erection surrounded by other naked bears playing around in the water. I'd *like* him to be there without me thinking he's an…yeah, okay, I'd like to take my boyfriend too. Otters do the salmon run too nowadays. It's more of an accepted thing that bears and otters mix; there isn't fighting over territories everywhere if you go to the right place. I want that kind of thing, Mom. But Dad isn't that kind of man. He probably *has* helped fight otters off.'

Natasha laughed. 'Your father couldn't fight his own shadow, Benjamin. He can't even fight when drunk. But I understand what you mean. We'll see what I can do about his issues. The best thing you can do is go back to college, with him thinking this whole Christmas has just been about friendship.' She looked at Orson. 'Thank you for not being a squeaker, whatever it is you were up to.'

'At least not while the family was in,' Ben said, as if attempting some revenge.

'Eeeeeeeee!' Orson went, turning the heads of a few diners, and then laughing at himself. *Revenge my ass.*

I'll always be the one who can make you glow under your fur more. I'm the guy who wii-moted the PM's little public school brat. I'm the one who can and should destroy his shitty parents who are never even going to eat salmon with him again, let alone go on a run in a nice holiday location. You're right, Ben. That's for the new family I'm now working on instead.

'I was asking for that, wasn't I?' Natasha said. 'Well, this affects you more than you think, squeaker. There's something that might just *really* make you do it. When John gets home this evening, we both need to talk to you. Benjamin, we want you there as well. The help you asked for the other night got John thinking. Nobody can help you move to this country easily, but John thought of a way to help give you a start at moving out of your parents' house. Tonight he wants to tell you about it. So be prepared not to hug your new boyfriend in too obvious a way or start to gush all your secrets if emotions take over a little.'

'Oooooh boy,' Orson said. 'What are we talking about exactly? Because I really didn't...' He squirmed on his seat now. 'If it's money, I really didn't mean to ask for it. I don't think Ben did either.' He looked at Ben. 'Did you know about this?'

'No!' Ben said. 'Mom, what the hell's Dad done?'

'Something nice,' Natasha said. 'With nothing expected in return. It's like I said: two sides. You're about to see the better one. The price you're both going to have to pay is that you keep your secrets and we do this the way we've been talking about this morning. So

286

try not to make too many jokes about Orson's pants or mention Ella's present. And definitely don't admit that those flushed condoms were from you two and that Cliff covered. Even drunk I knew something about that whole scene was out of place.'

Orson sighed. 'It was me, Dr B. I'm sorry.'

'Don't worry. I wouldn't have made you pay us back for the plumber and the cost of the water damage even if you could have. I thought it was funny. Before I was mouthy-drunk, I spent a good hour trying not to be laughing drunk.'

At least she thinks we're having protected sex, Orson thought.

'Are you two prepared?' Natasha said. 'Because you'd better be.'

Chapter Thirteen

Orson hadn't wanted a mass goodbye from the Barstow family in the airport, so on his behalf Ben told the family the best thing to do was have the goodbye in the house, and then Ben would drive him to the airport. Any kind of special goodbye was between them.

In other words, Ben thought Orson was going to start sobbing. He hadn't. He'd wondered if something would crack Ben, but that hadn't happened either. It had been a great big warm hug that had lasted for a good couple of minutes while they made their promises that if all else failed then next Christmas would see another reunion. Ben said he thought he could save up enough money to come to England.

'No pressure then, Snowbear,' Orson said, finally bringing himself to end their hug. 'Who's to say where I'm going to be calling home by then? What it's going to look like, who's going to be there, what I'm going to be doing to keep it...hold on, why am I even saying this when there's a totally obvious question: why the fuck would you want to come to England? It's a dump! Did you miss the part where I'm only going back there right now because I can't move here yet?'

'I've kind of missed fish and chips.'

'Urgh. I'll bring you some over next Christmas. They'll reheat okay after they've been in a suitcase on a plane, right?'

'Why do I get the feeling you really just might turn up with that and pee in your pants laughing when you explain it to my family? I can't even imagine how much your clothes would stink. I'm definitely coming to London. I know one answer to what you said though. What you're going to be doing. You're going to be a YouTuber.'

Orson sighed. 'Benji, your dad suggested I try that shit because he thinks I'll make an arse out of myself.'

'I actually don't think that's it,' Ben said. 'I think he wanted you to succeed. Why give you what he did if he just wants to see you fail? He's got nothing to gain from setting you up for that.'

'Unless he secretly still doesn't think I'm a good friend for you.'

'Don't *over*think it all, otter-brain. I still like how Ella called you that and Dad told her not to be rude. She really wasn't. That's just Ella. Dad changed his mind about you. Before you think it if you're not already, no, he hasn't clocked it about us. He's not even entertaining that thought as a worst-case scenario. He saw what he wanted to: you needed a new start. *Try* the YouTube thing at least. *I* think you'd get noticed. You're a better person than half the jerks who make a fortune off it.

Don't say you won't because you're not them. Say you might because you're you. Then who wins?'

Orson couldn't compete with that. He heard the number of his flight being called for boarding. 'Gonna kiss me goodbye then?'

Ben froze. Orson should have realised he would. 'Orson, I...I just can't. A lot of people go to and from this place for Christmas in New York. I know a lot of people and so do my family. You heard what Mom said. One wrong move and we could just sink everything before we've had a chance to actually not get a horror story out of it. I can't check around me like I could in the Waffle House.'

You set yourself up for disappointment, you dumb fuck. What else was he going to say?

He didn't kiss you there eith...

Orson barely saw it coming, until Ben's face was right up next to his. Their kiss lasted a good minute longer than their hug. Not that Orson had any concept of time. He didn't care if he stayed like this all day and missed his flight. When Ben finally came apart from him and he realised his headiness was because he hadn't been breathing normally for a good three minutes, Orson looked at Ben and didn't see any of the look he had a minute ago. He knew Ben hadn't been winding him up with a planned response. This was a spontaneous rush of bravery, and Orson could barely comprehend it.

'You know what, Orson?'

'What?'

Ben took a step towards him, grinned and leaned in to quietly talk in his ear. 'Fuck my parents too,' he said. 'Now go get on your flight and go serve yours what they've got coming.'

This time, Orson really couldn't compete. He just laughed, put his hands on Ben's bear-butt one last time, then went and boarded the flight.

* * *

Not crying in Ben's home or the airport was one thing. Not doing it once he'd taken off and was looking down at the city knowing Ben would be watching his plane up in the air should have been another, but now that he was doing it, Orson found it wasn't. Not after Ben saying those last words. He owed it to him to face this with his head up and his face dry.

Once the light that forbade electrical appliances went out, he got out the iPad.

Yeah, how about that? Of course John Barstow spent stupid money on stuff he never used, because that's what people in that industry did all the time, mostly to keep up with each other, flashing brand names and latest upgrades just like they did business cards. So of course John had an iPad to simply give away like New Year was another Christmas.

Orson hadn't known what to say apart from thanking both of Ben's parents, as they were both there with Ben to give the gift, and Orson knew it would be no use saying, 'Guys, really, are you sure it's me who should have this?' So he said it anyway, and that was where the talk began.

'Your parents don't know you have this,' John said. 'Don't *let* them know. So even if you surrender your phone to them every night, you still have a device.'

'Forget all that,' Orson said, managing not to go with the words he really wanted. 'I'm not surrendering anything to them. Not anymore. Especially not my phone.'

'Good,' Natasha said. 'That was going to be our next suggestion. But listen. John and I had a talk about the other night, and it turned out we're both afraid of you doing the same thing. They might not handle this well when you tell them. Especially not your mother. That's their problem. Yours is going to be if you don't handle it well back. Basically if you give them another version of what you gave us, and that's *not* a telling-off for the other night. We all thought it was legendary. We all liked...how did Benjamin put it? You ottering the place up. But Orson, I think you already know, starting your life over will be a lot harder to do if you're homeless.'

Ben was actually the one surprised. 'Mom, neither of his parents have the nerve to make their own son homeless. Besides, look who his dad is. The political fallout would be too big if the press who don't like him got hold of that, and you've seen Orson when he's in the kind of mood where he'd not just tell them, he'd full on yapper about it exaggerating. The homeless thing won't happen.'

John took over. 'It will if Orson storms out and tells them both what to go and do and then says he'd rather sleep in a doorway.' John looked at Orson. 'Tell us that wouldn't be you on your worst of days.'

Orson couldn't help but laugh. 'My worst of days? I'd probably trash their whole house too.'

'So just don't,' Ben said. 'Use self-control. I know you have it, no matter how amusing you find it to pretend you don't.'

'He gets it, Benjamin,' John said. 'That's what we've all been saying.' He looked at Orson again. 'Blowing off steam to us and the family was what you needed. Now you can take a look at everything you said that night and reframe it in a way that's not going to have you starting again from a doorway where someone will steal that new iPad, or do something worse. So, just in case you're looking at that, despite all efforts to do this better, do you have a place you could go?'

He knew what the question really was. He didn't want to answer it.

'Orson,' Ben said, knowing this was the moment that might break him long before an airport. 'Do you have any friends besides me you could actually trust if something like that happened? Would any of them be there? Okay, we know you've got Kingsley. He's good. But you can't live on an RAF base with him. He can't take you in. I'm not so sure his parents would do that for you either, or that you'd be able to live with them. They're demanding, and they're up their own backsides even more now that Kingsley's such a success. So is there anybody else?'

'I don't know,' Orson said, deciding it was better than saying no. 'I doubt it.'

'What about the stag you were talking to the other night on the PS5?' John said.

'That's Kingsley, Dad,' Ben said, enjoying his moment of knowing better.

'Okay,' John said. 'So is there anyone who you could get to do that for you anyway?'

Oh God. John had thought of this. Orson had thought of it too, daydreaming himself to sleep over the last couple of nights, wondering what could be different when he got back to London. The idea had entered his head, but he'd refused to consider it seriously. This conversation was better off over thought. The Barstows had to know he had something of a plan. Let them think he'd really do this.

'Yeah, okay, there's maybe one. There's a bit of making up to do, but the truth is it's more him than me. He'd do this because he owed me. And it might just be fun if that's where my parents knew I'd gone.'

'Are you talking about Syd Sheldon?' Ben said. 'Dad, that's a bad idea. Manipulating someone into keeping a roof over your head? That ends badly in every scenario. Especially if he's...well, vulnerable himself. This is complicated, Dad. Syd's not had an easy time either.'

'That's why this could work' Orson said, before John could. 'It's not manipulation if it's genuine. Maybe we need each other. Your dad's right. I could do with friends. Maybe I'll start with trying to make up with Syd. The truth is, Syd's actually a big pansy. He's had more than a year of probably feeling like shit about not owning up when I was the one getting dragged through it. If I ask him to open a door, he'll do it just to feel better about himself. That's good enough. He's probably in a good job now. I wonder if I could tap him for something else that gives me a better wage.'

'Atta boy,' John said.

'Orson's life isn't Wall Street, Dad,' Ben said.

'Why shouldn't it be like that?' John said. 'He's got everything to play for and not a great deal to lose right now. No offence, otter, but you *don't* have much. You could have it all though. Why be a waiter your whole life to people like me throwing money everywhere on a Saturday night when you could go back to college and learn how to make those games you play again? You didn't drop out because you didn't have the brains. You just used them the wrong way. Loads of kids do that with college. Second chances are possible when you're your age.'

It wasn't bad advice, Orson had to admit it.

'Come on, Benjamin, dream for your friend a little,' John said. 'You've seen how much he's enjoyed the last two weeks here. You think he doesn't want a place like this one day with a family and kids of his own? You've got to work for that. But dreaming helps you do it.'

'Does anyone want a drink?' Ben said, with the kind of smile that said he too wanted this conversation over. 'I'm going to have whisky.'

295

Orson realised he hadn't seen Ben drink hard spirits all holiday, but nor had Ben complained about the smell of it on Orson's breath every night they kissed.

All four of them drank whisky and toasted Orson's future. Ben knew John had spoken the toast before Ben could do it and call him Otterpants again.

Looking at New York disappearing below the clouds, Orson began to think about not going home at all. Why bother going to his parents' place again when he just about had what he needed to strike out alone anyway? That had been the real gift, right after the iPad, and right before the toast. Somehow, John had almost forgotten it.

'Before we do this, there's something else.' John poured the drink, of course. 'Orson, do you have your own bank account still?'

'Well yeah, sure. My wages have to get paid into something.'

'I mean do your parents control your finances for you or have access to it?'

It surprised Orson that they didn't as soon as he'd heard someone ask the question. Legally he'd always thought they couldn't do that without a court order, but knowing everything else he'd finally admitted two nights ago, he wondered if they'd secretly tried to get one. 'No. It's mine and they don't.'

'Good,' John said. 'Because I'm going to need you to tell me your account number so I can transfer you something. Just so you wouldn't feel guilty about taking it from me, I reached out to a Christian charity I sit on the panel for, one that helps prevent people from becoming homeless. I might have had to exaggerate your situation a little, but I was honest enough that my conscience is clean. It doesn't matter that you're not a U.S. citizen; homelessness doesn't know borders with these guys. That's how I knew they'd do this. What I managed to get for you will convert to around £1500. That should be enough for a deposit and the first month's rent somewhere close enough to where you said you work. *If* you want to use it that way. You could use it as the start of a college fund to start in September instead, if you can stick it living with your parents for that long. Then you could save your wages rather than spend them on rent and living.'

'You think I could convince them to let me go back to Sussex to do that degree again when it's computers?'

'There doesn't have to be any letting involved,' Natasha said. 'You're more than old enough that the choice has nothing to do with them. If it's what you want, *tell* them that's what you're doing and that you want their support. Then if you don't get it, tell them you're clearing out of their house and you're going to do it anyway. If they ask how, you needn't bother telling them where that money came from. Just do it. Leave them wondering. They might even respect that you found a way to do it.'

Orson decided he liked that idea. Going back to uni might not actually be the right thing to do, but by the time he landed, he was going to have picked something. That would do if he had nothing else.

He wanted his own PS5 back. That was the one smart thing he'd done when this all started. He let his father take it to the recycling centre, not knowing that he was following him. He couldn't buy it back, so he'd had to sneak in and take it, but he didn't consider it stealing when it wasn't really his father's to give in the first place. It had been hidden under the loose floorboards under the rug in his bedroom for the last year, dusted off occasionally even though he'd promised not to use it. He just wanted the feeling that he still owned something he wasn't supposed to. It needed to be plugged in. Uni wouldn't be a bad place to do it.

Neither would his parents' house when they weren't there. That was an odd thought; he'd ranted about how they were never there when he was growing up, but what had changed now? Even with the control they exercised, trying to retrospectively be good parents, they were fucking that up on a daily basis by simply not being there. He'd thought of breaking their rules behind their back as disloyalty he could no longer afford. Now he thought of it as taking back the life he needed.

Forget Syd though. That plan wasn't going anywhere.

Was it?

He logged in to the airline's wi-fi. He still remembered Syd's email address.

'Hey, I wanted to say...' Okay, fine, he could do it. '...I'm sorry things turned out so badly during that night on the town. I've got regrets. I'd kind of like to talk to you about them and see if we can work anything *out. I've been to New York. I'm on way back right now, flight 745216, due in at Heathrow 12:30 midnight. Any chance you can come pick me up? There's family shit going on with my parents right now. I'd kinda like to crash anywhere but theirs, even if it's on a couch.'*

Syd wouldn't go for it, Orson thought. But at least he'd tried. He'd managed not to say everything he knew about Syd now, just so Syd wouldn't think he was only doing this out of feeling sorry for him. Still, the text-silence wasn't reassuring. Orson ended up thinking about it so hard that eventually he fell asleep to the thoughts.

An hour later, he woke up from his nap to the sound of the iPad's alert tone on his headphones.

'I'll be there. You wouldn't believe the Christmas I've had either. I'll take anybody's company right now. I'm sorry about last year too. I don't know how much you know, but I've had a god-awful year and I've done a lot of thinking because of it. I'm lucky to be alive. It's made me re-think a lot. I'd rather say what I need to in person. Let's talk about it after you've crashed for a day or two. I'll make sure there's breakfast for you before I go to work tomorrow.'

'No fucking way,' Orson said to himself, shaking his head, not in refusal but in disbelief that what he'd said about Syd needing to feel like a good guy again was starting to sound true. Having breakfast left, no matter what the quality of Syd's taste in food, or god forbid cooking, or the quality of wherever he might be calling home now, seemed a better start than going back to his parents' house. Except to get that PS5, eventually. He thought he might walk out with it under his arm in plain sight.

Orson decided he had to take a chance. *'I know what's been happening. Kingsley got in touch with me the other day. People are worried about you. When we have our conversation, can you promise me you'll...'*

Orson thought for a moment, then deleted the last sentence and wrote, *'When we have that conversation, I promise I'll be sober. Can you do the same?'*

It took an uncomfortably long time, but eventually Syd texted one word. *'Yes.'*

Orson took a deep breath and sighed it out with relief. He started messaging his parents to say that he'd made other plans and that they shouldn't come to the airport to pick him up but then decided not to bother. They probably wouldn't come anyway. If they did, he could slip out unnoticed, because Syd was always ten minutes early for everything, if not more. Orson wondered why he'd hung on to that memory all this time and never thought of it.

Sober. Although it was obvious he'd meant alcohol and drugs, Orson wondered if Syd somehow thought he was talking about gaming. His thoughts wandered back to two nights ago.

'Tasha, can I ask you a bit of a blunt question? Do you really think someone who went where I did with gaming can control it if they go back? Or did you want me to get back to it because you're mad at my parents for being crap parents?'

Natasha looked a little troubled, and Orson knew it was more by the things she'd said before than his question. 'Let's reframe this. Your parents got certain parts of parenting wrong, and yes, it made me mad at them, but no, I'm not seeking any kind of revenge on them. It's about what *you* want. If you don't want to be a gamer, you don't have to go back to it just because this holiday made it happen. If you do, there's good information on how some people who've had a problem with it before manage it better going forward. Not all addiction treatment is about complete abstinence. That's what got my back up about your parents and you most of all. I doubt you were ever offered any kind of treatment apart from the one they made you have, or made aware of it.'

Orson sat quietly for a moment. 'I wasn't. I really didn't think it could be like that.'

'Exactly. I could show you what I'm talking about now though. We could find you some options to explore that would guide you to a happier path where gaming was still a part of your life. Would you like that?'

Orson had been thinking about it ever since keeping to his three-hour limit that night. 'Yeah. I think so.'

He still thought so. This time, he thought of the world he'd live in when he switched off the TV and the console. Ben would be in it. So would other people.

The East Coast of the USA was disappearing. Orson started looking at what Ben had sent him that had eclipsed the email from Syd in his notifications: package holidays to salmon runs in mountain ranges all over the USA. There was a picture of a naked bear modelling in one, with his legs positioned so they hid his dick and the angle so that you could just about make out the shape of his butt without seeing both cheeks. There were otters in the same picture.

It was strange – Orson still felt like he was glad he was heading for London instead of wanting the flight to turn around and going straight there instead. He had something to want in his future.

It was about time.

Afterword, and more books by Todd Aldrington

Thank you for reading *A Christmas Reunion*; out of all the furry books out there, I'm glad you chose this one. I'd like to promise you one thing though: not all my work is as silly as this book was! At one point I was going to edit certain parts of the humour out, but then I came to recognise that if it came out as daft as it did then maybe it was *supposed* to be a rather silly story, with enough seriousness to appeal to an adult audience, or perhaps kidults (I've come to increasingly like that word. Let's face it, I'm totally one).

Is there another book with Ben and Orson? Yes, I'm almost sure of it. There's more than enough potential for further drama. I can't promise when that will be; as of now I've several projects on the go and at least two other titles nearly ready for release, but what I've come to like about Ben and Orson is that they've been there when I needed them – namely for some comic relief at Christmas, creating a story that's really quite easy to write. I can't commit to a Christmas 2024 book with them, but definitely watch this space if you're after more.

In the meantime, here's an Easter egg for you: the book Ella gifts Orson, *Chasing Colton's Tail*, is one of my own titles. I couldn't resist that shameless self-promotion there, and anyone who's already read that book and its series doubtless rolled their eyes at that scene. Fox-boy Colton Vincent is probably my best-received character to date. If you thought Orson had a bad-boy side to him then Colton makes him look like Santa, and he's certainly not giving up his secrets as easily as Ben Barstow does. Todd 'Deacon Blue' Aldrington, the raccoon whose name I took for my author name, has to work pretty damn hard to get them out of him, and heaps of high drama follows, spanning from Arizona to New York to France to Tokyo, and several times back again.

Here's where to find it: most of my readers use Amazon, but you can also find it on Smashwords, Kobo, Apple, and you can get the .epub files that work on most e-readers from my Patreon page. (Note: epub doesn't work with Kindles; at the time of writing, I'm trying to persuade Patreon's tech department to accept the .mobi files to their store as well.)